"Is this a former girlfriend? A wife?"

Max followed Miles's gaze to where it rested on Winnie and forced a smile. "You know I've never been married, Chief. And Winnie, well, she's my best friend's widow. We lost Tom over five years ago—EA-6B Prowler crash. I was the CACO."

Miles shook his head and let out a low whistle. "Sorry, boss. That sucks."

"It's part of our business, isn't it?" Max rubbed his chin. "It did look like we might have something between us a while back. But it was only a lark."

"How long ago was that?"

"Ahh, let's see. That was the summer before I took the squadron on deployment, so…" His mind leaped onto an unexpected tangent with lightning speed.

No way.

"Boss, you okay?"

"Yeah, I'm...just figuring something out." *How old is her daughter? What's the time line?*

The tightness in his chest had everything to do with the reality of what Winnie had revealed to him. And what she *hadn't.*

Dear Reader,

I'm a navy veteran and navy wife, so the military has played a pivotal role in my life. Our family has lived all over the United States and the world, including Whidbey Island in Washington State, the setting for *Navy Rules*.

I have wanted to bring the dedication and sacrifice of military families to light in my work for a long while. I've been so blessed, as my husband, the father of my children, came back from war alive. Others have not been so fortunate. Husbands, wives, mothers, fathers, daughters, sons, sisters, brothers—the list goes on— have paid the ultimate sacrifice so that we may live in peace and continue to cherish our freedom.

Winnie is a navy widow and mother to two beautiful girls. Max is a battle-scarred war hero. They've known each other for years—Max was Winnie's Casualty Assistance Calls Officer, CACO, when Winnie's navy husband was killed five years ago. Their attraction to each other is unexpected after years of being family friends. It's further complicated when Winnie conceives their daughter, Maeve, after only one night together, two years before the story starts.

This story is dedicated to the strength and courage of all military spouses, men and women, who have to endure while their loved ones are in harm's way for the sake of freedom. To my U.S. Naval Academy classmates who made the ultimate sacrifice—I salute you and I salute your surviving families. May God bless and keep you.

Peace,

Geri Krotow

P.S. Please get in touch with me through my website, www.gerikrotow.com.

Navy Rules

GERI KROTOW

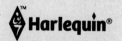

TORONTO NEW YORK LONDON
AMSTERDAM PARIS SYDNEY HAMBURG
STOCKHOLM ATHENS TOKYO MILAN MADRID
PRAGUE WARSAW BUDAPEST AUCKLAND

Recycling programs
for this product may
not exist in your area.

ISBN-13: 978-0-373-60710-5

NAVY RULES

www.Harlequin.com

Printed in U.S.A.

ABOUT THE AUTHOR

A former naval intelligence officer and U.S. Naval Academy graduate, Geri Krotow writes about the people and places she's been lucky enough to encounter. Geri loves to hear from her readers. You can email her via her website and blog, www.gerikrotow.com.

Books by Geri Krotow

HARLEQUIN SUPERROMANCE

1547—WHAT FAMILY MEANS
1642—SASHA'S DAD

HARLEQUIN EVERLASTING LOVE

20—A RENDEZVOUS TO REMEMBER

Other titles by this author available in ebook format.

For Kathy Coughlin and Ellen Stoner

You taught me what being a military spouse means.
I miss you both dearly.

CHAPTER ONE

WINNIE PERRIN ARMSTRONG stared at her computer screen while she stroked her dog's belly with her foot. Sam, a medium-size shepherd mix, lay under the desk in her bedroom while she indulged in her morning luxury of reading the news before the girls woke up.

The only light in the room came from the glow of the screen. Winnie read the national news highlights, then switched to the local news. She kept an eye on the time—the girls would wake up in the next ten minutes or so.

Former Whidbey Commanding Officer Gives Back to Community

The headline didn't surprise her. But the accompanying photo and its caption, Commander Max Ford Plans to Coach Youth Soccer, made her sit up straight and grasp her desk.

Commander Max Ford, USN, brought his EA-6B Prowler Squadron back from war. He saved dozens of the sailors from a suicide bomber attack just weeks before the squadron was due to depart from Afghanistan. Ford returned to Whidbey last month after a lengthy stint of rehabilitation at the Walter Reed National Military Medical Center in Washington, D.C. He has signed up to coach community youth soccer. With so many of our children's parents deployed, the soccer teams are in need of dedicated coaches. Ford leads the way for returning vets to fill the gap and help our young soccer players.

Good thing she planned to tell Max about Maeve—the result of their night together after the Air Show two summers ago...

Winnie looked back at the article and bit her lip. It didn't mention Max's wounds, no doubt out of respect for his privacy. She knew about his injuries because she and Sam were going to pay Max a visit today.

You should've done it ages ago.

Sam wagged his long, silky tail and she caught a glimpse of the blond fur beneath the black. It matched the fur that grew horizontally out of his pointed ears and in swirls on his belly.

"Good boy, Sam. You've got a big day ahead of you." The first Monday in March. Time to finally come clean with Max. And after she met with him, she'd have to talk to her parents.

So he was going to coach community soccer. Was that going to be another complication? *What if he coached Krista's team?*

Sam licked her hand as if he wanted her to know he understood. Of course he didn't; he was a dog and while his gifts of compassion and companionship were priceless, he wasn't the human partner Winnie had once had.

Tom.

She let a happy memory of them walking on the sand in Penn Cove wrap around her heart. It'd been more than five years since he died and she still missed him more than she'd ever told her family. Because they lived so close, less than an hour away in Anacortes, they saw her and the girls regularly. They saw how bereft she still was, yet they never pressed her about finding a new man. Even after Maeve was born last year. Winnie loved them for that.

"Mom!" Krista barged into her room, all arms and legs at thirteen. "Maeve's up and you forgot to dry my jeans again."

"I'll get her. Throw them in the dryer. They'll be done in time for the bus." Winnie got up and headed for the baby's room.

Krista let out a long-suffering sigh as she followed her into the hallway.

"Yes, I did, but, Mom, you've got to remember to dry things *right away* or they'll be wrinkled."

"Good morning, sunshine." Winnie ignored Krista's adolescent rant and took in every second of Maeve's tiny-toothed grin. The eighteen-month-old clung to the side of her crib and looked up at Winnie as though she were seeing a deity.

"Hi, baby sis." Even Krista was under Maeve's spell, talking to the baby while Winnie changed the soggy diaper.

Winnie put on Maeve's pants, picked up the baby and turned to Krista. "Let's go get breakfast before you start in on me about the laundry, okay?"

This was like the beginning of any other day in the Armstrong household. Except that today Maeve's father was going to find out he had a daughter.

Winnie was going to tell him.

No more excuses.

"Sorry, Mom." Krista was immediately apologetic and her sincerity made Winnie want to pull her close and squeeze hard. Krista had been through so much, not the least of which was accepting that her mother was having a baby two years ago. A baby by a man Winnie had told her "once meant a lot to our family, but can't be with us right now."

"I know you are, honey."

A few moments later, as Winnie prepared Maeve's breakfast, Krista suddenly asked, "Mom, are you ever going to tell me who Maeve's father is?"

Winnie dropped the knife she was using to spread peanut butter on a whole-wheat English muffin. It splattered peanut butter all over her slipper.

"Whoops! Thank goodness the baby's in her high chair!" Her voice was high and brittle as she struggled with an honest answer for Krista.

"Mom?"

"I heard you, Krista. As a matter of fact, Maeve's dad is back in town. And I plan to tell him about her soon. I'll fill you in after I do, okay? I can't thank you enough for being such a loving sister to Maeve through all of this, Krista."

Krista shrugged as she ate her toasted muffin.

"It's okay, Mom. You've had a hard time."

Winnie sighed. They'd both had hard times when Tom died. But that was more than five years ago. And then the unexpected pregnancy—by a man with whom she'd shared an unexpected attraction. That was something she could beat herself up about, but what was the point? She had a beautiful baby daughter and Krista had a baby sister. They were a family.

Still, living by her motto of being open with her children, unlike the way her mother had been with her, was growing more difficult as Krista matured. She'd already been wise beyond her years, but the addition of Maeve to their family had catapulted Krista from preteen to teenage older sister.

"Honey, life isn't all hard times. We've had more than our share, I admit, but there are people with problems so much bigger than ours. You do understand that, don't you?"

"Not many kids I know lost their dad in a Navy plane crash, Mom."

"No, but trust me, there are a lot of kids your age who have lost a parent to war."

"I know that, Mom." Krista drank down the rest of her milk. "I can't miss the bus and I still need to get my jeans on."

Winnie smiled. "You mean, you don't want to go to school wearing your airplane pajamas?"

Krista flashed her a grin before she disappeared into the laundry room. She was open with Winnie about her lifelong love of airplanes and flying, but at her sensitive middle-school age, she wasn't so quick to share all her dreams with her friends.

"Give me a hug."

A few minutes later, Krista allowed Winnie to kiss the top of her head before she bent down to pick up her overstuffed backpack.

"Bye, bye!" She wiggled her fingers at Maeve, who was in the step-down living room in full view of the kitchen, playing with her soft blocks. Sam sat near her, as if babysitting.

"Ba ba, sisseee!" Maeve was just like Krista had been at the same age. A busy chatterbox.

The front door closed behind Krista and Winnie looked at Maeve, who'd decided to return to the kitchen.

"Let's get you moving, too, girlfriend. Mommy's got a lot of work to do today."

THE REFRAIN OF "MY GIRL" came from her cell phone and she smiled when saw her sister's ID.

"Hey, Robyn."

"Hey, wait a minute, Winn. Brendan, put the hammer down *right now!*" Robyn said in her stern "Mommy" voice. Ten years older than Winnie, Robyn and her husband had undergone in vitro fertilization, which had produced the two-year-old who ruled his parents' lives.

"How did he get the hammer?"

"Doug and Brendan made a birdhouse yesterday and the tools are still on the workbench." Robyn's voice reflected impatience—at Winnie's constant nagging to be more mindful of safety or at Brendan's morning antics, Winnie couldn't be sure.

"So how did he get into the garage?" Winnie loved her sister but they raised their kids very differently. Winnie had been an organized parent from the start; it had seemed like a prerequisite for a Navy wife. Not to mention her sanity, which relied on tidiness. Even as a child Winnie liked to have all her toys and books organized.

Not Robyn.

"He's figured out how to open the doors."

"Ouch. Time for some sliding bolts, up high." Robyn sighed.

"Yeah, I think I'm headed to Home Depot with the little guy today. What are you up to?"

"The usual. I don't have any orders going out until next week," she said, referring to her fiber orders. Sales would pick up over the next several weeks, as retailers were beginning to order for the following season. She'd started the business from scratch four years ago when she'd discovered, by accident, that there were a number of private farms on the island that raised fiber-producing animals, including sheep, alpaca and llamas.

Winnie's lifelong love of knitting had led her to the few knitting and crochet groups in the area, where she met the farm-owners and listened to their wistful dreams of being able to market their own fiber. Winnie had dreamed with them until Tom's death—and the realization that she needed a means to provide for her and Krista. The insurance they'd received was more than generous, but

Winnie never looked at it as anything other than a
means to pay for Krista's future education.

Winnie had founded Whidbey Fibers with only
three sheep farmers. Today she had almost two
dozen clients not just on Whidbey but on a few
of the outlying islands like San Juan and Orcas,
too. Her fibers included merino, alpaca, llama and
angora.

Robyn chuckled.

"You always say you don't have a lot going on,
Winn, but you've got tons to do every day or you
wouldn't be the famous businesswoman you are."

"Yeah, right." Winnie brushed off Robyn's compliment. Robyn was talking about the attention
Winnie had received last season for taking her
business to the international level by procuring a
client in Victoria, British Columbia.

"I do have one important appointment today—
an assignment with Sam, up in Dugualla."

"When? Can you meet me for lunch?"

Winnie bit her lip. Despite her praise of Winnie's success, Robyn didn't really understand how
much work her fiber production business was, on
top of two kids, her volunteer work and no husband.

Robyn had always been there for her. Sometimes she just forgot Winnie's extra burden.

"I'd love to meet you but I have no idea how
long this one will take. I'm driving Sam out to a

residence—the client wants to be able to spend time with Sam but not at the base hospital or even on the base."

Please don't ask any more questions.

"You're a good soul, Winnie." Robyn didn't ask for more details—she knew that Winnie's canine therapy work was confidential.

Of all people, you can trust Robyn with who your new client is.

Robyn was the one person who knew the whole story, knew who Maeve's father was. Robyn had never betrayed her, even to their mother.

Maybe she *should* tell Robyn. But Robyn would kill her if she found out Winnie was driving up to Max's today.

"Oh, I forgot to tell you that the mother of the autistic boy I told you about wants you to bring Sam over at some point." Robyn was off on another tangent, nothing new for her sis.

"Have her call the base. Maybe there's another dog therapy team available. I only work with returning sailors at this point."

"I told her that, but she sounds desperate."

"She has to work through her pediatrician." Winnie sensed Robyn's frustration, and she wanted to help, but she and Sam could only be in one place at a time. Since she'd started dog therapy with Sam a year ago, requests for service work had increased tenfold.

She'd begun it with the intent of giving back to the Navy community that had so strongly supported her and Krista in the aftermath of Tom's death. The basic obedience and Canine Good Citizenship tests had been easy for Sam to pass. True to his German shepherd genes, he was incredibly intelligent and motivated to please his trainer, Winnie.

"Okay, then, I'd better go. Brendan is off on a tear!"

Winnie laughed. "Of course he is. I still say you'd enjoy a day or two on your own each week. For your sanity, you know?"

"Maybe we could just switch lives for a day."

Winnie understood what Robyn meant. Winnie had the girls taken care of, between school and day care. She had to—she didn't have a husband or partner to support her. But true to her oversensitive nature, Robyn panicked at the immediate silence on the line.

"Oh, Winnie, I'm so sorry. I didn't mean—"

"Stop it, Robyn. I know exactly what you meant. Please, *please* let it go." Robyn ran on guilt as much as caffeine, a trait both girls inherited from their devout Catholic mother. Whenever the three of them got together over a cup of coffee, their father accused them of sounding like a beehive in overdrive. Thank God for their father, whose patient nature made him a revered high school teacher and track coach, and had kept their family on an even keel when they were younger.

"All right. But if your day turns out differently, come and meet me for lunch, okay? We can get takeout and eat it while Brendan naps."

"Will do. Love you."

"Love you, too."

Winnie turned off her phone with a sigh of relief.

Thai takeout in front of Robyn's woodstove sounded like pure bliss. But the chances of there being enough time to drive up to Anacortes, the town north of Whidbey Island, and back again to get the girls from school in Coupeville, were slim.

She still had to finish her fiber inventory. Whidbey Fibers' success wasn't an accident. She'd taken the energy she'd focused on her marriage and put it into the corporation, client by client.

The farm-owners were, for the most part, great at raising livestock and producing viable quantities of fiber, but getting it spun into usable yarn was another story. Drawing on her business background, Winnie had recruited machine- and hand-spinners across the Pacific Northwest and became the liaison between the farmers, spinners and yarn shops. She'd begun receiving orders from Europe and Australia within eight months of start-up.

Her business model was unique in that instead of simply purchasing the fiber outright, she shared the profits of the finished product with the farmers. This increased their motivation to produce and created a camaraderie in the Whidbey Island fiber community that hadn't existed before. Instead of competing, each farm benefited from the success of *all* the farms. She also employed hand- and machine-spinners who transformed the fresh fiber into usable yarn.

As she walked by bin after bin of sheared wool and alpaca and checked off her inventory master list, Winnie's mind drifted back to her other commitment for today.

Her therapy-dog visit.

Max.

She'd accepted the assignment knowing full well that she risked losing the secure life she'd built for herself and the girls.

Self-recrimination washed over her. She took a ball of alpaca out of its bin and held the soft wool to her cheek. She should've told Robyn who her client was. When Robyn found out, and she *would* find out, she'd be furious that Winnie hadn't told her she was finally going to tell Max about Maeve. Rightfully so, as Robyn had been her support and anchor through the past five years. She'd never judged Winnie and had kept her deepest secrets *secret*.

Ever since Winnie learned she was pregnant, Robyn had been adamant that Winnie needed to tell Max he was a father. And it wasn't that Winnie disagreed. The timing had been hell, with Max headed to war. She'd planned to tell him when he returned, but then his deployment was extended.

Risking such a huge emotional upset to a man at war was not something Winnie would ever do.

Shivers of apprehension chilled her as she looked out the back window of her fiber studio onto Penn Cove. The gray sky covered the white-capped bay and she knew the waves on the western side of Whidbey would be even more powerful.

A spring storm was coming in from the Pacific. She hated making the drive up to the Naval Air Station on the slick black road, but her volunteer time at the base was one of the few sacrosanct commitments in her life, besides the girls.

She loved her daughters and wanted to cherish each moment with them. But she also relished her work and needed time alone to think about how to manage her burgeoning career without the neediness of a teen and toddler weighting her every move.

As she prepared to leave the studio, she paused in front of the window that overlooked the street. Her building sat in between the rocky narrow coast and a side road off Coupeville's Main Street. Winnie watched the rain begin to fall. When she came back from this afternoon's therapy visit, everything would be different.

She leaned her head against the studio's front door and closed her eyes. She tried to let the rain pattering against the window panes of the century-old building soothe her.

It hadn't been her choice to be a single parent to Krista. A mishap on an aircraft carrier had dealt a devastating blow to her life when it killed her husband and Krista's father, Tom, more than five years ago.

She'd had a choice, however, in how she made a family for Maeve, her baby. She'd deliberately refused to tell her family, except for Robyn, who Maeve's father was. Her parents had wondered if she'd used Tom's frozen sperm. She'd assured them that wasn't the case, but as they became more persistent she let them think whatever they wanted.

She'd told Robyn about Maeve's father—with instructions to tell Max if anything happened to her. But she needed to tell Max herself; he deserved to know before anyone else did that he was Maeve's father. Unfortunately she'd learned that a life can end with no notice, and that included her own.

While her parents had no idea who'd fathered Maeve, it was pretty clear soon after she was born—with dark, straight hair—that she had a different father than Krista, who shared Winnie's curly blond mane.

Maeve's father had moved back to Whidbey Island two months ago. In spite of her best intentions to tell him he was a father as soon as she could, she'd still procrastinated.

It'd been two years, three months and five days since she'd last seen U.S. Navy Commander Robert "Max" Ford. It seemed more like three minutes.

Especially when she looked at her beautiful baby daughter.

COMMANDER MAX FORD, United States Navy, sat on the deck of his dream home and stared out at Dugualla Bay. The Cascade Mountains were snowcapped, as they'd remain for most of the year.

As a junior officer, J.O., he'd idolized the Commanding Officer of his squadron who'd owned this place. When his Commanding Officer got divorced and the house was sold as part of the settlement, Max bought it. He'd rented it out while he was stationed in Florida, and eagerly returned to his prized home just under two years ago, when he took the Executive Officer/Commanding Officer, XO/CO, job in his squadron. He'd had his Change of Command party here last year and the world seemed to be his to conquer.

He'd been so much younger only a year ago. His Aviation Command of Prowler Squadron Eighty-One had been in front of him. He'd led over two hundred men and women into battle over Iraq and Afghanistan. They'd all come home intact.

Except him.

He raised his arms overhead to stretch his back, as the physical therapist had taught him. The shrapnel had been removed and the scars were healing.

Too bad his brain couldn't get stitched back up so easily.

"You have PTSD. You know the drill, Max. You're one of our Navy's finest. We'll get you a great job on Whidbey, shore duty, and give you time to heal. Then we'll see where it all falls out for an O-6 command."

His boss, the Wing Commander, had done everything Max would have done for one of his own charges. He'd been compassionate, honest, strong.

But having been a commanding officer himself, Max saw beyond the clichéd promises.

Max had seen the look of resignation in his boss's eyes. He didn't expect Max to return to a real Navy job. His operational days were done. No one came back whole from what he'd seen—the monster who'd appeared in the form of the suicide bomber he'd prevented from killing hundreds of fellow servicemen and women.

Instead of preparing his squadron for another deployment, during which they'd become the well-honed warriors they'd signed up to be, he was sitting on his deck, staring at the Cascade Mountains, waiting for some volunteer social worker to bring over a dog.

A dog.

It wasn't that he didn't like dogs. Max planned on having several once his Navy days were over. Hell, since he was on shore duty indefinitely, he could even consider going to the animal shelter in Coupeville and adopting himself a real dog. Something big and furry. He'd never been a tiny-dog fan. If the dog handler showed up with anything smaller than a bear cub he wasn't going to work with it.

His problem wasn't with the dog per se. Max's problem was with still needing therapy. He'd accepted the weekly meetings with the on-base counselor. He'd met with the PTSD support group and shared his feelings. Yet his therapist thought he'd benefit from some dog time. Dog *therapy* time.

He blamed himself for asking what else he could do to help the other sailors. It was getting too painful to go back to the base day after day and not be able to walk into a hangar that he'd practically owned. Not to face a squadron of courageous young men and women and know that he was leading the best team on the planet. Know that he was the CO they could count on to lead them through hell and back.

His therapist had suggested canine therapy.

"Do you mean so I can give therapy to other vets?"

"No, Max. So *you* can get some healing from the *dog*. The caretaker isn't a therapist, just a handler. You and the dog form the bond."

"But you mean I'll do this so I can then provide the same service to others, right?"

Marlene Goodreach, his therapist, had shifted in her seat. Her face was lined, no doubt because of the countless tales of horror she'd helped sailors like him unburden.

"Max. This is about *you*. You've done brilliantly—your physical wounds have healed, your memory is back. But you're still resistant to facing your own anger and disappointment over the change in your career plans. I think working with a therapy dog would help the tension you still have in your gut."

Max had learned that the price of throwing himself into his recovery and hoping to eventually help others was that his therapist got to know him too well. He didn't have the option of keeping his emotions from Marlene.

At least the counselor had agreed to let him meet the dog and its handler on his own turf, away from the looks of pity on base NAS Whidbey Island.

He clenched his hands around the porch railing.

Only when his grip became painful did he force himself to breathe and release his grip. He despised the well-meaning comments, the compassionate glances, the fatherly pats on the shoulder.

"Take care of yourself, Max. You've been through a lot."

"Hey, you've had command, you brought the team home, relax."

"You've earned this shore tour. Enjoy it."

"Why not retire after this, take some time for Max? You'll make O-6, what's your worry?"

He didn't even like working out on base anymore. Too many familiar faces. He flexed his feet. The soreness in his calves was a testament to the extra-long session he'd put on the spin bike he'd bought. He kept it on the glassed-in deck upstairs, so he could watch the sun come up as he rode in place.

He saw the sunrise every day. Sleep wasn't a given for him anymore.

The dark clouds threatened rain but so far only gusts of tropical warmth rustled the underbrush under tall firs that waved with the wind. Spring on Whidbey meant chaos as far as the weather was concerned.

He saw the approaching car before he heard it. A compact station wagon. As it neared he recognized the larger shape in back—the dog.

The woman in the driver's seat made him catch his breath.

No.

It was the same honey corkscrew hair, the same generous mouth under the too-round-to-be-classic nose.

Was this some kind of joke? The very woman he'd guided through the fires of her own hell when Tom died was here to reach a hand into *his* purgatory?

More importantly, the woman who'd rejected him and whom he'd avoided since his return.

He stood as she brought the car to a stop in front of his house. She stepped out and walked straight to the back. There was no mistaking her graceful gait, her purposeful stride.

Winnie always knew where she was going, save for that brief tortured time after Tom's death.

She opened the back of the wagon and commanded the dog down. It was a big dog but not a fluffy soft breed. The mostly black coat ruffled a little in the strong breeze.

Not a tiny dog, at least.

Max let out a sigh. The dog appeared to be tough and knowing as he trotted next to Winnie up the driveway.

She drew closer and he tried to stay focused on the dog, Winnie's muddy boots, her barn coat, her jeans. Anything but the face he had trouble forgetting… He'd prided himself on staying away from her since his return to Whidbey two months earlier. He hadn't even checked to see if she was still on the island—he assumed she was, or nearby, since her family lived in the vicinity.

But he'd kept her out of his life, away from the mess his mental state had made of it.

Until now.

She stopped a few feet away, close enough for him to make out the almond shape of her long-lashed amber eyes, yet far enough not to invite physical contact. No hello hug.

"Max." She'd known it was him; he saw that in the resigned line of her mouth. But she hadn't called first, hadn't given him fair warning.

Hell, why should she? She made her feelings clear when she didn't return your calls over two years ago.

He'd last seen her just before he'd taken the one-year position of Executive Officer, which had led into his next tour, also one year, as Commanding Officer.

"Winnie." He stood at the edge of the drive, his hands in his pockets. Her hands were busy, too— one thrust in her pocket and one on the leash.

He'd always loved her hands. They were warm, long-fingered, elegant.

If he thought the PTSD had robbed him of his sex drive, he'd been mistaken. The familiar surge of need he associated with Winnie made him clench his hands inside his jeans pockets.

Winnie seemed unmoved by their reunion except for the way she tossed a stray curl out of her face. He saw her do that just a few times before. When she'd heard Tom's will read by the Navy JAG, when he'd stopped by her house in the weeks after Tom's death and two years ago, when she'd agreed to meet him for a beer at the local microbrewery after the Air Show. If only one of them had said no that night. If only he hadn't given in to the surprising yet delightful sexual attraction that sprang up between them. If only they'd preserved their basic friendship, this inevitable meeting might not be so bone-scrapingly painful.

"This is Sam." She turned to Sam. "Good dog, Sam. Greet Max."

The dog sat and wagged his tail, an expectant look on his dark face. As Max leaned lower he could see the blond eyebrows and wisps of blond coming out of Sam's ears. He reached out his hand. "Hi, Sam."

Sam sniffed inquisitively before he licked Max's open palm. The dog sidled up to him and sat down next to Max's sneakered foot.

"He likes you." Winnie smiled at Sam while she avoided eye contact with Max.

His memory of that night two years ago was intact, always had been. She'd enjoyed their lovemaking as much as he had. She could have called him. But Winnie hadn't, as he'd known she wouldn't—it wasn't her style. She'd probably been embarrassed that she'd revealed so much to him that night. Physically, anyhow.

He'd already seen her inside and out on an emotional level when Tom was killed and he'd been her CACO, her Casualty Assistance Calls Officer. He'd been the one, along with the base chaplain, to knock on Winnie's door at six in the morning, to inform her that Tom was dead. He'd taken her through all the paperwork, the life insurance forms, the burial arrangements. He'd found child care for Krista when it was needed, when the proceedings were too grim for a seven-year-old child to partake in.

He'd seen sides of Winnie he'd never expected. The whiny wife he'd chalked her up to be, the woman who always wanted Tom to get out of the Navy, turned into a strong widow before his eyes. She didn't blame the Navy or Tom for his untimely death. Through the devastating grief, he watched her accept the unwelcome change in her and Krista's lives with dignified grace.

Her grace was one of the many things about her that attracted him. A more serious relationship with Winnie, however, had never been a remote possibility. His first allegiance was to Tom and the Navy, and he planned to keep it that way.

He had more work to do, as the counselor said. And not all of it concerned his PTSD.

"I have hot water for tea," he said. "Would you like to come in?"

Winnie lifted her chin and her gaze finally met his. The sparks in their brown depths took him back to that night with her, that one great night.

Before his life as a Navy pilot had been shattered.

"Okay, thanks." She offered him a smile, but it didn't come close to reaching her eyes. "We won't stay too long, just enough to make sure you'll be comfortable with Sam this weekend."

THE KITCHEN WAS SLEEK and modern, as she remembered. It had been "the" house when they were all so much younger. Before death had cast a long and early shadow across their lives. Winnie watched Max pour hot water from the stainless kettle into the iron teapot. She didn't dare look at his face. But then, staring at his masculine hands was awkward, too; as she remembered the last time she'd seen him.

When those hands had been all over her.

She sighed. *Not* dating was the only option for her at the moment but it had its drawbacks. Being acutely aware of her sexual attraction to Max was one of them.

"How's Krista?" His deep baritone broke the silence of the square house.

"Krista's great, fine. She's in middle school."

Her reply was as bare, as unadorned, as the house. She knew it and, judging by his raised brows, so did Max.

"She's a great kid. Tom would be proud of her." Her cadence was still too clipped. He was going to wonder why.

Stop it.

"I'm glad. Has she—" Max pulled out a strainer for the tea "—adjusted okay?"

"It's been almost six years, Max. It was a horrible time for her, but she doesn't remember as much of the awfulness of it as we do."

He poured the tea with practiced ease.

"I forgot you're a tea drinker." She'd grown up in Washington State where coffee was a staple. But Max's mother was from England and his father a Harvard law professor; tea was the drink of choice in his childhood home. Years ago, Tom and their aviation friends had teased him mercilessly about it.

"Yeah, some things stay the same. Honey?" His voice triggered her awareness of him. And took her thoughts back to the night of the Air Show when he'd whispered in her ear.

"No, just plain. Thanks." The kitchen counter stool was cold against her back. She had to focus on where she was today and stay away from memories of that night.

She had to get back to the purpose of her visit—telling Max what the fateful outcome of that night had been. Telling him he was a father.

But she couldn't do it. "You want to have Sam for the whole weekend?" she asked. Nothing about Maeve, only the dog. She couldn't strike the match that would ignite an explosion of feelings—recrimination, accusation, disbelief, anger.

"If it's okay with you. Yes, I thought that would keep my therapist happy and cause the least amount of trouble for you."

"It's no *trouble* for me, Max. I come back and forth to the base every week. This is only another ten minutes past there. I can easily bring him over daily instead of leaving him." She'd never leave Sam with a new client, but Max was hardly new to her.

"We'll work it out." He seemed distracted.

Tell him.

"Winnie, I owe you an apology. I was a real shit after the Air Show two years ago. I did try to reach you, but when you didn't respond I should've been more persistent. I was getting ready to go to war, and frankly, that took over my life. But I want you to realize I didn't take that night casually."

Her stomach felt as if it had collapsed inward and she fought to keep her demeanor calm and collected. Without knowing it, Max was making her need to take responsibility more painful.

This isn't about you. It's about Maeve and her daddy. He deserves to know. Screw up your courage and get it over with.

"Stop it—we're both adults. No apology needed." Yet her face grew hotter by the second.

Where was this reaction coming from? *She'd* decided to keep him out of her life, away from Maeve.

You're angry at yourself. *You've kept him from his daughter.*

"No, it was totally wrong of me on so many levels. I enjoyed my time with you, and that night, believe it or not, was special to me. But I went back to Florida, and then got the command posting here, the deployment orders to Afghanistan and, well, I figured you might have regrets and not want to talk about it. I never wanted to cause you any pain, Winnie."

"Max, please, drop it." She was terrible at lying.

"I tried emailing you, too, but when you didn't reply, I felt it was probably best for both of us."

She kept her eyes glued on the steel-gray mug she drank from, but the sense of being watched made her look up and into his dark blue eyes. Shame clawed at her and sent heat up her neck, onto her cheeks. She should have called him. But she'd found out he was going to war. Not a good time to tell someone he had a baby on the way.

"I want you to be able to trust me, Winnie." He set his cup on the counter and leaned toward her. She felt the warmth that radiated from him, smelled the scent that had imprinted on her mind two years ago.

"I trust you, Max." That had never been an issue between them.

"With your dog."

She blinked.

"I don't have a problem leaving Sam with you. I mean, as far as trust goes."

"But?"

Winnie shifted on the hard stool This really was a bachelor's home—it looked slick and modern but definitely lacked comfort.

"The girls and I rely on Sam for our weekends. He's part of the family."

"Girls?"

She winced and hoped it was inward.

God, please don't let me blow this. Not now.

"I have two children, Max. Krista and Maeve."

His expression went still. She saw his gaze on her left hand, watched as his eyes registered her bare ring finger.

"I didn't know you were with someone new."

"I'm not with anyone. But would it be such a shock? It's been a long time."

"Of course not. I was surprised you didn't move on more quickly." He had his back to her, rinsing out the teapot in the sink.

"Oh?"

"Your marriage with Tom was so solid. Most of the widows I've dealt with over the years remarry sooner rather than later if they had a strong first marriage."

She sighed and forced her hands to unclench the fists they'd become on the granite counter. She felt so stiff, as if warding off an attack, and here was Max giving her a compliment.

"No, I haven't remarried and I don't see any reason to. The girls and I have a good life, and the thought of bringing in a third party at this point isn't on my priority list."

A moment ago she was ready to tell him. Now she wanted to turn tail and run.

He nodded. "I hear you. When I was Commanding Officer of my squadron, before we deployed, most of my late-night calls, unfortunately, were domestic violence or child molestation—many at the hands of a boyfriend or second husband. It's scary out there."

She relaxed her shoulders. This was much safer ground. As much as she'd convinced herself she was ready to tell Max about Maeve, she was nowhere near prepared to deal with the storm of emotions it would inevitably release.

Emotions from a man who'd spent the past months doing everything he could to repress all emotion, just to survive. Who was still recovering from the effects of his own hell.

Stay focused, damn it.

"Yes, it is. I'm not willing to take any risks when it comes to my girls and their safety."

He sipped his tea and regarded her with steady eyes.

"There's one thing you haven't mentioned, Winnie."

Her breath caught, her mind beginning its all-too-familiar racing. What had she forgotten? How had she left the girls vulnerable? "What?"

"What do you do when you're lonely, Winnie? Who do *you* turn to?"

CHAPTER TWO

MAX EYED WINNIE as she clenched and unclenched her fists. He hadn't forgotten one nuance of her expression. He was going on pure instinct but he knew she was hiding something from him.

He supposed he should be relieved. The blast and resulting PTSD hadn't erased *all* his memory. Anything that had to with Winnie seemed to be etched on his brain. Probably on his heart, too, but he had enough soul-searching to do without adding her.

Max hadn't dared to hope anything would happen between him and Winnie again. But from the minute he saw her get out of her car, thoughts of having her back in his bed flashed across his mind. He swallowed a grin. For months he'd tried to fight off any kind of "flashes," especially flashbacks to the bombing. Now he'd love to relive one—of Winnie naked and begging him to push harder.

"You seem to be taking your time getting settled." She looked around the Spartan living room and nodded at the empty bookshelves.

He followed her gaze and smiled.

"I built them myself. Helped pass the time when I first got back and couldn't work full days yet. I just haven't gotten around to unpacking all of my books. They're still stacked in boxes, in the garage."

"I know you love your World War II history. It's hard to think of you without full bookshelves."

He felt a warm stab in his gut. Did he care that Winnie remembered something personal about him?

"I have an electronic reader and I tend to use that for straight history. But you're right, I miss my books. There's nothing like looking at photographs of vintage aircraft."

"I imagine you don't have too many extra hours, what with work. Are you back full-time, then?"

"No, not quite. I'm close, though. I just have to do this dog thing with you—or rather, Sam." Sam's ears pricked but he remained at Max's feet on the kitchen floor. "Hopefully my therapist will be satisfied that I'm ready to play like a big boy again and let me get back to a real job."

"This 'dog thing' can't be all that's keeping you from working full-time."

Same Winnie, same cut-the-bullshit attitude.

Instead of annoying him like they used to, her questions now seemed oddly comforting.

"No, it's not. You're right. I still have two more

weeks before I'll be released from the mandatory rest I had to take for my shrapnel wounds." Truth be told, he'd needed the two days off per week. Until about a month ago, he'd found the exhaustion the hardest part of all the injuries, physical and mental.

"Are you on meds?"

"Are you a medical doctor?" His reply cut across the unavoidable buildup of sexual tension between them.

"No. I'm sorry, Max." She did look sorry. And jumpy. When and why had she ever been jumpy around him?

She crossed her arms in front of her and stood in the middle of his living room. "We haven't, I haven't, we, um…"

"We haven't spoken in over two years." He finished it for her.

"No, and I don't know where to start, especially since—"

"The last time we were together we didn't have clothes on?"

Bingo. Red flush, bright eyes.

She's still attracted to you.

"About that—" she began.

"No, Winnie, stop. We don't have to go over any of this. It was two years ago, and like you said, we never spoke again. There's no sense in dredging it up now. But I am curious as to why you agreed to work with me. You must've known it was me before you came out here."

"Yes, of course I did." She raised her chin. "I thought it was the least I owed you after everything you did for Krista and me."

"You never have to thank me for that, Winnie. Tom was my friend."

"I know, and I know I thanked you back then and again two years ago." She paused. "But I can never thank you enough for all your help."

He held up his hand and fought the urge to come around the counter and gather her in his arms.

"It's over, Winnie. We're moving on. No more reliving all that history, okay?"

He saw her eyes cloud as she bit her bottom lip. He wanted to ease her obvious distress.

Old habits die hard.

She nodded. "You're right, Max. It's not fair to you, to either of us, to keep bringing up Tom and when he died."

Was this the same Winnie he knew? The woman who'd fought so hard for whatever she wanted from Tom, who'd all but ordered him to leave the Navy after his first tour?

He was reminded of why he'd been so attracted to Winnie two years ago; that night of the Air Show. He'd seen this quality in her then, recognizing the mature woman she'd been hiding under her younger, often self-centered, persona.

He drummed his fingers on the counter. "So that's that. Now tell me more about your new business and your life."

The relief in her expression was almost comical.

"I love the business I started. It's not really new anymore—heck, it's been almost four years and I've been turning a decent profit for the past eighteen months. Great considering the economy, you know?"

Her eyes widened as she regarded him and he couldn't keep his mouth from twitching.

"What, Max?"

"Winnie, we've known each other for how long—ten, twelve years?"

"Fifteen." Her answer was soft and swift.

"Okay, fifteen. I've seen you through your best days and your not-so-good days." He wouldn't say "worst," since they'd just agreed to keep Tom's death out of it. "The Winnie I used to know says 'hell' and doesn't make bullshit small-talk with her friends."

Her eyes narrowed and she bit her lower lip. A sensual memory of how he'd licked and sucked on that lip punched him in the gut.

"I—" she began, then shook her head. "I'm a mom now, Max. I don't swear in front of my girls."

There it was again. *Girls.* Plural. When had she become involved enough with anyone to have a child? Unless she'd been lying to him the last time he saw her, or had lied this morning, dating wasn't part of her life.

Maybe she has a friend with benefits.

He couldn't think about that, not now. Not when the woman he'd thought of all through the war sat there in front of him... He'd ask her who Maeve's father was some other time. Besides, she'd intimated that the man was no longer in her life.

"Fair enough. So how did you get started with canine therapy?"

Her eyes lit up and her face instantly looked ten years younger. The passionate Winnie he'd met when Tom brought her to the Navy Birthday Ball during their first tour on Whidbey Island was sitting in his kitchen. She tilted her head slightly to the left, eager to share her news with him.

"You remember my family and all their dogs? I grew up with dogs and always loved them."

"And Tom didn't. Not so much."

She hesitated, her mug halfway to her mouth. Damn it, he couldn't seem to stop talking about Tom. As though mentioning him would help keep Winnie at arm's length, safely out of his reach.

That didn't work the night of the Air Show.

He took a swig of his tea and waited.

"No, you're right. Not small dogs, anyway. Our first dog, well, *my* dog, Daisy, was that little Jack Russell, remember? She annoyed the heil out of

Tom because she'd ignore him unless I was out of the picture. Then she'd pee in his flight boots."

"I remember more than one sortie," Max said, referring to the Navy term for an operational or training flight, "where Tom bitched the whole way through about his wet boots. He knew that dog had got to them again, and it didn't matter where he hid them."

Winnie laughed and slapped her hand on the counter. "I forgot about that! One time he even put the boots on top of the bookcase—"

"But neglected to remove the smaller bookcase next to it. Daisy climbed up there like a cat and knocked the boots onto the floor."

"Where she—"

"Peed in them!" They spoke simultaneously and the unselfconsciousness of their shared laughter sideswiped Max.

Until their eyes met and he saw the depths of Winnie's pain and struggle of the past five years. There was joy, too, and something else he hadn't seen before. Something harder, older than he'd ever associated with Winnie.

Resignation? Bitterness?

"Well, back to my point." Winnie cupped her half-full mug and stared into it. "We had Daisy until two years after Tom died. Krista needed a pet. It was gut-wrenching to say goodbye to Daisy, in some ways harder than it'd been to say goodbye to her father." Winnie's hands stilled and she looked up at him.

"That sounds sacrilegious, doesn't it? But she was only seven when Tom died. Two years later she was so much more aware and so attached to that dog. Daisy was a living link to Tom. It killed both of us to put her down."

She sighed and shifted her gaze to the view outside his huge kitchen window. Her irises reflected the blue of Puget Sound and the shadows of the Cascades.

"My vet suggested getting a new dog right away. She'd been with us—with me—through everything, and she understood more than we did how a puppy would heal us. I thought I was off my rocker, and so did my family, but a couple of weeks after Daisy's death, Krista and I went to the animal shelter in Coupeville. We looked at all those dogs that needed a home and while we could have been happy with any of them, only one made an effort to get our attention and to keep licking our hands and faces."

She smiled down at the quiet German shepherd mix who lay beside Max's feet.

"I told you about him at the Air Show—" Her voice trailed off, and she must have assumed he didn't remember.

"I recall that you mentioned a new dog, but you didn't say anything about canine therapy."

"I'd just started to look into it. It's not something I would've been talking about at that point."

She didn't say it but he thought it—after they'd caught up on their three years apart they'd spent their time in his hotel room, and it hadn't been talking.

"I can't believe you got this purebred German shepherd from a *pound*. I know people who've paid thousands for purebreds."

Winnie laughed. The sound delighted him, like an unexpected gift. God, he'd missed her.

"Sam's no purebred. He's mostly German shepherd, sure, but his momma was a mixed-breed from Seattle."

"I didn't know you could find out lineage when you got a dog from a pound."

"You can get a DNA test done. But Sam was dropped off with a litter of pups that'd been brought to the shelter by a young woman who had a farm. She said the mother had been killed in a freak gun accident. This woman couldn't tend to the pups properly and manage her farm, so she brought them here, minus one pup she kept for herself. The mother had been her companion for six years and was a mixed breed. There was a purebred German shepherd guard dog from a local quarry who got out one night…"

"And they had love puppies," he said, grinning at his own joke.

"Pretty much, yeah. You'd think a farmer would know enough to fix her animals, but in this case, I'm glad she didn't. Sam is the best pet ever, and his talent for therapy work has made me wonder what happened to his littermates."

"Did they all get adopted out?"

"Yes, every last one of them, all on Whidbey. Whether they're still here or not, who knows?"

"So how did you find out he'd be good at this, uh, therapy?" He still had to fight a grimace as he said the word. As though not saying it would make him not need it.

As though the bombing had never happened and he was sitting across from Winnie whole and in control of his future. A future of Navy assignments and leadership instead of rehabilitation and retirement from the Navy, a lot sooner than he'd planned.

"Ever since he was tiny he seemed especially intuitive to my moods and Krista's. I've known a lot of dogs over my lifetime and I never met one that had such a knack for knowing whether you need a lick or a little nudge when you come through the door."

She smiled at him and he wished the smile was for him and not her dog. Still, he'd take what he could get.

"At first I took him to obedience classes with Krista. It was a family bonding time and it helped her with her self-esteem, which was shaky at best. That might have been due to my grieving and inability to bounce back from Tom's death as quickly as some people thought I should."

"Who thought you should have bounced back more quickly?" Maybe she'd never healed. Like him, maybe Winnie was forever affected by her loss.

"No one in particular, Max. It's just that after the first few months of understanding and compassion, people get worn out by the exhausting nature of grief. They mean well, but have to get with their lives. And they can—they're not the ones who lost a husband or father."

He heard no rancor or self-pity in her voice.

"The same people who claim they'll be there for you tend to fade away," she added. "That's been my experience."

At his silence he saw her hand jerk suddenly and her spine straighten.

"I don't mean *you*, Max! You were there through the worst of it and you left because of your job, not because you chose to."

He let her words hang there. He'd sought the assignment in Florida, unbeknownst to Winnie. He'd had to. It'd been time to move on. He'd needed a career change.

Still, looking at the situation through Winnie's

eyes, he saw that he'd faded away. He'd abandoned her and Krista.

"Winnie, I know it was a difficult time for you. I—"

"No, Max. Enough! You were there for me and you went above and beyond the call of duty. You are not who I'm talking about, period."

He didn't say anything else, simply allowed her to continue.

"So in an effort to continue the healing process, Krista and I went to more and more dog-training classes. Sam passed the basic Good Citizenship test from the American Kennel Club, and then I heard on National Public Radio that canine therapy was helping vets when they got back. The rest," she said with a flourish, "is history."

Max remained silent. He'd forgotten how much positive energy could be emitted by someone so enthusiastic about his or her vocation.

Bullshit. You've forgotten what it feels like to be around Winnie—to feel alive.

"You're the greatest, aren't you, boy?" Winnie cooed at Sam and the dog merely pricked his ears toward her. He still lay at Max's feet.

"How long did it take you to train him to behave like this?" He nodded at the dog.

Winnie's eyes widened. "Train him? Oh, no, Max, I didn't *train* him to do this. It's the intuitive streak I told you about. He knows who needs his comfort the most, and he knows when we're in 'work' mode. He's taken to you because he wants to, not because of anything I've done."

"So what does that mean?"

"What does it *mean?* I don't follow you."

"The fact that he's stuck to me like a barnacle ever since he jumped out of your car. Is he guarding you? Protecting you from me by keeping me in my place?"

Winnie leaned forward and placed her hands over Max's tense fingers. He involuntarily jumped at the awareness that shot up his forearms.

"Max, he's lying next to you because he senses you need him. And to be frank, judging by Sam's behavior, you're one of the neediest clients I've dealt with this year."

Her words slammed through him almost as quickly as his reaction to her touch. But they didn't elicit lust like her touch did. Instead, he felt only white-hot rage.

He pulled his hands out from under hers and shoved himself back from the table.

"F— Ah, shit, damn it!" He fought to control it, to control the cold stranglehold of fear.

He'd really wanted this meeting to go without a hitch.

CHAPTER THREE

WINNIE WATCHED THE cyclone of emotion twist Max's handsome face. The only thing recognizable as "Max" was the sharp hue of his eyes.

Crapola.

Big mistake. She'd thought that by putting the focus on Max and his work with Sam, she'd be able to push aside her reaction, the quaking that was a direct result of her attraction to Max. Wrong. Their physical chemistry still made her toes curl in her comfy shearling boots.

"Needy? So this is a *pity* call for you, Winnie?" Max snapped. She was almost surprised that spittle didn't shoot out of his mouth.

She sighed and grasped for the right thing to say. Like fired bullets, she couldn't retract her words or the damage they'd caused.

"I'm sorry, Max. I was speaking too freely. Sometimes my mouth isn't connected to my brain. I guess I'm still missing that filter you've always teased me about not having."

Her jibe at herself didn't work, either. He stayed silent, simmering with rage.

Pointing out their long-standing relationship and all its baggage—that was the stupidest comment she could have made. She needed to rely on their common bonds if she was going to salvage anything of their friendship once he knew about Maeve.

Double crapola.

He ran his fingers through his short hair. The same dark, straight hair Maeve had.

"Damn it, Winnie, I know I must still need some work or you wouldn't be sitting here in front of me—my doc wouldn't have suggested it. But I'm not *totally* mental. I've come a long way and what I've been through doesn't come close to what so many other vets are suffering. Hell, I feel guilty taking your time." His eyes shifted uneasily to Sam. "And this dog's time. There are a lot of sailors who need Sam more than I do."

"This is about *you,* Max. Sam sees plenty of other sailors, and there are other therapy dogs, too. You're not keeping him from anyone else." A white lie, as there was always another veteran in line, hoping to benefit from Sam's ministrations, but she needed Max to buy in to her rationale—and the value of her work—if it was going to help him at all.

"Why did you get involved with this, Winnie? You can't enjoy the constant reminder of Tom's death whenever you drive on base. For that matter, why did you stay in Whidbey this long? And why the *hell* did you agree to see me? Didn't you tell the social worker you already knew me?"

Take it easy. He's just angry at the situation, not you.

But his words hit home. They struck the part of her that she kept cordoned off from everyone. The Navy widow part. Where she hid the knowledge that she could never handle another trauma.

Still...she might have to. His anger wasn't personal yet, but when she told Max the secret she'd kept from him, his anger would be directed at her. He'd have every reason to accuse, convict and sentence her.

"You know why I stayed, Max. I love it here, my roots are here. I didn't want to move up to Anacortes, and I still don't. And I don't live in Oak Harbor anymore—I have a nice home in Coupeville, near my shop and office. If you saw where we live, you'd understand why I stayed."

"'*We*,' Winnie? Are you living with your daughter's father?"

"No, I already told you, I don't have a relationship with Maeve's father."

He didn't reply, but when she raised her eyes to meet his, she froze. He could look at her as no one else could.

He knows.

Dark spots floated in her vision and she realized she was holding her breath. She released it in a measured exhalation, trying not to let him see that she was distressed.

"I never took you for the casual-sex type, Winnie."

"Except after the Air Show two years ago?"

"We didn't have *casual* sex, Winnie. It was a surprise, a shock even, but not casual."

This is too close. He's going to ask, he's going to figure it out.

"Who says it was casual? Really, Max, at this point it's none of your business." Another lie, as Maeve was *completely* his business, but Winnie had to save that conversation for another time.

Drawing on what she'd learned during those first painful months after Tom's death, she looked for the next task she needed to do. She had to tell him about Maeve, but not at this moment. He was too stressed, too wound up. She couldn't risk putting him over the edge with his PTSD.

So now you're God? An expert at deciding when someone needs to know what is most definitely his business?

"Why don't we drop this, Max, and you and Sam go for a walk out on the paths?" She meant the myriad dirt walkways that snaked through the often-lush island vegetation. The water of Skagit Bay lapped against the rocky beaches and Mount

Baker stood off to the east, its aquamarine glacier visible on clear days.

She hoped that if Max and Sam went for a walk, the high emotion between her and Max would diffuse. Maybe she'd find the courage to do the right thing and tell him the truth, even if it was more than two years too late.

But Max wasn't finished with their conversation. His unhappiness was evident in his clenched fists, tight jaw and shallow breathing. She studied him and wondered how they were ever going to get past this tension.

Seconds later, he visibly relaxed his body by rolling his shoulders. He bowed his head, and she wondered if he was saying a prayer.

Max, a praying man?

She'd never met a pilot who wasn't a believer, but Max had never demonstrated a predisposition toward any particular religious faith.

He lifted his head, and his gaze rested on her, without the rancor she'd seen moments earlier.

"I'm sorry for acting out on you, Winnie. My control over my temper is still a work in progress, or so I'm told." His lips twitched and she thought he might smile, but it was obviously too much effort. He'd aged over the past two years; she saw it now in the resigned expression that made the lines on his face deeper than she recalled.

Max looked sad, she realized.

"It's fine, Max. Now let's get you out there with Sam."

"I move a bit slower than I used to. He's not going to pull me over, is he?"

She offered him her best smile. "Not if I can help it."

SHE WATCHED MAX LEAD Sam onto the path across the road from his driveway. They made an interesting pair, she had to admit. A tall warrior who moved with the gait of a man twenty years older than he was, flanked by seventy pounds of exuberant dog.

Sam could be trusted to stay close to Max and match his stride. It'd taken months of repetitive training, but she'd finally communicated to him the need not to pull, to allow whoever had his leash to be the alpha "dog."

Tears pricked at her lids and she turned her face up to the sky. She couldn't keep watching Max and Sam together or Max would come back to a puddle of tears.

The beauty of Sam's ability to relate to injured vets never ceased to move her. She often felt tears of pride and joy well up as the dog worked with a client, bringing out healing and survivor instincts that even the most highly trained therapists had been unable to reach.

But this wasn't just another client. It was Max,

and Max would forever be a part of her life. Not to mention Maeve's.

You have to tell him. Now.

CHAPTER FOUR

"HE NEVER ASKED how old Maeve is?"

Robyn's auburn curls sprang into her eyes and she brushed them away with an exasperated movement. Winnie sat with her sister on the sectional couch that occupied most of the family room in Robyn and Doug's traditional home in Anacortes.

"No." Winnie dug into her white container of Thai noodles and avoided eye contact with Robyn. Sam was curled up at her feet and she rubbed his belly with her toes.

Robyn was the only other person on earth who knew who Maeve's father was because Winnie trusted her, and Robyn hadn't let her down, which was a spectacular accomplishment considering the inquisitive nature of their family.

But Max's return to Winnie's life had put a knot in her stomach. Robyn had remained hands-off and kept her opinions to herself when Winnie had the baby and while Max wasn't in the picture. Now Robyn's impatience was reflected in her questions.

"I still don't get why you went over there *know-*

ing it was him if you weren't going to tell him about Maeve." Robyn fixed her with a stern look. "Which, by the way, you should've done two years ago."

Winnie stopped stroking Sam with her foot and swallowed a forkful of noodles whole.

"I know your opinion, Robyn. I don't need to hear it again. Don't you think I do a good enough job of beating myself up?"

When Robyn's mouth opened, Winnie held up her hand.

"I did go over there to tell him. And I *really* meant to. But then he started talking about things that upset him. He almost lost his temper and I sent him for a walk with Sam."

Sam's ears pricked up at the mention of his name.

She put down the container of noodles and leaned against the back of the red suede couch, pulling her knees up to her chest.

"I thought it would be easier to tell Max in his house, without Maeve there. I also want to be able to help him with Sam. I owe him."

"If you owe him anything, it's the truth. You're holding back the most valuable, important information of his life." Robyn's criticism chafed at Winnie's patience.

"He doesn't know that yet, Robyn. He was the best CACO at the worst of times. I'll always be grateful to him for what he did for Krista and me." In the aftermath of Tom's death, Max had taken on the duty of Command Assistant Casualty Officer. His duty had been to see her through every aspect of her new, unwanted status as a military widow. From the funeral arrangements to walking her across the chapel parking lot after the service to making sure she and Krista received all the survivor benefits due to them—Max did it all.

He'd also been Tom's best friend and had grieved for Tom more than anyone besides Winnie, Krista and his family.

"He got me through so much, Robyn. When I was acting crazy, trying to keep my mind off the pain. And when I found out he's the one who needs the canine therapy, I felt I had to return the favor." She paused. "No, that's not completely true, either. Ever since I found out he was back in Whidbey, I knew I had to tell him."

Winnie sent her sister a weak smile. Robyn's expression remained stern.

"I've completely blown this," she went on. "I would have, *should* have, told him I was pregnant, but he was on his way to war and I thought it'd be awful to contact him when I hadn't replied to his calls after the Air Show. His deployment was extended, and six months turned into nine. Then he got injured and was on the East Coast for rehab.

I couldn't tell him when he was going through so much, could I?"

"Of course you could have." Robyn could be so unyielding.

"I planned to go out there a few months ago, remember?" She'd decided to fly to D.C., find Max in the rehab center where he was spending his initial recovery period and tell him.

"Yes, I remember. But then you found out he was on his way back to Whidbey—it was in the paper. I've been here the whole time, Winnie. I haven't missed any of this." Robyn rolled her eyes. "You're taking the risk that he'll figure out about Maeve before you tell him. Then he'll *absolutely* never trust you again."

Winnie ignored the white-hot fear that pierced her gut, telling herself that Robyn had been the college drama major, after all.

"Don't be so melodramatic. I'm risking nothing. Okay, so Max might put two and two together. But will he want a future with us at all? With his daughter? Doubtful. As good a man as Max is, he's been a loner all these years. He's not going to change now."

"Are you really believing what you're saying, sis? We're talking about *Max*, the guy who would've given his left arm to keep you and Krista safe after the accident. Finding out you're a parent changes everyone, and Max *especially* would want to be part of his daughter's life. Plus, it'll take about a minute for Tom's family to come charging back in, looking for custody if they think that what you're doing isn't in Krista's best interests."

"They were acting out of grief. They're over it." Winnie's in-laws had initially suggested that Winnie and Krista move to Oklahoma after Tom's death, so they could be near their granddaughter. Never the most congenial of couples, they'd gone so far as to hint that there were legal steps they could take.

The Navy, namely Max, had come to her rescue again by ensuring that Winnie had complete legal custody of Krista. He'd made it clear to Tom's parents that Tom's wishes and Winnie's legal right was that she be the one to raise Krista.

Tom's parents had finally acquiesced, but not before implying that they'd pounce the moment they thought Winnie was doing anything harmful to Krista or to the memory of her father.

Winnie was grateful they'd calmed down once they realized that if they wanted to see Krista it would be at Winnie's discretion. They'd since had cordial visits together two or three times a year, either in Oklahoma or on Whidbey.

Robyn had never trusted them.

"They may have backed out, but they're lying in wait, honey, have no doubt. The minute they find out you're involved with someone else but not married, they'll ring their lawyer. You're lucky they never pressed the issue when Maeve was born."

True. Winnie knew the only reason Tom's parents hadn't made a fuss and hadn't tried to reopen their custody case was that they wanted to believe Maeve was their biological granddaughter, too. They'd picked up on Winnie's parents' theory that Tom had frozen sperm in case he died—always a risk with a military career.

Winnie had let them believe whatever they wanted. As long as it kept them off her back and out of court....

"Win, you need to tell Max. Maybe you should even consider stopping by his place again on the way home."

Winnie sighed and picked up her container of lemongrass chicken. "Don't worry about it, Robyn."

"Hey, you can't blame me for caring. Maeve's my niece. I'd die without her and Krista."

"As they would without you." Winnie and Robyn had grown so much closer through the aftermath of Tom's death, and Krista had bonded with Robyn as the safe, loving auntie. Maeve loved Robyn and her husband, Doug, but was more interested in the antics of cousin Brendan.

"So, are you going to do it?" Robyn's persistence was almost worse than sitting in Max's kitchen this morning, wanting to tell him, yet keeping her secret hidden.

"Do what?" She deliberately ignored her sister's urging.

"Come off it, Winnie! Are you going to stop at Max's on the way back?"

She put down her container. "No, not today. He's going to have Sam this weekend. That's soon enough, don't you think?"

"No, I don't. But you're going to do it your way no matter what I tell you." Robyn cocked her head, and Winnie heard her nephew's crying over the baby monitor.

"He's awake!" they both chimed in unison, then laughed.

"I'll say hi to the little guy and then I'll be going. Thanks for the lunchtime talk—I think." Winnie figured if she ignored Robyn's pointed looks, she'd be able to drive home without any temptation to stop at Max's home.

MAX GRUNTED AS HE BENCH-pressed half his weight. It still bugged him that he couldn't do as much as before, but he'd come far in the past few months. After the shock of losing his physical strength and fitness, he'd accepted what he had to do, even embraced it.

Work out harder than he ever had in his life.

He put the bar back in its notches and sat up, his

breathing labored and his heart pounding. Both were a comfort to him when he worked out, a familiar reaction.

Unlike the cold sweats that woke him and left him unable to catch his breath.

Yeah, he preferred a tough workout in the gym to his night terrors any day.

He used the gym's towel to wipe the sweat off his forehead before he lay back for another set. He raised and lowered the bar and, beyond that, focused on a small spot in the white tile ceiling.

A huge shadow obstructed his concentration.

"Boss!" The unmistakable voice of Chief Warrant Officer Miles Mikowski echoed through the weight room, and Max sat up. He offered Miles his hand.

"Warrant!"

Max was a Navy Commander, an officer, and Miles was former enlisted. The two of them were bound by a fellowship no one wanted to be part of—that of injured warriors. Max liked Miles because, like him, Miles was a survivor and still believed that he'd held the best job in the whole world as a U.S. Navy sailor.

"What are you doing, boss?" Miles looked at Max with one brow arched, his gaze raptor-sharp as usual. Max knew his friend didn't miss a thing, from his sweat-stained gray T-shirt to the amount of the weights on the bar.

"Weren't you in here yesterday, too, boss?"

"Yeah, but it wasn't enough. I needed to burn some more today."

Miles always called him "boss," even though he'd never worked for Max. It was a sign of respect that humbled Max. Miles had lost more than he had in the war.

"You should be doing cardio, boss. Too much lifting's not good, you know that." Miles might call him "boss" but Max heard the tone of an older brother in his voice. They were close to the same age—Max guessed that Miles was around thirty-eight, four years younger than he was. Miles had come into the Navy later in life, after college. But he hadn't originally sought a commission—since he'd wanted to become an expert in all aspects of Explosive Ordinance.

Miles and Max had gone through much of their reentry therapy together and they both knew that pushing too hard wasn't part of the combat recovery process.

Max was well aware that breaking down his muscles more than he needed to wasn't recommended by any medical professional. He knew the risks of wearing down his immune system. But he wasn't overdoing the weights, no matter what Miles thought. And even if he was, that was better than ending up with a panic attack over Winnie's reappearance in his life.

She's got another kid, for God's sake.

"I've got some extra steam to blow off. What are *you* doing here?" Max looked pointedly at Miles's weight belt. "You sure you put the right leg on?"

Miles gave him a wide grin and tapped his prosthesis. He'd lost his left leg on the same day Max had intercepted the suicide bomber. Also in Afghanistan, but Miles had been in a remote area conducting land-mine removal ops. The military medics were the best in the world but even they couldn't save a leg an IED had blown to bits.

"I'm trying this one out for the lab techs. The walking one is great, and the running leg lets me go for a good couple miles before I need to give it a rest. But I needed something sturdier for the weight room."

"You've got a bigger selection of legs than I do sunglasses, Miles." They smiled at each other. Miles had been Explosives Ordinance and Max an EA-6B pilot, but that didn't matter anymore. What mattered was that they were both still here.

If you tell yourself this every morning and click your heels together three times, maybe one day you'll believe it.

"What's got you worked up, boss?"

"Not going to drop it, are you, Warrant?"

"I wouldn't be a very good sailor if I let my

shipmate get away with doing the absolute worst thing for himself."

"There are worse things than overworking muscles."

"I'm not worried about your muscles, boss. It's your head I'm thinking about. What aren't you dealing with? More nightmares?"

Max sat up and looked across the weight room at the reflection of himself in the wall mirror. The image was familiar, but still fresh to him. It was the "new" Max, the one with more gray than brown in his hair and less body mass, as evidenced by the scrawny legs that straddled the bench. He'd never be as fit as he once was. Not just because of the war but because he was getting older. He wasn't twenty-five anymore.

Still, did forty-two have to *feel* so old?

"Nothing out of the ordinary. I did have a conversation with someone who knew me before." His voice cracked on *before* and he cleared his throat. "It's the first time I've seen her since I was, well, since before I went to war."

"How'd she act toward you?"

"Fine. No different, really."

"Can I ask, boss, is this a former girlfriend? A wife?"

Max forced a smile. "You know I've never been married. And Winnie, well, she's my best friend's widow. We lost Tom five years ago—EA-6B Prowler crash. I was the CACO."

Miles shook his head and let out a low whistle. "Sorry, boss. That sucks."

"It's part of our business, isn't it?" Max rubbed his chin. "It did look like there might be something between us a while back. But it was just a lark." Images of that Air Show weekend had been flashing across his mind ever since Winnie drove off with that dog.

"How long ago was that?"

"Ahh, let's see. That was the summer before I took the squadron on deployment, so…" His mind leaped onto an unexpected tangent with lightning speed.

No way.

"Boss, you okay?"

Not possible.

"Yeah, I'm…just figuring something out."

One of the condoms broke. Did you forget that?

Miles's strong hand wrapped around Max's upper arm. "Buddy, you sure as hell don't look okay."

How old is her daughter? What's the timeline?

"I think I've done it again, Miles. I've been shoving so much down—"

"And now your gut's spewing emotions everywhere, isn't it?"

Max couldn't help laughing. It eased the tightness in his chest, a tightness that had nothing to do with bench presses and everything to do with what Winnie had revealed to him.

And what she *hadn't* revealed.

"Yeah, you could say that." He wrapped his towel around his neck. "I'm good, Miles. Thanks for sitting with me. Now I've got to go burn this off in a healthier way. You're right about that."

"Anytime, boss, anytime."

Max walked out of the weight room with a feeling he hadn't had since before the suicide bomber leveled the spirit he'd taken for granted. He didn't have to report to anyone else, didn't have to ask what he needed to do. He knew his next move.

He was going to Winnie's. He'd get her address and if it was unlisted, he'd drive through Coupeville house by house if he had to.

Winnie had some explaining to do.

CHAPTER FIVE

"Stop it, Maeve, those are *my* chicken nuggets." Krista's tone resembled a mother's more than an older sister's as she chastised eighteen-month-old Maeve, who had a penchant for stealing food off her older sister's plate.

"Mine!" Maeve's baby voice was irresistible to Winnie but annoyed Krista.

"No, *these* are mine." Krista covered her plate with her hand and pointed with the other. "And *those* are yours, on your Fancy Nancy plate."

"No!" Maeve screeched the word and her lower lip jutted out in warning.

"Krista, knock it off. We use our dinner manners now. Right, Maeve?" Winnie fought to keep from smiling as she stared at Maeve.

Maeve's huge blue eyes reproached Winnie and, not for the first time, Winnie felt Max's presence reach out through his daughter's eyes.

You blew it today. You should've told him.

She had told him too much about her life— without telling him what she should have.

She tried to convince herself that she'd wanted

to avoid his questions until he wasn't so upset
That she thought it was better to wait.

That was all crapola and she knew it. Not only
was she betraying Max, but each day she kep
him from the truth, she kept Maeve from knowing her daddy.

Maeve.

Maeve needed her father, a father who wasn'
dead like Krista's. He'd survived a war, for God':
sake, and was living and breathing just a drive up
the road.

You are a class-A chicken.

"Maeve, don't look at Mommy like that. You
have to be a good girl and eat the food on your
own plate, not Krista's."

Maeve's expression reflected her inner-toddler
struggle. Winnie knew she was hungry, and the
cut-up chicken nuggets on her Fancy Nancy plate
were just as tasty as her sister's. But it was so
much *fun* to annoy Krista and to get her attention. Tears shimmered in Maeve's luminous eyes
and her chin worked frantically to keep her lower
lip in a pout.

No doubt due to Maeve's hunger, sanity pre-
vailed and she picked up a nugget from her own
plate and shoved it carefully in her mouth.

Winnie expelled her breath. It'd been a long afternoon with both girls arriving home in cranky
moods.

These days she was never sure who'd have the bigger fit after school—Maeve or Krista. At thirteen, Krista had started wearing a training bra this past summer and she'd shot up three inches since Christmas. She wore the same shoe size as Winnie, although Winnie didn't think that would be for long. Krista was going to be long and lean, as Tom had been.

Maeve, however, was Winnie's "mini-me," except for the shape and color of her eyes and her mop of straight brown hair—clearly inherited from Max.

He's going to know she's his the minute he sees her.

"Krista, how much homework do you have tonight?" Her voice shook and she knew that her anxiety wasn't going away. Not until she came clean with Max.

"I already told you when I came in, Mom. I finished it on the bus."

"Good." Krista probably had told her, but Winnie had been distracted since she walked through the door. Her thoughts had stayed in Dugualla Bay....

The same sense of inevitability she'd had once she'd started labor with each of the girls filled her stomach with dread. Now, just like then, there was no escaping the pain to come. No going back.

Then, it had meant the baby was on her way out; now it was the truth emerging.

With no guarantee of a happy outcome as far as Max was concerned.

Life doesn't come with a warranty.

She'd betrayed Max, the one person who'd seen her at her best and her worst, from her and Tom's life together, through the crash and then her short stint as a psycho-widow, when she'd tried to pick up an addiction. Any addiction—she hadn't been fussy.

Drinking, men, shopping, whatever would take "hold" she'd tried to cling to. But Max had stepped in before anything could consume her and tear her from her life with Krista. His words to her the night he'd dragged her out of an Oak Harbor bar and dumped her back in her house had ended her quest for self-destruction.

"You can abuse yourself all you want—the hurt will still be there, and Tom won't. He's not coming back, Winnie. You have a daughter to raise. This isn't the time to let Tom down."

He'd left her alone in her empty house. Her parents had taken Krista for the weekend, which was the pattern for the first several months after Tom died, to give Winnie a break and Krista time with other family. Instead of using those free hours to heal, Winnie had been hell-bent on dousing the firestorm of pain.

Max had saved her. Ultimately, he'd saved Krista, too.

He'd never mentioned that time again. Wouldn't comment on it if she brought it up, either.

Even today, when he was spitting angry at her stupid comment about his being a charity case, he hadn't reminded her of when *she'd* been in need of charity.

Of all the people to deceive, she'd picked Max.

Crap on a cracker.

"Okay, Krista, could you play with your sister for a few minutes while I get the dishes done?"

"C'mon, Maeve, do you want to play kitchen?" Krista expertly unsnapped Maeve from her booster seat and lifted her down to the hardwood floor. Maeve took off with a squeal, her bare feet slapping the oak planks.

"Slow down, Maeve," Winnie admonished while she cleared the table and took the plates to the sink. She looked through her garden window and sighed. The clouds were just as gray and the trees bent—almost as though they were doing yoga. The windstorm promised to continue all night.

The first time she heard a rapping out front, she thought it might be a branch. But the second time, Sam barked and she realized someone was at the door. She looked at the clock. They weren't used to visitors this late on a school night.

"Keep an eye on her, Krista." She glanced at the scene of domestic tranquility. Krista was helping Maeve make plastic pies and cakes in her toy microwave.

"I *am*, Mom." Krista's tone had changed overnight into that of a know-it-all teenager, and Winnie didn't like it one bit. She missed her easygoing daughter, who'd delighted in the simple things like baking cookies and fitting a jigsaw puzzle together.

Sam trotted to the door with her, but instead of his usual bark he stood still and wagged his tail. He gazed at the door with a look of expectation.

Winnie peered through the beveled glass and recognized the shape of a man. A man who immediately made her stomach tense.

She opened the door to a rush of wind—and Max.

"May I come in?" It wasn't really a question, since he'd already walked into her foyer and shut the door behind him. He wore a hoodie, and his T-shirt underneath was sweat-stained. His hair was damp and his eyes—oh, his eyes.

"Sam." She started to command Sam to remain in place but she didn't have to. He'd sat down and waited patiently for Max to acknowledge him with a pat.

"Come on in, I'll make us some tea." Winnie

spun on her heel and headed toward the kitchen in her stockinged feet. But Max was quicker.

His hand wrapped around her wrist. "Not yet. We need to talk."

Winnie looked down at her arm, and at his hand. In spite of her heightened anxiety, his touch elicited a warm throb of excitement. She dared to look up at Max's face.

His eyes blazed and his mouth was set in a straight line. The years seemed to fall away as she looked into his eyes.

"Of all people, you were one I thought I could trust."

She eased her body around to face him and leaned her back against the wall. She couldn't trust her legs. She willed herself to meet his eyes and to answer him truthfully. No matter what he asked.

"And now?"

"Where are the girls, Winnie?" He stared at her but not *at* her. He was obviously distracted by his inner demons.

"In the family room. But don't you think we should talk about this first?"

He gave her a look of derision and released her wrist. But he didn't move. She felt the nearness of his body, the scent that was uniquely Max. She remembered him like this from before, the night they'd made love.

And made a baby.

"Is there anything you'd like to tell me before I walk into that room, Winnie?"

She swallowed. "Apparently I don't have to."

He leaned in and she thought, maybe some part of her hoped, that he was going to kiss her. Erase the years, the trauma, all of it. With a kiss.

"What you've done is unforgivable, Winnie."

Shivers shot down her neck and spine as his breath swept across her ear, but the desire she'd felt fled as quickly as it had come.

He'd hate her forever.

MAX PUSHED BACK FROM the wall and strode down the hall, pausing at the entry to the family room. She heard the girls' voices in their singsong play and Maeve's giggles, which she saved for her time with Krista.

It was impossible to take her gaze off Max's profile. Max, the warrior, who stood on the threshold of his new life. Once he walked into that room and got a full look at Maeve, he'd know the truth.

That he was a father.

From her own experience, Winnie understood that when you became a parent, any previous presuppositions, ideas, intentions, were irrelevant. All that had mattered to her was her child. Max would be no different. It wasn't in him to do anything halfway, regardless of what she'd said to Robyn.

"Maeve, do you want to wash the dishes now?" Krista asked.

"Wheeee!" Maeve's accompanying giggle was infectious. Winnie usually laughed along with her baby girl, but all she could do now was watch the rise and fall of Max's chest. The way his nostrils flared and his hands rested on his hips. He was still in sweats and there was mud on his running shoes, as though he'd run here on foot from the Air Station gym, the soreness of his shrapnel-ridden body be damned.

The girls' chatter died at the same moment Winnie saw Max's lips move.

"Hello," he said.

Silence. Plastic falling on the play kitchen counter. Then Krista's voice.

"Uncle Max?"

She remembered him. She'd called her godfather "Uncle" from when she was a baby. But she hadn't seen him since she was seven, since Tom died. Winnie had wondered if Krista had forgotten him and Winnie never brought him up. She made it a rule not to bring up specifics about the time of the accident. If Krista wanted to talk, she did, and she asked questions as she needed to.

Their talks about Tom were daily and loving. But Max and the time right after the crash had never been discussed. Winnie figured the questions might eventually come, when Krista was older and mature enough to wonder about those days and months, to peel back the layers of memory and take a more detached look at the heartbroken little girl she'd been when her daddy died.

"Yeah, it's me, Uncle Max. Are you going to give me a hug?"

Winnie walked up to the threshold and did her best to smile at the girls.

"You recognized your Uncle Max! Do you remember him?"

"Of course, Mom. I just said hello to him, didn't I?" Krista muttered in teenage bemusement as she stepped forward and offered Max a hug. He embraced her, his eyes closed and his face impassive. He opened his eyes and held Krista by the shoulders as he studied her.

"You've grown a yard or two, Krista!" He smiled and Krista's face lit up while a blush crept over her cheeks. Other than her uncles and grandfather, she didn't get a whole lot of male attention. A bittersweet pang of regret hit Winnie as she thought about how much Tom would have loved Krista, how he would've been the one to light up her face like a Christmas tree.

"Thanks, Uncle Max."

"And who's this?" Max kept his hands on her shoulders as he looked past Krista toward Maeve, who kept playing with her plastic fruits and vegetables, oblivious.

"My sister, Maeve. Mom says she's our miracle baby."

"She sure is." Max walked farther into the room and knelt down in front of Maeve. Maeve paused, her thumb in her mouth and a plastic bunch of broccoli in her other hand. She stared at Max unblinking, as if she'd never seen a man before.

She's never seen her father *before.*

Winnie's throat constricted and she swallowed. This wasn't about *her,* it was about Max and Maeve. About Maeve meeting her father.

Her daddy.

"Hi, honey. How are you?" Max's voice was gentle in spite of its deep timbre. He was patient as he waited for Maeve to respond, and Winnie held her breath. She was acutely aware of Krista's sharp gaze on the pair, as well. Winnie stood still as Krista met her glance. Krista finally knew who Maeve's father was.

Maeve lifted up the plastic broccoli and Winnie's pride welled. Maeve was such a sweetie—she was going to give her toy to Max, a man she'd never met. But somewhere deep down, she must've known Max was her father.

"Noooo!" Maeve hurled the broccoli at Max, who didn't move. It hit him in the nose and he didn't wince, but from having been on the receiving end herself, Winnie knew it hurt.

"Whoa, sweetie-pie. It's okay, I don't like

strangers, either." Max stood and smiled at Krista. "She's tough like you, isn't she?"

Krista laughed. "Yeah, she's pretty crazy."

Winnie cleared her throat.

"Max, did you eat? I have some leftovers from dinner. I was just cleaning up."

"I'm not hungry. But I'll take a glass of water."

Winnie went to the kitchen and filled a plastic tumbler with water from the fridge. Her hands shook and she put the cup on the counter for a moment.

"Breathe," she whispered in the quiet kitchen.

"It's not so bad for *you,* trust me."

She whirled around and stared at him.

"Max, I don't know where to start."

"*When,* Winnie." He came toward her. "Not *where.* The question is *when* should you have started? How about the first time you missed your period after the Air Show?"

"I was in denial for weeks. Months. I couldn't believe I'd gotten pregnant after just one time— and with you."

"It was more than once, Winnie. Three or four times, if my memory serves." He continued to look at her with that unyielding glare. "It's not like we'd never met, like we were a one-night stand."

"But we'd never, we'd never—" Her hands gripped the counter behind her at the panic that threatened to stop her breathing.

"We'd never what, Winnie? Made love?" His palpable anger seemed to shake the air around them. "True, but speak for yourself. *You* never looked at me, saw *me* as more than Tom's friend."

"Of course not—"

"I *saw* you, Winnie. From that first happy hour at the O Club when we were J.O.s."

He couldn't be talking about the night they'd all met. She, Tom and Max. Could he? She'd been intimidated by Max and his silent presence from that first moment. Tom was affectionate, loving, respectful. He put up with what she knew now were her immature demands.

"You never liked me, Max, not from the start. You even tried to keep Tom from proposing to me."

"I didn't like the way you behaved, Winnie. The way you treated Tom, as if he was supposed to do what *you* wanted with no regard for what *he'd* worked so hard for. He was my best friend. Of course I was going to warn him if I thought he was making a mistake. But that doesn't mean I didn't find you attractive. It just wasn't ever an option."

They were inches apart. His gaze wasn't on her eyes anymore. His chest still heaved, his anger still simmered. But he stared at her lips and she felt his desire as if it were her own.

"But this isn't about me. It's about *you,* Winnie.

I have a child and you didn't tell me. How the hell am I supposed to take this?'"

"I'm so sorry, Max. I never meant to hurt you."

"Just as you never meant to hurt me by not returning any of my calls or emails after the Air Show? Weak, Winnie, even from you."

"I didn't want you to feel you owed me anything for that…that night." Of course, that was before she'd realized she was pregnant.

"That's not why I was calling you, Winnie."

His windbreaker rasped as he lifted his hand to her face and tilted up her chin with one finger.

Winnie looked into his face and prayed that her knees wouldn't buckle. His eyes, red-rimmed from anger and probably the wind, reflected something she never expected from Max once he learned about Maeve.

Interest. Desire.

"I wanted to be with you, and not just on that night." His gaze shifted to her lips again and she willed her defenses to kick in and push him back.

Instead, she met him halfway.

She felt the instant shock of recognition as the smoothness of his lips touched hers. His kiss ignited the fuse that always lay between them.

She knew she shouldn't be doing this, she should be concerned about the girls in the next room, somehow fighting this need to have his mouth on hers. Coherent thought wasn't an option with Max's tongue in her mouth and his hands wrapped around her head.

His hair was wet at his nape and she liked how the short strands rubbed against her palm. Her other hand was on his shoulder, but instead of pushing him away, she was holding on for her very sanity.

"Tell me you didn't miss this, Win," he whispered as they both sucked in air, then reached for each other again.

A verbal reply was impossible. Her self-loathing—for keeping Maeve's existence from him—came up against the hard fact that she was still incredibly attracted to Max.

Another thing to beat myself up for. Great.

She'd made a commitment to herself that she wouldn't bring another man into their family. At least not while the girls were so young. If she needed to date she would, but definitely not another Navy man. Not even Max.

Pulling away was what she had to do. But as long as she was kissing Max she didn't have to face *his* recriminations, either.

"Mom?"

Winnie broke free, stepped back from Max.

"Krista!" Winnie looked toward the open stairway and winced at the expression on Krista's face. Comprehension, incredulity and teenage disgust.

"Um, never mind." Krista fled from the hallway but not before Winnie saw the red flush on her pale face.

"Oh, crapola."

"That was so not cool." Max rubbed the back of his neck.

She let go of a shaky breath. "Understatement of the year."

She watched the emotions play across his face. Remorse, frustration, elation. He had been given the gift of a daughter tonight. A gift she'd kept from him for too long.

He looked at the floor, then shook his head.

"What?"

"'Crap' is right. This is not the way I want to start being in the girls' lives. I'll talk to Krista next time I see her."

"No, Max. I'm her mother, and I'll talk to her." She released another shaky breath.

"We can't do this again." She had to know he agreed with her on that. It couldn't be part of their new relationship.

"You're right, Winnie. Absolutely—this can't happen again."

"Momma?" Maeve had toddled into the kitchen. Krista had let her, no doubt in an effort to avoid getting totally grossed out for the second time in one evening.

"Honey girl, what do you need?" She bent down

and picked up her baby. Maeve nuzzled against her neck. "You're sleepy, aren't you?"

Max was still in the kitchen with them and his gaze unnerved her. She looked at him over Maeve's straight, dark hair. *His* hair.

"I have to put her to bed. You're welcome to stay until I get her down, but it usually takes a while."

"Mom, I can put Maeve down." Krista walked into the kitchen.

"That's okay, honey. Uncle Max is getting ready to go."

He turned his face away from them and took a long swallow of the water she'd poured for him. He emptied the tumbler, placed it in the sink and wiped his mouth with the back of his hand.

She could still feel the hot imprint of that hand....

"Your mom's right, Krista. I've got to get back." He turned and took a step toward them. They all stood there for a moment, unmoving, and their silence said what none of them could put into words.

Strange as it seemed, they were linked together now, in one way or another, whether they wanted to be or not.

"It's good to have you back, Uncle Max." Krista offered Max a shy smile, apparently still embarrassed by Winnie and Max's embrace.

Winnie felt her shoulders relax, even with the

weight of Maeve growing heavier as the baby fel
asleep against her.

"It's great to be back, Krista." Max opened hi
arms and Krista walked into his hug as thoug
it'd been a day since they'd last seen each othe
and not several years.

When they pulled apart, Max smiled down a
Krista. "We need to catch up, kiddo. Do you stil
like playing soccer?"

"Yes! Spring season starts this week." Krist
smiled at Max but kept her eyes averted. Winni
tried to ignore the panic that pummeled her chest

"I know, I'm one of the coaches. I get my tean
list tomorrow."

Max turned back toward Winnie. His face wa
calmer but the glint of anger in his eyes was jus
for her. "You'll still bring Sam by on Friday."

Her muscles snapped with tension and she tool
a deep breath. "Of course." It would be easier t
leave Sam there than to be too close to Max th
entire weekend.

"Bring the girls with you, too, if you can."

"Krista's in school until three. Do you wan
Sam earlier than that?" As if he knew he was th
subject of their conversation, Sam's ears perke
straight up as he lay on the braided rug next to th
stove. He'd followed Max to every room he wen
to. Winnie wanted to believe the dog was guard-

ing her and the girls, but Sam had cast his verdict on Max within minutes of meeting him.

Sam liked Max and trusted him.

"No, late afternoon is fine. Come by with the girls any time after three-thirty."

Why did Max think he could order her around like a sailor in his squadron? She knew she'd been in the wrong in keeping Maeve from him, but she didn't deserve to be talked to like a subordinate.

So why was she letting him get away with it?

Because you owe him.

Tears burned behind her lids but she would not allow them to fall in front of Max. "Fine. See you on Friday, then." She spoke around the lump in her throat.

"Bye, little one." Max ignored Winnie as he brushed Maeve's cheek with his index finger. His gaze lingered on his daughter's face before he turned and ruffled Krista's hair.

"See ya, Krista."

"Bye, Uncle Max." Krista's eyes shone and Winnie felt regret pull at her.

Max didn't say anything else as he walked down the hall and out the door. Sam's nails clicked on the hardwood as he ran to sentry position at the window. He whimpered for a few minutes. When he quieted down, Winnie knew Max had driven out of sight.

She hugged Maeve and closed her eyes.

"Isn't it great that Uncle Max is back, Mom?" Krista's voice was filled with awe. Max had that effect on women, no matter what their age.

"Sure, baby." She opened her eyes and stared at her older daughter. Krista's hopeful expectation was reflected on her face. Regardless of her own deepest fears and her reluctance, Winnie couldn't keep joy from either of her daughters.

"He's Maeve's dad, isn't he?"

"Yes, you've figured it out." Exhaustion washed over her but she stayed where she was, despite Maeve, warm and heavy, in her arms. Krista needed her here.

"So, are you two going to get married?"

"What? No, no! We're not getting married—or even dating. We've known each other for a long time, but we don't have—"

"The love you and Daddy had. I get it, Mom. But you were kissing him—why are you doing that if you're not hot for him?"

"Krista, where did you learn to talk like that?"

"Like what, Mom? Jeez, give me a break. I'm thirteen not three! I know people still like to kiss after they've had a baby. Or," she added with a wicked smile, "even if they haven't."

Winnie smiled back. She'd been about to say that she and Max didn't have any plans to be to-gether, that it wasn't meant to be for them. But maybe Krista's interruption was a blessing in disguise. A relationship with Max, another Navy man, was *not* a good idea. After a while, she'd see how they could all be family friends without Winnie and Max being a couple.

"Okay, Krista. Yes, you're right. Adults do have needs, even though that probably seems gross to you now. Someday you'll appreciate it."

Krista rolled her eyes and Winnie could almost hear her thoughts. *No way.*

That was fine for now. Let Krista think romance and physical intimacy were overrated.

CHAPTER SIX

WINNIE FIGURED SHE had two choices. One, despair over Max's involvement in her life. Two, feel despair, but get on with it. She no longer had complete parental control over Maeve, but Max wasn't going to upset the good life she'd made for herself and the girls. It was a life she'd learned to rely on. Her daughters and her fiber business filled each day.

At least she had a few more days until she had to face Max again. She felt as if she still hadn't caught her breath after her two charged encounters with Max on Monday.

Her wireless device in her ear, she spoke to her mother as she prepared to drive up to Oak Harbor, where they were meeting for lunch.

"Hi, Mom. I'll be up there in forty minutes. And I need to stop at a client's on the way up."

"Take your time. I'm having a blast in the garden shop at Walmart." Barb Perrin's voice, so like Winnie's, sounded blissful. Mom loved her plants.

"See you soon."

Sam's bark startled her, and Winnie realized she

was still in her world of Max, even while speaking to her mother.

"No, you can't go with me today. You'll be fine." She never made a big deal of leaving because Sam had had a serious bout of separation anxiety as a puppy. She'd crated him until he was almost eighteen months, for his own protection as well as her furniture's. He'd matured into a regal watchdog and companion, but he still acted jumpy when she went off without him.

"See you later, puppy boy." She threw on her coat, wrapped a paisley green scarf around her neck and went out the door. She reveled in the scent of cedar, fir and ocean. It was going to be a good day.

Maeve was in preschool until noon; after that, Winnie's friend Katrina would pick her up for a playdate with her daughter, Lily. Katrina was also a single mother but through divorce. Her Navy ex-husband had a fondness for naive younger women who were wowed by his uniform and didn't care if he was married or a father.

Katrina was bitter and an avowed man-hater but a loving mother to Lily. She and Winnie had become friends for pragmatic reasons—it wasn't a relationship of confidantes or one of meeting for coffee regularly, but they offered each other a break by taking turns with playdates.

Winnie was free until she had to pick Maeve up at three.

She made herself focus on the swooping bald eagles and farm animals she saw during her drive. She'd spent enough time thinking about Max and her self-blame for not telling him about Maeve.

Her cell phone rang but she ignored it, despite having her wireless earpiece on. She preferred to wait until she was parked. Winnie knew she tended to be overvigilant on safety issues but she couldn't risk even the tiniest slipup. She was all the girls had left. Well…not anymore. *Max is here.*

She parked in the lot in front of Applebee's, her mom's favorite lunch spot, and checked out who the caller had been. It was a new number. She returned the call, in case it was about one of the girls.

"Hello." A deep male voice.

Max.

"This is Winnie. Did you call?" Of course he'd called.

"Hi, Winnie. Can you meet me for coffee today? In Oak Harbor, if it's convenient for you. I'm in meetings at the base most of the day but I have an hour and I wanted a chance to talk to you alone before I see you and the girls on Friday."

"You get right to the point, don't you, Max?"

"I think I'm allowed to, Winnie."

Winnie didn't know if she hurt from old wounds

Max was opening or if they were new gashes. The self-recrimination she'd carried for keeping Maeve from him ballooned within her.

"Do you have time today?"

"Yes. I'm meeting my mother for lunch at Applebee's, but then I'll have about forty-five minutes before I should get back home."

"Where is Maeve?"

"She's at day care, and then my friend's picking her up for a playdate."

"Who's your friend?" The possessive note in his voice annoyed yet satisfied her motherly instincts.

"She's trustworthy, Max. Do you think I'd turn my daughter over to a freak?"

"No, but our daughter is my concern now, too."

What could she say to that?

"Winnie?"

"I'm here. I'll meet you at the coffeehouse by the theater at two."

"Two o'clock. Got it." He disconnected.

Sadness washed over her. It was no surprise that Max was angry; she'd expected it. The relationship they'd once had was severed, though, and that hurt more than she'd realized it would.

After Tom died, she'd learned to rely on Max as a good friend. She knew she could ask him for anything without any sense of "owing" him, but in her heart she'd be forever indebted to him. He'd never crossed the line of their friendship, never demanded more from her.

Of course she hadn't known that he'd seen her as anything other than Tom's widow at that point. No matter what he said about noticing her before, when she and Tom were just starting off as a couple.

She and Max had trusted each other. Even after that night of lovemaking, she'd known their friendship would always be there—if she wanted it to.

She'd destroyed it. Max would never trust her again.

Winnie pulled into the long drive that led up to Alexa Howard's alpaca and sheep farm. Alexa was one of the widows who'd lost her husband in the same crash that had killed Tom. She'd recently built a fiber mill in an old barn on her property—a cornerstone for Whidbey Fibers. At least with clients like Alexa, Winnie was able to completely be herself and enjoy her work. Right now, she needed to immerse herself in something other than worries about Max or her mother, if just for a few minutes, before she drove into Oak Habor.

"ROBYN SAID YOU were over on Monday." Barb stirred a sugar substitute into her iced tea while she kept her laser gaze firmly fixed on Winnie.

"Yeah, I had a half hour to spare after a

client appointment and you know we both love our Thai takeout."

"*I* was home."

"Sorry, Mom. Sometimes we need sister-only time, you know."

"It just seems like it's *always* sister-only time with you two."

Winnie hid her frustration by sipping her herbal tea. She loved island coffee as much as anyone but didn't need caffeine before her meeting with Max. She was on overdrive already. Mom wasn't helping her nerves any, either.

"How are the girls?" Barb sounded like she hadn't seen Krista and Maeve for eons when they'd all had dinner on Sunday. They met at Barb and Hugh's big water-view home every Sunday afternoon.

"Great." She deliberately left out any mention of Max as she relayed the events of the past two days to her mother, detail by detail.

"Maeve is so much more like you every day. Krista's got Tom's common sense and steady balance in her approach to life. But Maeve, she's a firecracker!"

Winnie laughed. "Yes, she is."

"Are you still glad you did it, Winnie?"

"Mom!" They'd been over this time and again. She wasn't going to give her mother the information on Maeve's father until she was ready to.

"I have a right to know, Winnie. Maeve is my granddaughter, too."

"Mom, please—does it always have to be about you?" Tears sprang up. Tears of frustration and anger that she'd never shed in front of her mother rolled down her cheeks before she could swipe at them with her napkin.

"I'm sorry, honey, I didn't mean to upset you."

Of course you did.

"Don't worry about it, Mom."

Barb didn't respond but picked up her fork and dug into her Penn Cove mussel salad.

Winnie took several shaky breaths and tried to focus on her fish chowder but it was useless. Her appetite was gone.

"Your brothers will both be here this weekend. They finagled some time off and are coming home to see us on Sunday. Isn't that great?"

Her brothers were both studying medicine in the Washington D.C. area.

"Yes, Mom."

BARB REMINDED WINNIE about Sunday dinner before giving her a quick hug and drove off in her Mini Cooper.

Winnie loved her family and knew she owed them more than she'd told them about Maeve, but the girls needed some boundaries and Winnie was the one to enforce them. After having all her emotions exposed to the world after Tom died, she'd desperately craved privacy. Anyway, Barb would know who Maeve's father was soon enough. She wanted—no, *needed*—to tell Max first. It was the least she owed him.

She'd never seen herself as a victim, not after the initial period of grief and shock. So she hadn't indulged in any "poor me" thoughts after Tom died. But she had to admit, if just to herself in this windy parking lot, that keeping Maeve's father's identity from everyone, including Max—especially Max—was perhaps the most self-centered thing she'd ever done.

Max could have died in Afghanistan and never known he'd been a father. Never seen Maeve's eyes, identical to his, stare back at him.

At the time, she hadn't had a choice. She couldn't risk Max's life by letting him know something so fundamentally life-changing when he was in the middle of fighting for his life, for the squadron's safety.

She'd made that fatal mistake with Tom.

Max had been injured, anyhow, despite the care she'd taken not to confuse him with such shocking news.

You couldn't stop it from happening.

Short of putting on running shorts and shoes, Winnie did the only thing that could ease her pain. She walked toward the beach.

Although the wind bit at the tips of her ears and neck, by the time she reached City Beach the water was calm and tranquil. On the eastern side of the island, it was as smooth as glass compared to the side that took in the wind as it swept through the Strait of Juan de Fuca. She sat on a hollow log washed up from the storm surge. Ducks splashed about in the shallow shore waters while cormorants dove for their lunch just yards away, where the water was cold and deep.

Sam usually accompanied her on her trips to the beach and she longed for the distraction of playing fetch with his floatable ball.

Distraction.

That was her motto for the years after Tom's death and then again after Maeve was born. She had no regrets about the girls and the way she was raising them. While building a solvent business and developing her community volunteerism as a canine-therapy handler she'd enjoyed each minute she could with her kids.

Maeve was only eighteen months old; she'd grow up thinking she'd always known her father.

Krista was more fragile. She needed time. She'd been furious and downright disgusted when she'd caught them kissing in the kitchen. Yet she loved Max and appeared to take the fact that he was Maeve's father in stride.

Winnie kicked at rocks on the beach with the

toe of her leather boots. It was almost too warm out here with the sunshine and shelter from the harsh breeze. She turned back. She had to walk over to the coffee shop and Max.

MAX GOT THROUGH HIS business with the base support staff with only a few minutes to spare until his meeting with Winnie. He worked three days per week as the Administrative Support Officer for the base. Full-time was in his near future— he just needed a final approval from his therapist and his assigned Flight Surgeon.

He felt crushed that as a senior Navy Commander on active duty, he had to get medical clearance for every damned step he took. No one trusted *his* judgment that he was ready for full-time.

He made it to the coffee shop in record time and pulled his Jeep Cherokee into the sole empty parking spot in front. Even though Oak Harbor was a small town, its favorite places stayed busy all day, every day.

When he entered the shop, the bell that hung on the door tinkled next to his ear. His gaze homed in on Winnie immediately. She sat straight-backed in one of the cozy booths, studying the menu. He knew better. She was trying to give him the impression that she was oblivious to him.

He looped his khaki uniform cover—*hat* to a

civilian—under his belt and walked over to the table. She raised her head with that stupid pretend-blank look on her face.

"Oh. Hi, Max."

"Winnie." He slid into the seat opposite her.

"What can I get you folks?" A college-age girl with multiple facial piercings stood, hands on hips, waiting for their order.

"Winnie?"

"I'll have an Americano, cream on the side."

"Same, but black."

"Be just a minute." The girl turned and went back to the espresso bar.

Max studied Winnie for a long moment. Her blond hair was curly as always and she had it styled in a sexy cut that framed her face. A few stray curls, however, sprang out from behind her ears. Her white blouse hinted at cleavage with the buttons just a tad too tight across her breasts.

He remembered how full and soft they'd been under his palms. He'd sworn her skin glowed in the pearl moonlight of the hotel room where they'd spent that night.

"What?" Her impatient tone reminded him that he had no business thinking of Winnie as a lover anymore. How could he ever make love to the woman who'd kept his child from him for nearly two years? He'd never even seen her pregnant, her belly swollen with his baby.

No, Winnie was not an option as a lover.

You'll never be able to trust her.

He'd have to live with his body's conflicted feelings about that.

"I'm still trying to process why you kept this from me for so long. I know we lost touch, and that's my fault. I should've kept calling you after the Air Show, should've come back here to see you."

"It wouldn't have mattered, Max."

"What do you mean 'it wouldn't have mattered'? I would've gone to war knowing I had a daughter to come back to!" He leaned back from the table and gazed out on the parking lot. He was using every tool he'd learned over the past six months in therapy and rehab to keep his emotions in check and stay focused on what really counted.

Maeve. Krista.

"I would never have told you before you went to war, Max. You didn't need the distraction."

"Still playing God, Winnie?"

Her eyes widened and the familiar red crept up her neck. He'd hit his target.

The jolt of satisfaction he'd anticipated didn't occur.

"Look, let me start over." He put his hands back on the table.

"After our night together, I felt that maybe we'd rocked our worlds a bit too much, and the last

thing I wanted to do was pressure you into mor
than what we'd had that night. I was at the end o
deployment workups and ready to take off for A
ghanistan for the first time. I didn't think it'd b
fair to you or Krista to push you for more."

She eyed him with a measured look that h
wasn't used to seeing from her. The look of
wise woman, not the girl he'd met all those year
ago in the O Club.

"What, Winnie? Tell me."

The waitress brought their coffee and he grate
fully wrapped his hands around his mug. He didn'
care if it burned his palms.

Winnie offered him a half smile.

"I think it's clear that I'm the one who's don
the screwing up around here." Her voice wasn'
full of self-pity but regret. He saw the wistfu
glimmer in her eyes.

"I told you I'd denied the pregnancy as long
as I could. But when the second month went by
I bought a home pregnancy test kit." She waved
her right hand and looked at him.

He nodded.

"I still thought it was some kind of mistake
I mean, we'd used protection and only had tha
one…problem." She didn't say that one of the con
doms had broken in the middle of the night. The
both knew it. "I wasn't even ovulating then, fo

heaven's sake. I really believed we were in the clear."

"You told me we were. I assumed you meant you were on the Pill. The condoms were for safe sex more than birth control, I thought."

"The Pill? No, I stopped taking it years ago. Tom and I had been trying to get pregnant—" Her mouth clamped shut. He hated that the ease between them was gone. Had been since the night he'd decided to go to bed with her.

Looking back, he would've expected to wish they hadn't made love, hadn't ruined their friendship. But that had been one hell of a night, and it'd produced what he felt was going to be his greatest accomplishment. His child. His baby daughter.

Their baby.

"I'm not going to pussyfoot around this, Winnie. You didn't tell me about Maeve, which, as I expressed last night, is unforgivable. It will no doubt forever be a wedge between us. But the one thing that matters more than anything that's passed between us is Maeve. Maeve is my daughter and I have every intention of being a father to her."

"And I have every intention of helping you make that happen. You're going too fast, though. Relationships take time to build. Just because I messed up by not telling you doesn't mean we should rush things. The girls need to be eased into this, especially Krista."

"I don't plan to come in like a bulldozer, Winnie. Give me a break, will you? Of course I'll include Krista in everything with Maeve. It occurred to me that she hasn't had much of a father figure, has she? Your brothers are scattered all over and your sister's husband is probably too busy with his own child. There's your dad, of course, her grandfather, but—"

"How do you know about Robyn's son?"

"I may have not have seen you since I got back, Winnie, but I do have eyes and ears in my head. Word gets around on this island as quickly as it ever did." He glanced at her.

"I'm surprised I didn't hear about your baby."

Her dumbstruck look made him want to hug her discomfort away and he almost swore out loud at himself. Damn it all, she'd held back the most important information of his life!

Deliberately.

Yet as he sat across from her, he felt—along with the anger—an intense desire to go to bed with her again. Had his PTSD taken away his pride?

He ignored that thought. From the feelings that looking at his daughter had stirred in him last night he was doing A-OK in the emotions department.

"I just heard about Robyn and Doug through the grapevine." He paused, then added, "However, I didn't hear anything about you. And Maeve."

"Oh." She blinked. Her chest rose and fell as though she was taking deep breaths before swimming the length of a pool underwater. Her face shone with perspiration and the color of her skin matched her white blouse.

Her guilt is not your problem.

"Look, Max, like I said, I've screwed up horribly. I don't just mean in not telling you about Maeve, but also with the dog-therapy program. I understand that you've lost your trust in me and I'll withdraw my name as your canine handler. There are other therapy teams at the base and any one of them would be able to help you."

"Whoa. I never said anything about that. I know I still need to check the canine-therapy box and I will. With Sam." At her mewl of protest he pushed harder. "You can't abandon me on this one, Winnie. I don't want to do any more therapy as it is. But I've got to show my therapist I'm willing to stay with it, keep improving. I'm finally close to getting back to work full-time."

He knew he'd reached her when she looked down at her cup of coffee and then back at him, her eyes moist. "Okay, I suppose it's the least I owe you. But the girls—Maeve—aren't part of the therapy package, Max. If you want to get to know them and spend time with them, we'll have to figure out something else."

I already have.

"Fine. We can talk about it on Friday when you bring Sam over for the weekend."

"I've been thinking about that, Max. I don't want to bring the girls. It's not right for them to be mixed up in your work with Sam."

"Point taken. The girls shouldn't be there when we're working together. But as for bringing them when you drop Sam off—I don't see the harm in that, Winnie. He's their dog, too."

He looked at his watch and then back at her. "I've got to go, and you do, too, don't you?"

She gasped when she looked at her own watch. "I had no idea it'd gotten so late! I don't like Krista being alone for more than a few minutes. I've got to go." She stood so fast that she knocked over her empty coffee mug with her scarf. She reached into her purse and pulled out a bill.

"No, it's on me. I called the meeting." He closed his hand around hers, folding the bill back into her palm. Her skin was as soft as ever and her hand jerked in his.

Whether her reaction was caused by anxiety over needing to get to her girls or any remaining attraction she felt toward him, he didn't know.

I can't afford to care enough to find out. This is the woman who betrayed me.

She tried to smile but it looked more like a grimace. Still, her face was stunning. Even through his rage at having the truth kept from him, he saw her beauty.

"Thanks, Max."

"See you Friday." He watched her hustle out of the shop and hurry toward the station wagon she'd driven up to his house in.

They were going to see each other a lot sooner than Friday, but he'd let her find out on her own. She wasn't the only one who could hold her cards close.

CHAPTER SEVEN

KRISTA LACED UP her soccer cleats and put on her shin guards. She loved soccer and she loved the mud of the new season. Her dream was to make the travel team, but so far her dream always ended at the local tournaments. Just once she'd like to be on an important team....

"Krista, will you get me Maeve's diaper bag, please? I left it in her room."

"Okay, Mom!" she yelled back. Then she went into Maeve's pink room to retrieve the flowered bag. She liked helping with her baby sister and loved Maeve like crazy but sometimes she just wanted to be the only kid again.

She looked around her sister's room and saw the bag in the far corner. Grabbing it, she headed back downstairs to go to soccer practice.

"Do you have your headbands?" Mom didn't even glance at her as she changed Maeve's diaper on the sofa. One of Maeve's favorite cartoons was on TV and Maeve was hypnotized by the sing-songy graphic characters.

Had *she* ever been so easily amused? She doubted it.

"Yes, Mom, and you're welcome for the diaper bag." The words shot out of her mouth faster than she'd meant, and she knew from Mom's wrinkled forehead that she'd messed up.

"Watch the tone with me, Krista."

"Sorry, Mom." She wanted to try to explain why her mouth ran away with her, but she didn't know why. Just like she didn't get why her mother was acting so ridiculous lately. She'd acted like a jerk in front of Uncle Max, which was strange. If anything, Mom was usually too friendly to everyone. And she hadn't been paying attention to Krista at dinner the past few nights. Krista wasn't stupid; she could tell if Mom was listening or just doing the "yeah," "oh, really?" and "that's super, sweetheart!" routine.

Mom finished with Maeve's diaper and pulled her tiny sweats over her rump. Maeve's feet hit the ground and she squealed happily when she saw Krista.

"Hey, little sista!" Krista ran her fingers through Maeve's cornsilk hair, while Maeve wrapped both tiny arms around her leg. Krista thought Maeve was the cutest little creature on the planet. She didn't tell Mom this, though. She still liked getting attention as the Older Sister Who Sacrificed For the Family.

"Let's go, then! Did you have something to eat?"

"I already had a banana. There's still juice boxes in the car."

"Okay. We'll have the chili when we get back." Mom threw on her green coat and Krista wished she'd buy herself a new, more stylish coat like other moms had. They weren't poor, and Mom could be really pretty if she took the time to put on some makeup and buy some nicer clothes.

They hurried out the door, Maeve's hand in Krista's, and Krista felt a surge of excitement at the new soccer season race through her.

They chatted on the drive to the field as the sun slanted bright rays across the road. Krista loved this time of year and enjoyed her rides in the car with Mom. She vaguely remembered her dad being with them when she played on the younger teams, but most of her memories of him were like dreams now. She missed his hugs and the way he smelled, but didn't feel any kind of major sadness when she thought about him. The only time she felt sad was when she saw Mom get sad. Which wasn't too much anymore.

Mom had been cranky and stressed since Uncle Max came over the other night. And ugh, the kiss. She hated remembering it. Talk about *awkward*.

Maeve's dad was Uncle Max. Krista wasn't sure how she felt about that. It was a relief to know that Mom hadn't had sex with some random stranger—*gross*—and she was glad to finally learn the Big Secret Mom had kept from her.

She wasn't naive; she watched TV and knew that grown-ups didn't have to get married or live together just to have sex. There was a little part of her that wished she was young and naive again so she could at least pretend Mom and Uncle Max could get together and give them a real family again.

She squirmed in the backseat of the car. She knew what Mom and Uncle Max's kiss meant. They still wanted to have sex. With each other. Disgusting. *So* not cool.

They pulled up to the grassy landing and Mom drove the car over the mucky parking lot. It would be hard and dry by the end of soccer season, but right now it was icky. Krista hoped she didn't lose her cleats in the mud like she had last year.

"Oh, Mom, did you bring the soccer packet that came in the mail last week? It's got all the forms you need to sign."

"Oh, no, honey, I thought you had it in your soccer bag." Mom turned to scan the back of the car. "I guess I forgot it…." She sighed. "Just ask your coach for a new one and I'll sign it tonight."

"But I don't know who my coach is."

"It's probably Coach Ted again, isn't it?" Mom had that distracted look on her face.

"I don't *know,* Mom. I've had a different coach every season for the past three years. They don't tell us who it is until the first practice."

"Don't worry, okay? They'll announce the teams. If you don't hear your name, just go ask one of the coaches. They'll be able to help you."

Krista wanted to scream. "Can't you come with me?"

"Maeve and I will be in the car for a bit—it's too cold and raw for her to be out there the entire practice. If you need me I'm here, okay?"

"Okay, Mom." Krista opened the door and climbed out.

"Wait! Did you remember your water bottle?"

"Yes, Mom, I've got it."

She slammed the door shut and pulled her hoodie up over her head. The wind smarted her eyes, but her sweatshirt was warm and cozy and her pants were the windbreaker kind. She saw where the girls were lining up and went to join her teammates from last season.

"Listen for your name and then go to the coach who calls it." One of the volunteer mothers used a megaphone to announce the procedure. At least Mom had been right about this; she'd find out who her coach was without any trouble.

Krista waited with Holly and Meg, her friends from soccer and school. Two teams had already been picked when a familiar figure walked up and took the megaphone.

"Hey, I think we'll all be on the same team again!" Holly's teeth chattered as she jumped up and down.

"Yeah, we're the only ones left in our age group." Meg stood still, the more serious of the three of them. She played goalie.

"I know him!" Krista's words came out of her mouth before she had time to process it.

Uncle Max had said he was coaching!

"Who?" Meg's question went unanswered as all three girls were called to line up behind their new coach.

Krista looked closely as she walked by him, to make sure. He caught her stare.

"Welcome to the team, Krista." He smiled at her.

Uncle Max was her soccer coach! This was going to be the best season yet.

Wait until she told Mom!

"DO YOU WANT TO READ a book together?" Winnie's options with Maeve grew fewer, since they'd already played peek-a-boo, done a wooden shape puzzle and listened to some children's music. She'd have to bundle both of them up and go out into the chill wind.

She couldn't see the selection process from

where she'd parked, due to the snack shack blocking her view, but now she saw that the girls were all headed out to separate fields. There was Krista, easy to spot in her neon green hoodie. She was walking with a couple of other girls Winnie hoped were Meg and Holly from last season. The three girls were tight, and she remembered how much it had meant to her at that same age to compete on the same team with her buddies.

The tall man leading them didn't look like any of the previous coaches she remembered.

But his gait, his posture, his profile even from this distance, were not unfamiliar to her. Her initial hunch when she read the news article about Max coaching soccer was right. He was Krista's coach. Why the hell hadn't he mentioned it this afternoon?

"Crap! Are you *kidding* me?"

Didn't he have shrapnel wounds? And how good was this for his PTSD? What if one of the girls got hurt? Would that catapult his mind back to the war zone?

That's not what's really bothering you about Max coaching Krista.

"Crap! Crap, Mommy!"

"Oh, sh— I mean, shoot, Maeve baby. We don't say that word, okay?"

"Crap, crap, crap." Maeve chimed the word over and over as if she'd found a new toy. Winnie put a woolen hat on her tiny head and tied it under her chin. She knew she had to ignore Maeve's chant or her use of the word would only be reinforced.

"C'mon, baby girl. Let's go see your sister play."

"Krista! Wheeee!" Maeve wriggled in her arms until Winnie cleared the parking lot and set her down on the wet field grass.

They walked together in the dimming light, Winnie's head bent against the wind and Maeve bouncing beside her. Winnie wished she was wearing a hoodie so that Max wouldn't be able to see her expression.

She needn't have worried. When they reached the sidelines Max was in full coaching mode, showing the girls which drills to do and giving constant feedback on their form.

Winnie breathed slowly, the way she'd learned early on after Tom died. Deep breaths helped keep her panic down to a minimum.

Max wanted to know Maeve better but didn't want to leave Krista out; she got that. And the soccer field was fine with her. It was a chance for Max to spend quality time with Krista and get to know her on her turf, so to speak.

So why didn't he tell me this when we met for coffee?

She swung Maeve up in the air and laughed with her baby girl. As she lowered Maeve and straightened, her gaze landed on Krista's face. The girl was raptly focused on her coach.

Max.

This is too fast.

"Crap, crap, *crap,* Mommy!" Maeve screamed at the top of her lungs as she ran back toward Winnie.

"My thoughts exactly, honey girl."

AT THE END OF THE NINETY minutes, Coach Max called them together and told them all to practice their drills at home if they could. "Even if it's only for five minutes after school. The player who knows her skills makes the winning moves."

Krista had never had such an awesome practice. It was great to be back out on the field and *so cool* that Uncle Max was her coach.

He dismissed the team and when she jogged past him she said, "Thanks, Coach," and he stopped her. "Good job, Krista. Are you okay with me being your coach?"

"Yes, it's fine."

"Great. I'll always be your Uncle Max, but on the field I'm Coach."

"Sure, Coach! See you next practice." She turned to run to the car but saw her mom and Maeve a few yards away. Mom had that frown on her face again. The one she had whenever Krista did something to disappoint her. But she wasn't mad at Krista; she was staring at Uncle Max.

Time to disappear.

"Mom, can I have the car keys? I want to start doing my homework."

Mom removed the keys out of her sweatshirt pocket and handed them over. "Please don't turn on the radio. It'll drain the battery."

"I have my music with me."

Before she could get to the car, though, Uncle Max walked over to Mom. Maeve wriggled in Mom's arms so much that Mom let her slide down her leg. Maeve saw Krista and made a beeline for her.

"Hi, baby sis. Are you having fun?"

"Crap! Crap, crap, crap!"

Krista giggled. "Where did you learn that?"

She turned toward Mom to tell her, but Mom was already talking to Uncle Max. The look on Mom's face was so stern Krista wanted to tell her to chill. Couldn't Mom see that her bossy ways were going to scare off Uncle Max like they had Meg's dad?

Meg's dad was so nice. His wife had left the family when Meg was little, right around the time Dad died. He'd tried to be friends with Mom, but Mom would only allow Krista to be friends with Meg. She didn't want to "encourage" Mr. Norton, she'd told Krista in private. Krista and Meg had dreamed about being real sisters, dreamed about their parents falling in love, but it hadn't happened. Then Mom had Maeve, and Mr. Norton didn't even try to be her friend anymore.

"I don't need your permission to become a community soccer coach, Winnie."

"Of course, you don't. You could've told me you were coaching Krista, though. You sat across the table from me yesterday and never said a damn word about it!" The wind made Mom's words hard to hear but Krista saw the expression on her face. She was really pissed off. She'd be pissed off if she knew Krista ever said "pissed off," too.

Now Uncle Max was talking, but his voice was so much lower than Mom's Krista couldn't figure out what he was saying. She couldn't see his face because he had his back to her.

"Hungee!" Maeve pulled on Krista's hoodie string and Krista grabbed the opposite end just in time, before it disappeared and she'd have to use a safety pin to get it out again.

"Okay, okay. Stop pulling on my string, okay?" Maeve answered with a wail.

"Mom!" Krista did her best to shout over the wind and Mom and Uncle Max's conversation.

They both turned and looked at her like she had three heads. Jeez, couldn't a girl get her mom's attention without getting everybody upset?

"What?" Mom's eyes were wide and her hair

was blowing all over, making her look crazy. Krista's gut told her that Mom was feeling a little crazy at the moment, too.

"Maeve's hungry. We both are."

Krista braced herself for her mom's wrath, but instead her expression relaxed. Was Mom relieved?

"Sure, honey. Go to the car and I'll be right there."

Krista turned to head off, but was stopped by Uncle Max's voice. She turned back.

"I meant what I said, Krista. Good effort out there today."

"Thanks, Uncle Max." She put Maeve down and held on to her little hand.

"C'mon, Maeve, let's race to the car!"

Maeve answered with a squeal and started to run on her toes. Krista pretended to run with her and they made their way to the car.

Krista glanced over her shoulder once, halfway to the parking lot. Mom and Uncle Max were no longer talking and Mom was walking toward them. She couldn't see Mom's expression but something told her it wasn't a happy one. She wasn't sure why, but for some reason Mom wasn't thrilled about having Uncle Max around.

CHAPTER EIGHT

MAX HAD SEEN WINNIE in every kind of situation. Or so he'd thought. But he'd never witnessed the instinctive, primal force that every mother held deep in her heart. No one ever saw it unless that mother's child was threatened.

Winnie had changed a lot from the grief-stricken widow he'd stood next to five years ago, not to mention the young bride she'd been ten years before that. Her control-freak ways hadn't changed much, though. He knew he could've told her that he'd volunteered to coach Krista's team when they'd had coffee.... He hadn't because he'd wanted to keep the focus of their conversation on Maeve.

He was still trying to control the intense betrayal he felt at her withholding his own daughter from him. But his attraction to Winnie was only growing stronger, regardless of what she'd done. His desire for her was really starting to get on his nerves.

He supposed he hadn't told her about the coaching position in an effort to control at least one damn thing in his life.

Winnie wanted to fight him on it, but her guilt wouldn't let her and he was taking advantage of that.

"Too damn bad, Winnie," he murmured to himself on the drive in to work the next morning. Fog clung to the road and he had to be careful around the bends. As familiar as the route was to him, nothing was a given with the ground fog rolling in off the sound.

She'd caught his eye the moment he'd met her, more than fifteen years ago. He'd never told her. What would've been the point? She and Tom made the perfect couple—and, truth be told, Max hadn't been ready to settle down back then. His priorities had been typical for a young pilot. They'd been all about himself and what was in it for him.

But if he'd pursued Winnie he would have destroyed his friendship with Tom. It was a no-go from the start. You don't betray your shipmate. Winnie had fallen for Tom, and he for her, and that was that.

Besides, if he'd had a family to care for while he was at war it would've been hell on all of them. Just in the few days he'd known about Maeve he'd felt the unbreakable bond of connection and protectiveness toward Winnie and both kids. He couldn't deny it, even to himself.

"What's done is done," he murmured. He had no power over the past or Winnie's previous decisions about Maeve. Pulling his Jeep up to the base security gate, he rolled down his window and held out his military identification card.

"Morning, Commander." The sentry took the ID card with fingerless gloved hands and shot his infrared gun at it. At the *beep* he passed the card back and saluted.

Max saluted back. "Have a great day."

He drove onto the base and let the myriad emotions wash over him. Pride at serving, regret at not being able to follow through with his squadron tour, gratitude that he was still alive.

The survivor guilt that came with being alive when so many had made the ultimate sacrifice was still there, but it didn't grip him as it had in the early days after the bombing. He supposed if any of his squadron had been injured or killed, he'd have had a harder time with it. Thank God they'd all returned alive.

The wing hangar came into view, and he noted that a P-3C Orion was taking off while an EA-6B came in for a landing on another runway. It was a clear day and the squadrons needed to get their training hours in.

His former squadron was still on its at-home cycle and not due to deploy for a few months. He'd accepted that he wasn't going with them the next time; he wouldn't have even if he hadn't had the mishap, as his Command tour would already be over. In reality it ended only three months early with the explosion in Kabul that had changed his life.

Yet nothing compared to meeting his daughter. He had to get on Marlene's appointment book pronto and make sure he handled this right.

Becoming a father was one thing he didn't want to screw up.

Once parked in his reserved spot in front of the hangar, he took the long way to the office. He liked to greet the maintenance people no matter which squadron they were from. Most were young, under twenty-five, and worked tireless hours on aging aircraft, performing miracle overhauls every day. As a pilot he'd put his life in their hands each time he went up, and they'd never let him or any of his aviators down.

"Hey, guys, how's it going?" He walked under the belly of a Prowler and stood next to the ladder on which a young aircraft mechanic sat, wrench in hand and goggles on her eyes.

"Morning, Commander. We're checking out her fuses again. The early-warning light keeps going off even when she's at 10K." The early-warning radar was supposed to alert pilots that they were flying at too low an altitude, which was certainly not the case if the craft was at ten thousand feet.

"You'll find it."

"Yes, sir."

He walked about the massive hangar and learned what some of the other mechanics were up to. Max had been a squadron Assistant Maintenance Officer during his junior officer tour, the tour they'd lost Tom on. Morale had sunk to nil after the crash and the only way he'd roused the mechanics had been to visit them several times a day, assuring them that the crash had nothing to do with their work. It had been a bad call by the aircraft carrier's Air Boss, period. The Air Boss was responsible for directing the incoming aircraft to continue their landing on the ship or, if circumstances were too dangerous, to wave them off. In the latter case the pilot would forgo the landing on the carrier deck and fly back out and around until he or she could land the plane safely on deck.

Tom should have been waved off, but wasn't. He followed the rules and did as the Air Boss indicated. He went to land his plane. Only too late did Tom see it would be impossible to grab an arresting wire with his tail hook. He powered up in an effort to swerve off on his own, but his aircraft plunged into the ocean. There was no time for any of the crew to eject; they'd all been lost.

As much as Max was used to the familiar twist in his gut when he thought of Tom's death, it still gave him pause. One bad call and Tom, along with three crew members, was gone. Forever.

Focus on today.

He had to—it was how he'd recovered from the worst of his PTSD and how he'd be able to help the young sailors on their way home with it. This was his new purpose. To reach out to anyone else who needed a helping hand after coming back.

He looked around the huge hangar. He'd earned the title of Maintenance Officer during his Department Head tour, which had directly resulted in his being selected for a Command tour. Its familiarity made him feel warm nostalgia for the hours upon hours he'd spent in hangars—leading other sailors or preparing for preflights.

These old hangars had been good to him.

MARLENE LOOKED AT him over her reading glasses. He noted that she didn't even have his file pulled. A positive sign—she didn't think she needed to add anything like "patient is definitely on a backslide."

"Max, you've got to be kidding me. There's no formula for raising a child. No proven way to know you're doing everything right. Patience, love and more patience are the only surefire things. A child isn't a *mission,* Max."

"I disagree. It's the most important mission."

"Okay. If you're so certain about this, why

didn't you call Winnie right after you had unprotected sex? To make sure she wasn't pregnant? And why hasn't Winnie been a subject of our work until now?"

The questions were typical of Marlene's get-to-the-root method, but this time Max felt as though she'd kicked him in the gut.

"I didn't see the need. It wasn't unprotected sex, except when one of the condoms broke. I did think she was on the Pill and she gave me no reason to believe she wasn't."

Marlene's silence meant what he hated—he had to dig deeper.

"I suppose I could've continued to call her after the Air Show, after I went back east." He sighed. "I was going on deployment, and honestly, shouldn't she have returned my calls? I left the ball in her court..." His voice trailed off and he heard what a pathetic excuse that had been. "Shit."

"Max, this isn't about berating yourself over what you did or did not do two years ago. It's about today—what are you going to do *today*? If you cling to your resentment over being kept in the dark, I don't see how it's going to help you or your future relationship with your daughter."

"Maybe not, but Winnie had a huge role in this. I can't ever trust her again."

"That's fair, but it's not what I'm getting at.

What have we spent the past few months talking about in here?"

He waited for her to supply the answer, but Marlene remained silent. There was a reason she had such a great reputation as a counselor. She was compassionate, honest and, when needed, a brutal ball breaker.

This qualified as one of the brutal sessions.

"Acceptance, living in the moment. Not projecting about the future." He grunted the words and knew he sounded like an adolescent but didn't care.

"*Why,* Max? Why is acceptance so important *now?*"

He sighed and rubbed his eyes before he answered. "Because I can't change what is. I can't go back and undo the first eighteen months of Maeve's life. I can't redo my actions the night she was conceived or after."

The silence went on, and Max felt the tension leave his shoulders. This was the part of therapy that had initially bothered him the most. The quiet. He never knew what visions or memories would burst in and slam him back to the battlefield.

The intense flashbacks had eased. Now the silence and his revelations signaled the prelude to a new level of understanding. "Real growth" as Marlene and his flight surgeon often called it.

"I've got so much learning to do."

"With your daughter or her mother?"

"Both. All three." He looked up at Marlene. "There's also my daughter's older sister, my god-daughter."

Marlene's brows rose. "It seems we still have some digging to do here, Max. Why don't we go back to once a week for a few weeks, to get to the heart of it?"

"Do I have a choice?"

Marlene laughed. "You've always had a choice, Max. Fortunately for both of us, you've always hung in there and, every time, you've done the next thing needed to get better."

"Yeah, I'm sure I'm getting *way* better, Marlene."

"Why's that?" she asked, obviously recognizing his sarcasm but pretending to ignore it.

"Because I feel like shit again."

"WHY DIDN'T WE SEE Uncle Max for so long? And why were you guys fighting at the soccer field, anyway?"

Winnie looked up from her laptop and the financial spreadsheets. Krista stood in the office doorway, her gaze fixed on Winnie.

She gave the baby monitor on her desk a glance. Maeve was asleep, as evidenced by her soft snores.

"I thought you were getting ready for bed."

"I already did." Krista walked into the office and sat beside her on the worn sofa that was pushed against the wall. "See, all clean." She shook her wet hair at Winnie.

"Okay. Nice pajamas, by the way." Winnie poked fun at Krista's faded monkey-patterned pajamas that she'd outgrown in height, but insisted on wearing.

"I love these, Mom."

"I know, but maybe we should take a shopping trip off island sooner rather than later." Winnie loved talking with Krista but knew this conversation was going to get deep.

"So why didn't we see him more?"

"See whom?"

"Mom!" Krista's exasperation was second only to her persistent inquisitiveness.

Winnie didn't know which to handle first—Krista's questions or the heavy weight on her chest that she thought a quick stretch might ease. One look at Krista's face told her she wasn't going anywhere until they'd had this conversation.

"It was hard for *all* of us after your daddy died, Krista. Uncle Max had been here day and night for quite a while—two months or so. It was his job to help us with all the details of being a Gold Star family."

Krista knew what Gold Star meant. They weren't the only family on Whidbey Island who'd lost a loved one to war. But they were one of the few who'd decided to stay. They were also one of the few with extended family on or near the island.

"Why did he go away?" Krista was on a roll.

"He got orders and he was stationed in Florida. He went there for two years before he came back here and took command of an air squadron, like the one Daddy was in. Uncle Max took a squadron to the war in Afghanistan."

"Wow! Is he glad to be back?"

"I'm sure he is, but you'd have to ask him yourself. I imagine he might have some interesting stories to tell you."

"Wow." Krista-code for "neat, that's interesting and not what I expected."

"As for why we were arguing, well, Uncle Max is rather protective of you, since he was, I mean *is,* your godfather. He feels he's related to you through your father, because he and your daddy were best friends."

"But why were you arguing on the soccer field?"

Winnie sighed and turned to face Krista as they sat together on the sofa. "It's me, honey. I'm a control freak, I admit it. And Uncle Max, uh, forgot to tell me that he was going to be coaching your team. And now that he knows about Maeve, he wants to be around her and you a lot more." Winnie paused and looked away.

"It's too much all at once," she said a moment later. "Seeing Uncle Max again, telling him about Maeve—"

"You didn't tell him, Mom. That's what you were fighting about when he came over the other night."

"You're right, kiddo."

"Yeah, but—"

"Krista, you have to understand that Uncle Max and I go way back. We knew each other when I met your father, before you were born."

"That long ago? Really?"

Winnie couldn't hold back her laugh. "It wasn't *that* long ago, honey. Just wait until you're my age and I remind you of this conversation."

Krista wasn't to be distracted. "But, Mom, if Uncle Max is so worried about me, where has he *been?*"

Leave it to a kid to cut right to the painful crux of the matter. "Well, he was here after your daddy passed away." Winnie rubbed Krista's back, but it remained stiff under her touch. She put her hand back in her lap.

"Then, like I said, he got orders to Florida and had to move. He came back twice over the years. His most recent job was being in charge of a squadron and deploying all over the world. He hasn't had a lot of time to spare."

"Huh."

Winnie wished she knew what Krista's mono-syllabic reply meant. Judging by her furrowed brows, the conversation wasn't over.

"I realize it's hard to understand, but sometimes people need time apart after such a hard thing happens."

"Didn't you want him to know about Maeve sooner?"

"The timing wasn't good, Krista. He had to get ready to take a squadron to war, and he was on combat missions, too. I didn't want to distract him in any way. It was more important that he get back safe and sound."

"You were afraid he was going to die, like Daddy."

Ouch. "I didn't know. It was…possible." Her words came out in a quiet rush. That was the truth; she didn't know if Max was going to come back alive.

"Hmm." Krista-speak for "I don't get it but whatever." Then, just like that, Krista was on to her usual after-school narrative. "In Life Skills class today we had to make pasta and some icky white sauce."

Winnie focused as best she could on Krista's chatter while telling her own demons to pipe down. Krista had every right to know the circumstances of her younger sister's birth—and why Winnie hadn't told Max sooner.

In truth, Krista was only asking what anyone would want to know after reuniting with a family friend who'd meant so much to her but had been out of the picture for a long time.

Too long.

Winnie's remorse remained a heavy weight on her chest. It'd been easy to ignore when she knew Max wasn't even on Whidbey Island, or if he was, it was for a short period between detachments and deployments.

Krista finally paused long enough for Winnie to urge her to bed.

"Don't listen to your MP3 player, okay?" she added. "It's too late."

"Okay. Love you, Mom," Krista leaned in and let Winnie embrace her while she wrapped her arms around Winnie's waist.

"Love you, too, sweetheart." Winnie planted a kiss on Krista's head before her daughter went upstairs. "See you in the morning."

"Night, Mom."

As soon as she heard Krista go up the stairs, Winnie placed her head in her hands. Her well-intentioned decision to not tell Max sooner had been a mistake. She'd done the right thing in protecting Max from any upset when he had to be at his most focused as a military professional. If only she hadn't nagged Tom the weekend before he'd left on his last detachment. If only she'd been

more supportive of him as a Navy pilot… Sh
wasn't to blame for his death, of course, and y
the guilt was intense. Her haranguing him sur
hadn't helped.

She rubbed her temples. Yes, she was positiv
she'd done the right thing for Max. But now he
holding back from Max was affecting Krista, to
Maeve seemed oblivious, except for the fact tha
she'd appeared to be in awe of Max the two sho
times she'd seen him. Winnie knew it was just tha
Maeve wasn't around men a whole lot, and Ma
was the kind of guy kids loved.

It's more than that. She feels the connection.

If Winnie wasn't attracted to Max, this woul
all be so much easier. When he was with her, sh
couldn't stop her defenses from going on full aler

If they hadn't recognized their mutual attrac
tion, more than two years ago, Maeve wouldn
be here.

Unthinkable.

It's not about you or Max, she told herself. It
about the girls.

The girls she'd vowed to keep safe and lov
with all her heart.

She stood and stretched. Sam did a downwar
dog stretch beside her.

Max wasn't the only one who could take ac
tion here. She might have been slow in telling hi
about Maeve. So be it. She couldn't change that

She could, however, take action to make sure things didn't spin out of control again. If Max was going to be part of their lives—from the soccer field to time with Sam to family meals—it was going to be on *her* terms.

"MAX AND MILES FINISHED their run side by side. They'd taken the dirt jogging path that took them from the gym, past breathtaking views of the ocean, through a stretch of woods and then a campground.

"It's not just about getting your head and your body back in sync," Max was saying. "It's about remembering why you joined the Navy in the first place. That helped me figure out what I really love to do, what I can still do, no matter what."

"I hear you, boss, but it's hard to finally accept that I'm never going to be climbing out of a helicopter again. No more Ordinance Disposal missions." Miles knocked on his prosthesis.

"You can train the new guys and gals to go out there and do it. I'll never command a squadron again, or anything else. My flying days are done because of my seniority. I can still *physically* fly but there aren't any jobs left in the Navy that require me to fly. I could be bummed about it, and I'm not saying I've never felt that way, but it's forced me to decide what I feel I can't live without—what I want to keep doing."

Max stretched his legs out in front of him on the bench. They sat alongside the running path; they'd completed their run, then taken a cool-down walk back to this quiet place with its stunning view of Puget Sound. The water was deceptively calm. The only movement was the flickering of the wings—the seagulls and circling bald eagles hundreds of feet above them.

"I can do without flying, the constant moving, the challenge of hard times in a third-world country. But what I can't do without is knowing I'm part of a team, knowing we respect each other, equally. The camaraderie that only comes from being with others who share the same values."

"You're right, boss, I know you are." Miles ran his fingers through his short blond hair. "But I won't be working next to people who'd give their life for their country if I join a big corporation."

"Who says it has to be big? Or that everyone has to be willing to sacrifice it all for Uncle Sam? Good people serve our country every day, and most of them aren't in a uniform. As long as you find a job you can be passionate about and do it to the best of your ability, you're serving your country. Does that make sense?" Max rubbed at his left thigh where microscopic pieces of shrapnel still lay, unreachable by the tiniest scalpel.

"Is it bothering you, boss?" Miles asked. His

gaze showed no sign of pity, just frank inquiry. He'd chosen to ignore Max's question.

"Oh, yeah." Max shrugged. "It's amazing to me that I survived it, sure, but the fact that there's still these tiny pieces of that psycho's bomb inside me—let's just say there was a time I wanted to tear them all out by myself."

"When you first got back? When you had the night sweats?"

"You got it. You still get them?"

Miles remained relaxed, his face tilted upward for maximum exposure to the sun.

"Not so much anymore. Sometimes I still wake up and think I have my leg. Sometimes it seems to hurt like it used to, in my knee—right before a storm front comes through."

"Like that one?" Max nodded toward the horizon. The wind had picked up and there was a long dark line of clouds out on the horizon.

Miles laughed long and slow. "Yeah, Commander, like that one." He shook his head. "Guess I gave myself away this afternoon, didn't I?"

Max smiled and lightly punched him on the shoulder. "Rare is the day that I outpace you, and I did feel you hold back a bit when we made our second loop. Right after the cedar bridge."

"I was hoping my leg would stay the hell on!" Miles's grin broke the tension of an otherwise unfunny conversation.

"You should've said something. I was almost at the end of my lung capacity."

"Sure you were, boss."

They sat and spoke for another ten minutes until Miles suddenly looked at his watch and jumped up. "I've got to be at the other base in twenty minutes. Same time Friday?"

"Sure. What's cooking tonight? A hot date?"

"Hell, no. I can't work this leg on my own, much less worry about what to do with a woman right now. I promised I'd help with an animal rescue—the cops raided a home near Dugualla with over a hundred puppy-mill dogs."

"That's out by me. I wondered why there was a roadblock on the way up to Blueberry Point."

"Got to go. Call me on my cell if you need me sooner than Friday."

"Okay." Max rubbed his neck. "Oh, and Warrant?"

"Yeah, boss?"

"Don't even think about bringing me a puppy."

Miles laughed all the way across the parking lot.

Max sat and soaked up the sun and clear air for a few more moments. Once the storm front came through, it could be cloudy for days. He needed more light; the slowly returning daylight wasn't enough.

Marlene said that just a few minutes of direct

sunlight each day would boost his serotonin levels and improve his brain chemistry. He didn't doubt it, but he also understood that there were other ways to get endorphins—from exercise and developing bonds with other people, people like Miles.

Sex is good for altering moods, too.

He frowned. He hadn't intended to go so long without sex. In fact, his old girlfriend had called, wanting to get together. Since their relationship had always been more about physical reasons than emotional ones, he'd surprised even himself when he told her he was too busy.

She'd heard he was back and wanted to spend some time with him. It should've scared him how fast he turned her down. As if he had another relationship brewing...

With Winnie.

He snorted, then shook his head to clear it. Shit, he'd made a mess of things. Whether you looked at the night he and Winnie made love as simply poor judgment or considered him rude for not calling her or blamed Winnie for her mistaken assumption that he wouldn't be interested in his own child—it all came down to one thing.

He and Winnie had a daughter together.

He was also Krista's godfather. Winnie had settled here with both girls, and he was done with his constant Navy moving.

Nope, Max wasn't going anywhere.

CHAPTER NINE

WINNIE WAITED OUTSIDE city hall as Max had asked. She was supposed to meet him here at eleven forty-five. Problem was, it was going on noon and still no Max. Not usual for a military guy like him.

What business did he have with the town, anyway? He hadn't shared his plans for life after the Navy with her. Did he intend to stay on Whidbey? Start a company of some kind? Buy a franchise?

Why do you care?

What Max did or didn't do after he retired wasn't her concern. There was only one thing that was relevant to her—what his plans were to be involved in the girls' lives. Because of that, she wanted him to remain a friend but nothing else.

She could stay in the limited parking area, she supposed, provided she didn't get out of her car. But honestly, how long could it take Max to get whatever he needed done at city hall?

"Easy, Sam."

Sam, sitting in the backseat, whimpered in pure spoiled-dog mode. He preferred to be in a moving vehicle or up front with Winnie. Instead, the car was stopped and he was banished to the back.

"I hear you, boy, but it's not going to make any difference. We have to wait for Max."

Fifteen additional minutes stretched into twenty, and Winnie had an unsettling thought.

What if Max had already been here and left?

He wouldn't do that. No, not Max, who'd made sure every one of Tom's funeral details was taken care of, who'd ensured the proper military flyover for Tom's burial.

Could she ever stop associating Max with Tom's death?

You did two years ago. And again when he kissed you earlier this week.

Sam whimpered once more and Winnie looked through the windshield to see Max walking out of the Oak Harbor city hall doors. He was dressed in jeans and a windbreaker. The usual fall/spring "uniform" for Whidbey residents, but on Max it took rugged to a new level.

His long stride, the slight tilt to his head, were familiar. Unmistakably Max. But she noted, the few times she'd seen him, that his stride grew shorter, his movements less fluid, at the end of the day. When they'd exchanged those angry words on the soccer field, she'd wondered if he'd been gritting his teeth not just in exasperation with her but in pain.

When he approached the car, she opened the door and got out. The wind whipped away her breath.

"Sorry I'm late, Winnie."

"I was afraid I'd missed you. So, what's up?"

"I wanted you to be the first to see this." He thrust a folder of papers at her.

"Careful, I don't want them to blow away. But you need to know my plans, Winnie."

Oh, God, was he seeking custody of Maeve? Surely he couldn't get more than partial custody but even that…

"Hold on a minute, Max."

"Winnie, calm down. Look at the paper. The top one."

She opened the folder and braced herself to see a petition for custody. Instead, she read Application for a Retail Business in Oak Harbor. Her hunch had been correct. He was starting his own business.

"But…you're still on active duty. And what kind of business is this going to be?"

"A flying business, Winnie. I'm going to provide charters to and from Seattle, and a local float plane tourist service."

"Oh."

Why bother getting out of the Navy if he was going to continue engaging in such dangerous work?

"Let's go grab a cup of coffee." His brusque

manner angered her. As if she could be so easily pacified!

"Are you going to leave Sam in the car?" He was even acting as though Sam was *his* dog.

"No, he can come with us. He's allowed in the coffee place—technically he's working with you."

Heat fanned her cheeks. She had to get over her physical attraction to Max.

"Out, Sam."

The dog jumped obediently from the back cargo hold to the sidewalk.

"Good boy."

Sam eyed Max and wagged his tail, showing his teeth in a way that could only be interpreted as a smile.

"Hi, Sam." Max came closer and leaned over to scratch behind the dog's ears.

Sam rubbed his head against Max's open hand, then lay down and rolled onto his back, exposing his belly.

"You traitor!" Winnie couldn't keep the laughter out of her voice. While always loving and affectionate with clients and approved strangers, Sam never displayed his belly to anyone except her and the girls. It was the ultimate gesture of vulnerability—and trust.

"He just knows a sucker when he sees one." Max's hands made Sam's belly look small. She'd always loved his fingers, their length accentuated by the dark hair that grew down his forearm and on his knuckles.

Hands of a warrior and her one-night lover.

The father of your daughter.

"Where are we headed, Max?"

He looked up at her and squinted against the sun that warmed her shoulders.

"I mean for coffee," she added.

Max kept his gaze on her as he knelt next to Sam.

"I know what you meant. We can go to the Coffee Klatch."

Where he planned to tell her he wasn't just going to retire and stay on the island but that he was going to launch his own business.

A very dangerous business.

He stood. "Shall we?"

She nodded and gave Sam's leash a snap. He jumped up, alert and ready to go. The leash was her means of communication with him; it had served almost as a kind of umbilical cord when he was a puppy being housetrained. Now it reminded Sam that she was at his side.

"Are you pressed for time?" He glanced at her as they made their way up the curve of the road.

"Am I in a hurry? A single mom with my own business? Are you kidding? All the time."

Instead of being blown away by a gust, her

words felt as though they lingered in the air between them.

She stiffened but not against the wind. Her words had sounded so harsh, even to her.

Stay focused on your purpose. Make the rules about time with the girls loud and clear.

Max ignored her retort as he matched her stride and walked on her left, protecting her and Sam from the traffic. She never thought of herself as the type of woman who needed a man to keep her safe, so it surprised her when a warm thrill of awareness spiraled through her.

Really? Have you survived widowhood and single motherhood only to be bowled over by your hormones?

"I'm glad you agreed to meet me." His tone was genuine, and the deep rumble of his voice heightened the sense of intimacy.

"Um, sure. We still have a lot to work out, Max."

He laughed. "With you, Winnie, there's always 'a lot to work out.' I'll bet you've made spreadsheets and calendars of exactly how and when I'll get to spend time with the girls. One of whom is my daughter."

Winnie opened her mouth, but then shut it. She frantically searched for a humorous reply and found none. Max knew her well, right down to her need for organization.

Robyn called it being a control freak. Winnie didn't disagree but preferred to describe it in different terms—that she was simply more deliberate in her choices than others.

She and Max walked in silence for nearly a block.

"Does he always obey so well?" Max nodded at Sam, who trotted with his head up, eyes forward.

"Yes. Well, no, not at first." A laugh escaped her throat and it felt good, laughing with Max instead of fighting him.

"He was a very exuberant puppy to say the least. It's hard to believe this is the same puppy we found on the dining-room table eating the Easter ham, sniffing through the laundry basket to find the smelliest clothes to tear apart or digging up dozens of tulip bulbs I planted."

"So what changed him?"

"Lots of obedience training and time. He's always had a very intuitive side. All dogs do, as far as I'm concerned. But Sam not only knows when one of us is upset, but how we need to be comforted." She hoisted her purse higher on her shoulder.

"If we were feeling down because of the weather or missing Tom," she went on, "Sam would do something to make us laugh. If Krista was sad over not being invited to a classmate's birthday party, he'd lie next to her and just give her his presence."

"Sounds more like a shrink than a dog."

She laughed again. "If they allowed dogs to be licensed, I'd never have to work another day in my life. Sam could provide for all of us."

They'd walked several blocks on the road that joined the main street until they faced the entrance to the coffee shop. At the pedestrian crosswalk, the three of them stopped and looked both ways.

"He even crosses the street like a person!" The amazement in Max's voice made her smile as they stepped out into the road.

"I—"

What she'd been about to say was cut off by the hard shove Max gave her just before a pair of motorcycles raced behind them and turned the corner in an illegal and potentially deadly fashion. She felt the *whoosh* of air the bikes' engines blasted over them as they actually rode up over the curb.

"Ooof." Her knees hit the edge of the cement curb and her hands stopped her from falling the rest of the way. Sam was beside her even though she'd lost her grasp on his leash. Max's left hand was on her back, the other on the ground near Sam.

"Are you okay?" Max's voice reassured her.

"Yes, yes, I'm okay. Thanks to you." She straightened up and turned around. "How did you know they were coming? I never heard them until it was too late."

"Instinct." His lips were pressed in a thin line and his fists were clenched.

"Here, let's get up on the sidewalk." She grabbed his upper arm and pulled him toward her. She caught her breath at the look of sheer determination on his face. The fact that Sam was whimpering to get Max's attention didn't help. Sam had behaved this way once a year earlier—moments before a client's epileptic seizure.

Max was struggling with his PTSD demons.

"Max, it's okay. We're all okay." She dug her fingers into his biceps and pushed her sunglasses on top of her head. When she looked into his eyes she didn't see his usual impenetrable gaze. The vacant look she saw shook her and simultaneously moved her to action.

"Stay with us, buddy."

"I'm with you, Winnie. I just have to catch my breath. Leave me alone."

"No." She wrapped her arm around his and urged him forward.

"Sam and I need to walk. So do you. Let's go." It was half a block to the café door. If she could get him in there, get him some hot coffee, she'd bring him back to himself. She had to make his war recollections stop.

Max didn't argue. Their walk to the shop was

slow and stilted. Winnie wondered if she needed to call anyone like his doctor or therapist.

"I'm not an invalid." His monotone frightened her. "I'm just stiff from falling over and moving so quickly."

She'd witnessed the effects of PTSD countless times while working with returning sailors and their families. Certainly she'd seen worse. Young men and women who couldn't even function outside of their hospital rooms.

Max's had been triggered by the backfire and the reckless actions of the motorcyclists. His quick reflex had saved her and Sam—and proved that he still was on alert the way he'd been in Afghanistan.

She sneaked a quick glance at him and saw the stress and exhaustion etched in each line of his face. He had to get past that time in his life or it would age him rapidly.

He is getting past it. He's agreed to work with you and Sam. He has a daughter to live for.

"Okay, here we are." They got to the restaurant and she opened the door for Max. "We're right behind you."

As Max passed through the double glass doors, Winnie bent next to Sam on the sidewalk. He sat still as she tied the "canine companion" scarf around his neck. The owners of this café knew her and Sam, so she didn't expect any resistance

from the staff but sometimes clients had issue
with an animal being in a place where food wa
served. The scarf ensured they'd have minima
friction from customers.

When they went inside, she saw that Max wa
seated by the huge window overlooking Cit
Beach, staring at the water.

She walked Sam over to Max and handed hin
the leash.

"Watch him while I order our coffee, okay?"

Max didn't reply, merely taking the leash in hi
hand. Sam happily sidled up to him and laid hi
head on Max's lap. Agitated though he was, ever
Max couldn't resist the blatant quest for affection
He buried his hands in the fur on Sam's head an
around his ears.

"Hi, Winnie!" Justin, the college kid wh
worked the coffee bar to pay for school, greetee
her as if she was still young and in college herseli

Winnie laughed. "Justin! How's it going?"

"The frother crapped out, but I have these lit
tle battery whips so I can still make your cap
puccino."

"Great. Can I have two, skim milk with nut
meg on top?" She had no idea what Max liked bu
maybe the tang of the spice would distract him.

"Right away." He started spooning the espressc
grounds into the holder, tamping them down, anc
nodded at the glass case. "Louise made her sticky

buns today. They're done with whole-wheat flour and pure cane sugar."

"No, thanks." She answered automatically before she took the time to really look at them. The buns were large curled pinwheels of what promised to be soft dough with a caramelized syrupy coating. "Wait a minute—I'll take two."

Justine grinned and shook his head. "I knew you'd think twice when I told you the ingredients." She smiled back at him. She'd decided to buy them to help both Max and her out of the shaky mood their near-miss had precipitated.

Once back at the table, two warm sticky rolls with cappuccino between them, she finally looked directly at Max. "How are you doing?"

His gaze, still on the water, wavered and he blinked.

She thought that was a good sign.

"I'm okay." He picked up his coffee cup. She noticed the strength in his hands as he brought the brim to his lips and sipped.

He put down his mug and sighed. "I'm sorry you had to see that, Winnie. I'm not the man you knew." The depths of his pain still echoed in his eyes.

"I can go weeks now without any hint of the PTSD. At night there's always the chance of nightmares, less often over the past month. But during the day I still get sideswiped by it every now and then."

She covered his hand with hers. "Max, even people without PTSD would react to almost being run over by two crazy motorcycle drivers."

He pursed his lips. "Perhaps. But they wouldn't still be thinking about it days later. I guarantee you that those bikes rounding that corner, just the sound of them, will replay in my mind for the next few hours."

"What can you do to stop it or prevent it? You're going to counseling. What else is there?"

"Medication. Therapy. Time." He said the three remedies as if he'd memorized his reply; he'd obviously struggled with the hope of his own permanent recovery.

"You *will* get past this, Max. It's not forever."

"Sure feels like it." He glanced down at the dog. "Doesn't it, boy?" Sam gazed up at Max in complete canine adoration.

"Don't forget where your food comes from, Sam," she whispered into the froth of her cappuccino.

"Mmm?" Max looked at her with a question on his face.

"Nothing. Just thinking out loud…."

He didn't respond and went back to stroking Sam's head. She wished those long fingers were stroking her—and not on top of her head. How sick was *that?*

"It's mind-blowing," he said thoughtfully, "no pun intended. In an instant I'm back there, powerless."

"But you acted, Max. You saved so many lives. And today you saved all three of us from what could've been a nasty accident. Not to mention the jerks on those bikes—they're lucky they didn't end up flat on the pavement."

The lines around his mouth deepened. "In Afghanistan, it was pure luck, Winnie. A nanosecond later, a slower reflex, and I would've lost members of my squadron. All those young kids."

"But you *didn't* lose them." Winnie took a sip of her coffee and forced herself to look away from Max's grim expression. The water on this side of the island was calm and tranquil. She'd spent hours staring at it after Tom died.

"I read the news, Max. And while I'm not a therapist I've worked with a lot of guys and gals who've come back from the edge of insanity. You will, too. You *have.*"

Max sighed and moved his hand from Sam's head to the table. Sam remained seated, but Winnie noticed that he was resting against Max, validating what she suspected. Max hadn't stopped beating himself up over his PTSD yet. When he did, he'd be rid of the worst of his torment.

"Yeah, I suppose I have. Until the next couple of bikes race around a corner and I think I'm going to die."

Winnie kept silent and occupied her hands with her coffee mug. It was an original hand-thrown Whidbey piece of pottery, cerulean blue, from the shop near her office in Coupeville. Just one of the many charming touches that made City Beach's Coffee Klatch one of her favorites.

Max leaned over and briefly touched her forearm. "Enough about my crap. What I want to talk about is how I'm going to get you to trust my motives with the girls."

"As long as we—"

He held up his hand. "Let me finish, Win."

Win.

He'd called her that the night Maeve was conceived.

CHAPTER TEN

THE NIGHT HE'D called her "Win" as he made love to her would forever be part of who she was, no matter how many times she said that they were over. He'd whispered her name in her ear; he'd shouted her name when he came.

The night his hands had brought her to a fever pitch she'd never experienced before. She never compared it with her and Tom's lovemaking—that wouldn't have been fair. But as much as she and Tom had shared a tender, loving relationship, she'd never felt the pure chemistry she did with Max. The sense of primal connection she experienced every time their eyes met. It was still a shock that after years of seeing him only as Tom's friend, her physical need for him was so voracious.

Like now, when he watched her steadily as he stated his case.

"I understand if you're concerned about leaving me alone with the girls—you're a great mother and you should never trust anyone right off the bat, regardless of how long you've known them. I'm sorry for pushing so hard just after you told me. I want to get to know my daughter. I want to help raise her. She happens to have a sister I care about, as well—and I'm Krista's godfather."

He glanced out the window before he returned his gaze to her.

"I screwed up, Winnie. I should've kept in touch with Krista after I left, and I sure as hell should've been more persistent about getting hold of you after our night together. It doesn't erase the fact that you didn't tell me. You realize I could have died in some godforsaken hellhole and never known my daughter? That I even *had* a daughter?"

If I'd told you, you might have died because of the distraction it caused you.

"How many times do you want me to say I'm sorry, Max?"

"It doesn't matter—it'll never change what you did."

"Wow. Just sucker punch me now." She didn't get the slightest smile out of him—but then, she didn't deserve to.

"I *am* sorry, Max, that this has caused you so much hurt."

"Why do I hear a *but* in there, Winnie?"

She remained silent. It wasn't the right time to tell Max that she still believed she'd helped keep him alive by not telling him sooner.

If she'd only been as wise with Tom. She would never have complained about his job, not once.

"Look, we've both made our choices and we can't undo what's been done. We *do*, however, have control over how we go forward."

"Control—we're both good at control, aren't we, Winnie?"

She couldn't tell if he was playing it straight or yanking her chain. She chose to believe the former.

"Exactly. So we agree to keep this on an even keel, to take it as slow as the girls need us to?"

His grin chased away the tension that just minutes earlier had stamped worry lines on his face.

"Agree to what, Winnie? To seeing Maeve and Krista only when you say so?" His tone was deceptively light. "Not to show them I care and I'm here for them? It would be nice for you if I agreed to your idea of my relationship with the girls, wouldn't it? But this isn't about you."

There it was again. The sucker punch to her gut.

"My biggest concern is that you'll get close to them and then have to transfer again. Where will that leave the girls? They've had too much loss in their lives already."

"Didn't I just show you the work permit and business license I'm getting so that I can have my operation up and running by the time I retire this summer? Are you going anywhere, Winnie? How can I be sure *you* won't move?"

"Of course I'm not moving!"

"Great. So we'll both be here to raise Maeve, and I can be active in Krista's life from now on, too. We each have our own lives, that's a given. We'll work it out, Winnie. It's what divorced parents do all the time."

She sat up straight. "No, this isn't like divorced parents, Max. We were never married or even in a relationship."

His lips twitched and she wondered what the hell was so funny.

"Relax, Winnie. It's clear that you've made a great home for the girls and that you're near your family. I assume that unless you marry a Navy man again, you're staying put, correct?"

"I'm never remarrying. Certainly not while the girls are young."

His right brow raised and she saw a tiny spark in his irises. "Whatever—that's your business." He folded his hands in front of his coffee mug. "I'm here for good, too. Like I said, I'm going to retire after this shore tour. The girls won't have to worry about me ever deploying or being in combat."

"No, they'll just have to worry about you in a tiny plane with the crazy weather here!"

"I didn't realize you cared so much, Winnie."

His sarcasm humiliated her, and she couldn't look at him. She thought of herself as an independent woman who'd be perfectly happy without another husband in her lifetime, at least not anytime soon, but his questions stoked a simmering pain that she'd been able to distance herself from. Until now.

Until Max came back.

"Are you sure you want to retire and stay here, Max? Why are you going into such a dangerous business?" She avoided his eyes. "You shouldn't make such a big decision right after a trauma," she murmured.

Max's laughter chafed her pride.

"Nope," he said, "neither of us has any control issues whatsoever."

Slowly she allowed her smile to come out. "None at all."

"Yes, I'm sure about staying here, Winnie. It's almost a year since the…accident. I've gone through extensive physical therapy, as well as counseling. Even though I still have moments like the one you just witnessed, they really are fewer and farther between." He looked out the window, apparently transfixed by two sandpipers chasing each other in the parking lot.

"This isn't a knee-jerk decision I made because of discovering Maeve." He looked back at her.

Winnie wiggled her toes in her shoes, trying to hide her discomfort.

"I've been thinking about it for a long time, actually. But it didn't gel until the past couple of weeks. And then our meeting, finding out about Maeve—it's all come together."

"But you could still make Captain, right? Don't you want to put your hat in the ring for Commodore?" The Commodore position was coveted. Only the top officers were picked to command the wing of AE-6B squadrons. It was a stepping stone to Flag rank, Admiral.

"You're kidding me, aren't you?" Max rubbed his chin.

"No, I'm not, Max. You're the best the Navy has."

He stared at her and she saw the light in his eyes, magnified by...tears. Max, crying?

"Thanks, Win. Your support means the world to me."

He took a breath, and she was moved by his sincerity.

"Getting command of a squadron has always been my goal. I've achieved it. Anything operational past squadron level is too political for me. Too much paper-pushing and not enough real-world. I'm done flying. As far as I'm concerned, I'm done being a Naval Aviator at this point." It went without saying that he'd always consider himself a naval officer, first and foremost.

"I understand what you mean about not flying anymore. Tom used to say that when the flying jobs were gone, it was time to find another one—in CIVLANT." She referred to the acronym given to the civilian world after the Navy. The civilian side of life was one that most sailors and marines didn't like to think about until they left the service.

"Exactly."

"But we're not that young or dumb anymore, Max. The employment situation is grim at the moment. You can see all the home foreclosures on Whidbey Island alone—enough to scare anyone off. How will you pay for your house?"

"I'll have a decent pension, Winnie, and I've been saving for that proverbial rainy day. The business should prove profitable within two years."

"I have my own business, Max. Fiber gathering and production is far more niche than a transportation company, but I do know how difficult it can be to start over on this island."

He stared at her, both hands clasping his mug. "You've succeeded, Winnie. Give me the benefit of the doubt that I will, too."

Heat flushed her neck and she wished she could take off the fleece pullover she'd grabbed on her way out the door. She was too young for this "power surge" to be hormonal. It came from being bested by Max. Again.

"So let me understand this—you want to get to know my daughters better, spend time with them, and you're getting out of the Navy and staying put on Whidbey. But you don't want me to plan any kind of visitation schedule at all?" She shook her head and stood.

His arm shot out and he grasped her hand. "Don't do this, Winnie. Don't make the five-cent issue into a million-dollar one."

She glared at him and when she couldn't take his scrutiny anymore she shifted her gaze to his hand, still holding hers. He didn't budge.

"What you're missing, Max, is that my children, my daughters, are the biggest issue here."

He let go of her and leaned back. "Of course they are. But it's not just about *your* daughters, Winnie. One of them is mine. And the other might as well be, because I've known her since she came into this world."

Damn Max and damn his ability to dig up the memories she'd struggled to bury. Her mind's eye saw the look of wonder on his face as he met Krista, right after her birth. Tom had been out on a mission and had made it back ten minutes too late. Max was in the neighborhood and had driven Winnie to the hospital on the Naval Air Station.

It should've been Tom she'd shared that moment with. But there was no denying it had been Max.

Max had been Tom's best friend and flying buddy.

And now Max had fathered her second daughter.

He'd been part of her life for so long she couldn't remember life before Max. And he appeared to have every intention of remaining part of her life, not only in the near term but the future, as well.

She could hardly breathe. "I need some space," she muttered.

She turned on her heel and walked across the café and out the door. The cool air felt good on her cheeks. She'd barely escaped an all-out panic attack in there.

About ten paces down the street, she heard his all-too-familiar voice.

"Winnie! You forgot something."

She took a deep breath and turned around. Max held Sam's leash as the pair stood in front of the café.

At any other time she'd laugh in disbelief at her absentmindedness. Had she really walked out of that coffee shop without her best friend, Sam?

Max got to her like no one else. He'd always intimidated her, even when she'd been in love with Tom. He had that steely persistence, the quiet and steady presence that she couldn't shake.

She walked the ten steps back to him.

It wasn't the easiest thing she'd ever done but she met his eyes. No censure, no anger. Only warm amusement simmered in his expression.

"My walk of shame." She sighed. "I'm sorry, Max. I let my temper get the better of me, which gave my anxiety a chance to take over." She accepted the leash handle he held out to her, careful to make sure their fingers didn't touch.

"Two apologies from you in one day. Are you sure it was your temper and not me, Winnie?"

"Trust me, Max, my temper doesn't need any help from you *or* your PTSD." She deliberately kept the focus on him.

He raised a brow. "I'm not talking about my PTSD. I'm talking about the tension between us."

Her throat felt scratchy and she couldn't meet his eyes.

"I get that you're not interested in being involved with anyone, especially me with my baggage," he continued. "That doesn't eliminate the chemistry between us. But we can't let it get in the way of me having a relationship with Krista and Maeve."

"You know, Max, maybe you're right. It is time for you to leave the Navy. Maybe you've missed your calling—why don't you become a psychotherapist?"

He ignored her outburst.

"Let's talk again soon, Winnie. At the very least, I'll see you on Friday."

She nodded. "Friday."

CHAPTER ELEVEN

"YOU'VE GOT TO BE kidding me, sis. You real[
think you can spend all this time with Max a[
not get emotionally involved?" Robyn stood [
Winnie's kitchen as the Wednesday-morning su[
shine slanted across the oak cabinets.

"I'm not the one who's going to be spending t[
time with him—the girls are. And it's good f[
them to have a positive male influence that is[
strictly our family."

"Sure, but he's going to be family to all of yo[
not just Maeve, if you go down this path. Y[
know that, right, sis? Is it what you want?"

Anger roiled and Winnie turned away from t[
coffee she was preparing for them. The girls we[
at school and day care. Brendan was with the[
mother, so Robyn had the day to herself and h[
stopped to see Winnie on her way to the Clint[
ferry; she was going to Mulkiteo on the mainlan[
From there she had a short drive to malls and t[
outskirts of Seattle. It would've been quicker ju[
to hop onto I-5 from Anacortes but she'd wante[
to see Winnie.

"I appreciate that you've stopped by to see me, but honestly Robyn, do I look helpless to you? Do you really think I've learned nothing in the past five years?"

"More like the past *two* years, you mean," Robyn said, prodding Winnie about the night of Maeve's conception.

"So I screwed up—literally—one time. I have a beautiful baby girl as a result and a sibling for Krista. Now the father's involved—which *should* have happened sooner. Millions of unmarried parents raise kids in perfect harmony."

"But millions of people haven't sacrificed their husbands to the Navy. Millions haven't had Max in their lives as long as their husband. It drives me nuts when you generalize about your life like this, Winnie!"

Winnie turned back to the coffeemaker to hide her expression from Robyn. She didn't trust her ability to be unreadable. Especially where Max was concerned.

"He was Tom's former Academy roommate and best friend," she began. "He was Tom's best man when we were married. He saw Krista before Tom did. And, oh, yeah, he fathered Maeve. But he's not, never was and never will be anything more to me, Robyn. Yes, we have connections, maybe even a bond after going through Tom's death, but that's it! Our one night together was…an aberration."

"Trying to convince yourself, sis?" Robyn continued to lean against the counter, her gaze serene on the trees outside. As if they were talking about the garden and not Winnie's judgment.

Winnie cursed under her breath. Tears stung her eyes and her knees shook.

The touch of Robyn's hand on her back, between her shoulder blades, was warm and welcome, and Winnie finally released her breath.

"It's okay, Win. You don't need to have everything all figured out. Sometimes it's better just to go with whatever happens."

"That's my point, Robyn. *Nothing* is going to happen. Timing and fate brought us all back together. Max deserves a relationship with his daughter, and I'm not going to keep him from getting to know Krista again. But, but…"

Weariness washed over her, despite the good night's rest she'd had.

"But you're not going to let him into your space?"

"I can't, Robyn. I can't ever risk going through what I've already suffered. Not again." She wiped her eyes and stood straight.

"Not every partner dies early, Winnie. You have to recognize that."

"I'm giving all I have to the girls. That's it. I

don't have anything left for anyone else. And if I did, I could never be with Max. No matter what he says or thinks, deep down, I'm still Tom's wife to him. The Navy bond between colleagues is bigger than a one-night stand, even if it did create my beautiful baby daughter."

"Tom's gone, Win. How can he still be a hurdle?"

Winnie sighed and threw up her hands. "Navy rules, Robyn. Max can't see me as anything other than a responsibility, if that makes sense. Add in my betrayal over Maeve and it's a done deal."

"Answer this for me, Win. How many times have you seen him this week? And how many *more* times will you see him before Friday?"

Winnie took a deep breath. "I saw him Monday. Then Monday night. Tuesday, tonight there's soccer practice again, and then I drop Sam off at his place on Friday evening." She left out the incident near the coffee shop yesterday and Max's PTSD reaction. Listing the other times that she'd seen him in only two days was unsettling enough.

"It's only Wednesday, sis. I'd say that Max isn't going anywhere soon—but I also want you to take it easy."

Winnie offered a smile and hoped her sister didn't see her hands shaking.

"Thanks, hon." She turned her head to look at the mugs on the counter. "Skim or regular milk?"

"Do you have two percent?"

"No. Just zero and three point two. Make your choice, lady."

Robyn laughed. "What the hell—I'll have the full fat. It's my day out and I need energy to get to the mainland."

"You're a wise woman. You never know how long the ferry wait will be."

"Exactly."

Robyn kept the rest of her conversation light and threw her arms around Winnie in a fierce hug before she left to catch the nine o'clock ferry.

"You know I'm a pain in your butt because I love you, sis," she whispered, her coffee-scented breath hot against Winnie's ear.

"I know, I know. Come back when the girls are here and say hi."

"Not today—I'll be out until late, so I'll just go home on the interstate. But maybe next week, if that works for you."

"It's a date!" Winnie gave her sister her best "I'm okay" smile and waved her out of the house. Robyn waved back over her shoulder before she got into her tiny hybrid automobile.

Since Robyn had gone green she thought everyone should and bemoaned Winnie's gas-guzzling SUV. But it had been Tom's, and that was back before hybrids and electric cars were as common as they'd recently become. It was the last remaining thing of Tom's that she used every day.

Winnie had her newer station wagon for town trips and client visits with Sam, but the full-size SUV was unbeatable when she had to haul fiber from farm to factory.

She watched until Robyn's taillights winked in the distance and stood on the porch for a moment to absorb the freshness of the morning. Then she walked back into the house and the chaos that her workday often brought.

The mist was still hovering in patches on the field across the street, but the morning sun promised to burn it off before noon. Nothing ever stayed fixed on the windswept island.

She wiped a tear from the corner of her eye. It wasn't grief or joy; it was the fear of a new beginning, a new way of living.

She felt a curl of anticipatory delight as she thought of Max....

Yeah, she was in too deep already. But she wasn't going to keep digging her own emotional grave. Max was off-limits for so many reasons. Her heart still ached at how her nagging, her emotional blackmail, had added unnecessary stress to Tom's job. Even if the accident had been proven to be a faulty call by the Air Boss, she couldn't help feeling a measure of responsibility—a measure of guilt.

Max would never stop flying. And Winnie would never stop worrying, trying to control. So their fate was sealed, despite their chemistry and their connection through the girls.

She hugged herself with both arms and smiled. One thing she'd learned from Tom's death was that while she couldn't actually control anything, since there were always other people and other factors, she could take the initiative. She chose to put her heart into raising her girls. She chose to devote her professional energy to a business that not only supported her family but had the potential to put Whidbey Island on the map of world fiber centers. She helped other farmers and single parents make a profit from their small farms.

She chose not to be involved with Max as anything more than a coparent.

Her satisfaction at having made that decision—the smart decision—soothed her and she went back into the house. As soon as she stepped inside, Sam trotted up from the family room to greet her.

"I'd forgotten about you, boy." She scratched Sam's ears and murmured, "I want you to do your best work with Max. He needs you, and I need you to fill in where I can't."

Sam wagged his tail.

ON FRIDAY AFTERNOON, Winnie was working on the business accounts. Her concentration shattered with the slamming of the front door.

"Krista? I'm in the office."

Krista's flushed face was framed by the curls that had escaped her ponytail. "When are we going to Uncle Max's?"

"Hi, honey. How was school today?" Winnie shoved aside her annoyance. Krista's fascination with Max threatened her resolve to stay emotionally clear of Max. She'd done well at soccer practice last night, in spite of Krista's constant chatter about how "epic" a coach Max was.

"Fine, Mom! When do we leave? Where's Maeve?"

"She's at her playdate. We'll pick her up on our way north. After we drop Sam off we can go out for dinner."

"I thought we'd go to Grandma and Grandpa's," Krista pouted.

"Not tonight. I'm tired—it's been a long week. And we've been wanting to go to the new Thai place. You love the Thai iced tea with coconut milk."

"Okay." She tilted her head. "Maybe Uncle Max will come out with us."

Winnie sighed inwardly at Krista's hopeful expression. Krista's hero-worship of Max wouldn't last forever, she was certain. But it was going to be excruciating while it did.

"Honey, we're dropping Sam off for Uncle Max. They need to spend time together. Leaving Sam by himself in Uncle Max's house right away isn't fair."

"Sam could stay in the car when we go out to eat. Uncle Max can meet us at the restaurant."

"No, Krista. Not an option."

"Lighten up, Mom," Krista grumbled under her breath as she flounced off.

Winnie usually called Krista on disrespectful behavior but this time she held back. The less she made of these moods and especially those involving Max, the better. For all of them.

Winnie finished her work, and she and Krista got Sam into the car. Once they'd picked up Maeve they drove to Oak Harbor and then onward to Dugualla Bay.

As they passed the row of chain restaurants that lined the highway, Krista groaned.

"I'm so hungry."

"Hungee!" Maeve screamed from her car seat next to Krista.

"We're going to eat soon. Let's just get Sam dropped off. Krista, will you look in Maeve's diaper bag and see if I remembered to put in some string cheese? There should be one for each of you."

Krista rummaged noisily through the bag and Winnie silently cursed herself for not taking Sam to Max's place earlier this afternoon. But between her schedule, the girls' schedules and Max's work,

she hadn't had much choice. They could also have
arranged to meet on base, saving Winnie some
time, but she insisted on taking Sam directly to
Max's, because she felt that was better for the dog.

She exhaled a sigh of relief as they turned onto
the black asphalt road that would take them along
the side of the bay to Max's home.

"I can't find any cheese, Mom, and there's nothing else for Maeve to eat."

Maeve promptly screamed, "Huuuungeeee!!"

Winnie took in a deep breath. "Krista, distract
your sister, please." Krista was well aware that
Maeve would react to her words with a scream.
Winnie knew it was inherently good that Krista
and Maeve shared a deep bond. They regularly
used each other to either express themselves or
get their way, which was great for a lifetime of
sisterly love but not so hot for the single mother
raising them.

"Look, Maeve, see the cows? Mooooo. They
make milk for ice cream and milkshakes."

"Wannn eyezzz keem!"

"Krista, can you please keep it off food for now?
Just let me drop Sam off and we'll be at the restaurant in no time." They might not make it to the
Thai place, after all, she figured. All their stomachs, but especially Maeve's, demanded nourish-
ment ASAP.

Winnie sighed again. She considered it a personal failure when she had to resort to the drive-through for a meal. She liked to treat the girls and herself to a nice dinner out once a week. They ate healthily the rest of the time and fast food once in a while wouldn't kill them, but she preferred to make their night out a real meal, not something eaten out of a waxed paper bag in the car.

Lights blazed from Max's house as she turned into the drive. Once she'd parked in the back, she stepped out, taking a moment to admire the view. Purplish mountains with white tops loomed in the distance as the Cascades reflected the last of the sunset. The sky above was a shade of pink and the water below looked inky. Winnie took in a deep breath. She'd never tire of the natural splendor of the Pacific Northwest.

Although the night was calm, it was chilly outside. She walked up the path to the door and rang the bell. Sam sat next to her on the small porch, with the girls standing behind him.

Max opened the door with a flourish, and his grin was reflected in the twinkle in his eyes. "Hey, come on in! You haven't eaten yet, have you?"

Winnie entered with Sam and was almost overwhelmed by myriad aromas that floated down from the upstairs kitchen.

"Hi, Uncle Max!" Krista stepped around Winnie and gave Max a huge hug, her arms tight around his waist.

"Hungee!" Maeve toddled over to Max and held up her arms.

Max lifted her up, slowly but surely. Winnie watched for any sign of pain or strain but detected none.

Max caught her gaze over Maeve's tiny shoulder. "I just have to make sure I use my core muscles so my back and legs don't cramp."

"Sure, whatever." She didn't mean to sound flip, but it was all she could do not to scream. Why did her whole family have to be so crazy about Max? Couldn't he just get to know Maeve a little at a time? Couldn't he see Sam for one hour per week like most other injured vets?

"Why do you have to always go for everything full-throttle, Max?"

She didn't realize she'd spoken aloud until he put Maeve back down and straightened, never taking his gaze off her face.

"I said that out loud, didn't I?"

"Yes, you did." He smiled instead of frowning at her and she found the sudden intimacy uncomfortable. "It's okay, Winnie. I know there's been a lot for you to digest this past week. As much as I hate to admit it, it's been tough for *both* of us."

Guilt hit her hard and she fought not to grimace or complain. This was her doing. She'd agreed to see Max this week, and she'd known where it would lead.

"I have no right to tell you that you're coming on too strong with your daughter, Max. Since I'm the one who kept Maeve from you."

"Yes, you are." He gave her no quarter and she didn't seek it. Facts were facts.

But their chemistry was another matter. From the moment she'd walked into Max's home, she'd been conscious of the intense awareness between them. Would it always be like this? Would they ever be comfortable old friends?

"Back to planet earth, Winnie." His playful comment grounded her.

"What smells so good, Uncle Max?" Krista homed in for the kill.

"Are you hungry?" Max asked.

"Hungee!" Maeve shrieked.

"Starving. But——" Krista turned to Winnie, a question on her face. "We're going out to dinner at the Thai place after this."

"That's a shame because I have homemade Neapolitan pizza upstairs." Max looked at Winnie and she didn't miss the amusement in his expression.

A laugh escaped before she was able to stop it. "I forgot about the pizza oven in the kitchen here. It still works?"

"Perfectly. And since my tour in Naples I pride myself on my pizza skills." This time he looked at Krista and Maeve. "Girls, give your mom and me a minute, will you?"

Krista glanced from Max to Winnie and back, probably trying to figure out if they were going to do anything "disgusting" again.

"Sure. Can we check out the pizza?"

"Go right ahead, but keep Maeve away from that hot oven, Krista." Max issued the directive as if he'd been in charge of kids his entire life.

"C'mon, Maeve. Wanna go see where the pizza is made?"

"Pizzaaaa!" Maeve loved pizza and Winnie's heart sank. No way were they getting out of here anytime soon.

Once the girls were out of earshot, Max turned his charm on her. His eyes alone were enough to sink her, but his smile and the way he clasped her hand left her defenseless.

"Winnie, please stay for dinner. I was hoping you would. The girls will get a kick out of homemade pizza."

Focus on his words and not how warm his hand is.

"Max, we've been over this. You've just started with Sam, and you and I are already getting in too deep."

"What's 'deep,' Win? We've known each other for years. Even if we hadn't made that beautiful baby girl, we'd have reason to enjoy a meal together. Even if I didn't need Sam and your talents it'd be perfectly natural for us to spend time together. I'm Krista's godfather and I've been so negligent in those duties."

She felt she was seeing him for the first time. Gone was the happy-go-lucky young pilot she'd met fifteen years ago. He wasn't even her protector anymore, as he'd been during his months as her CACO after Tom's death.

In front of her stood a tall, strong, battle-hardened warrior. Despite or perhaps became of his fight for his life, he was reaching out and asking her to grab a moment of joy. To share it with him.

"I'm not asking you for the world, Winnie. Just to join me for a pizza and soda. You owe me that much. Besides, it's an easy way for Maeve and me to get to know each other."

She broke their eye contact and nodded. "Okay. But, Max, this can't be a habit. I don't want the girls—"

He sighed. "I get it, Winnie. But don't expect me to worry about your feelings too much. This isn't about you."

No, it wasn't about her—as he kept pointing out.

CHAPTER TWELVE

KRISTA'S STOMACH GRUMBLED at the sight of the pizza fixings on Uncle Max's kitchen counter. She held Maeve up to see the different colors of the tomatoes, sauce, basil, cheese and dough.

"See, Maeve? We're going to make our own pizzas!" Mom had to agree to it. Uncle Max would convince her, though. Uncle Max knew how to have fun and she was so glad he was her soccer coach, but being able to hang out with him in his house was *really* cool.

"Cheeeeze." Maeve pointed to the pile of shredded mozzarella and Krista laughed.

"Yup, it's cheese. Want a teeny bite?" Krista reached out for a few white strands and passed them to Maeve. Maeve's hands were so tiny and cute. The cheese was the perfect size.

"What's this? You're not picking at the food, are you?" Mom and Uncle Max were standing behind her. Mom always sounded sterner than she ever really was. Krista hoisted Maeve higher in her arms.

"Maeve was starving, Mom. I just gave her a little bit."

"Nommmm." Maeve had half her fist shove in her mouth, along with the mozzarella.

"Sorry, Uncle Max."

"No problem. So what do you like on you pizza?"

Mom was wearing that awkward little smile sh had whenever she was uncomfortable but Krist was thrilled. They were staying for dinner!

"Can I roll out my pizza dough, Uncle Max?

"Better yet, you can toss it. Let me show yo how."

WINNIE WATCHED MAX as he showed the girls ho to knead the dough and then toss it to the perfec thickness. The girls giggled and had a blast try ing to do it themselves.

"Lemmeeee! Lemmeee!" Maeve squealed i complete bliss as Max made her a toddler-siz piece of dough to "toss." Which she did, right int Sam's waiting mouth.

"Drop it!"

Sam's ears went back at Winnie's command and he promptly dropped the now-soggy doug onto the black tile of Max's kitchen floor.

"Good boy. Leave it." Winnie bent to pic up the dough and noticed the sudden quiet. Sh looked up.

Three pairs of eyes were staring at her. Four, you counted Sam's. "What?"

"Can't Sam have that little piece of dough?" Max asked.

The room was too warm and she blamed it on the pizza oven. Max's glance slid down to her throat and cleavage, revealed by her bent-over position. Her nipples reacted as if he'd physically touched her breasts.

"No, he can't. Dogs aren't meant to eat processed human food, raw yeast dough especially. It can expand in their stomachs and make them very sick."

Krista rolled her eyes.

"Don't be disrespectful, Krista."

Krista wasn't ready to let it go so easily. "Mom, Uncle Max is right. What would one bit of dough hurt?"

"No, your mother's right." Max spoke up. "I'm sorry, Winnie, I'm not well-versed on what is and isn't good for a dog. If I had Sam, I'd be feeding him chips and beer."

The girls both giggled at his tone. Krista's expression relaxed and she mouthed "I'm sorry" to Winnie, behind Max, out of his view.

Winnie let her tension go; they gave her no choice. She managed a smile and said, "No beer for Sam, okay?"

The girls laughed again and then Max got them focused on their pizza-making.

Winnie studied his movements and her gaze

left his hands to wander over his backside. He was
clothed in a white T-shirt and jeans. His butt and
legs shouted power and sensuality. She was going
to have to get a grip or she'd beg him to knead *her*
before the night was over.

*Knock it off, Winnie. It was only one night and
it's not happening again.*

"Can you uncork the bottle of red I have on the
table?" His gaze was back on her as he threw the
request over his right shoulder. Their eyes met and
she saw the question in his.

The question that had nothing to do with wine.

"I won't have any. I'm driving."

"That's fine, but *I'd* like a glass with my pizza."

His lip twitched, and she knew he wanted to
smile at her. No, laugh at her. She must seem so
self-centered....

Amusement at her own ridiculousness bubbled
up as she turned to go to the dining room and
uncork the bottle that sat on an Italian ceramic
coaster. She noted the label and suddenly regretted that she was indeed driving.

"Do you like Montepulciano?" His breath
fanned her nape.

"Yes, I had some when...when Tom was deployed to Sigonella." She'd flown to Sicily to meet
him and then they'd take the train up north to ex-
plore the rest of Italy.

He nodded.

"You were there, weren't you?" An image of Max in his green Navy flight suit appeared in her memory. Tall as now but a bit lankier, not as filled out. Not nearly as sexy.

"Yeah, I was. I remember how excited Tom was when you agreed to meet him. Anyone would've thought you'd given him the world."

Max was talking about Tom's absolute joy that she'd flown across the "the pond" to come and see him. They'd been married, what, two years at that point? So long ago. A lifetime. She'd been working as an assistant in the local yarn shop, a stop-gap measure until she could realize her dream of owning a yarn shop in another location on the island. That dream had turned into the lucrative fiber business she owned today.

She'd always believed they'd conceived Krista on the night train between Palermo and Rome— the timing was right.

"I didn't think I liked wine, especially red wine, until that trip. We stayed at this little place in Tuscany where they had a vineyard and wine cellars on the property. I'll never forget it."

Tears moistened her eyes and she sought reassurance in Max's glance. Instead, she saw a brief flash of some emotion she couldn't identify before his expression reverted back to its neutral state.

"I picked the Montepulciano because I still have three cases of it, even after moving however many times once I finished that tour. The wine's kept amazingly well, considering I never took any precautions with it during transport. It still tastes wonderful."

"I can't believe they let you ship it!" Usually the Navy movers and their packers forbade alcohol in a change-of-station move.

"We're allowed a wine shipment from Europe. People ask for it all the time. I'm surprised you didn't know."

"How could I when I've never lived there? Besides, I've been busy with the girls and Whidbey Fibers."

"Nothing else?"

There was that damned enigmatic look again.

"What are you getting at, Max?"

"Are you dating, Winnie? Have you dated anyone besides me?"

Her stomach jumped as his words registered and she prayed he didn't notice her eyes, reddened by her restless nights.

"I don't see that it's any of your business, Max."

"Sure it is. I want to know that you're not bringing just any guy around my daughter. You're keeping her and her sister safe. But I also wonder what you do for release, Winnie. We all need to let off steam."

His deep voice lulled her as much as she fought it. "Like I said, that's no concern of yours, Max.

If I need someone to help me with my, uh, needs, I'll take care of it." Her voice was steadier than her shaky knees. Unadulterated awareness warmed her, and it felt like she had no vestige of privacy where Max was involved.

"Don't worry, Win, I'm not handing you my résumé."

Anger overrode her guilt. "Look, we need to deal with each other for the sake of the girls. But let's keep our private affairs out of it. This is my life, Max. Not Tom's, not my parents' or sister's or yours—just mine."

"Not entirely. Not when you're the mother of two beautiful girls that I care about. Certainly not when one of those girls is my daughter."

"Are you threatening me, Max?" Her neck itched and she wanted to hit something.

"No threats here, Win. I'm just someone you can count on."

KRISTA LIKED TO WATCH Mom and Uncle Max talk to each other. She was seeing a different side of Mom, one she hadn't seen before. With Uncle Max she had this tough-girl act that Krista wondered about.

Was this the "chemistry" her Honors English teacher had talked about? Like in *Romeo and Juliet,* which her class was in the middle of reading. Krista didn't care for the old English words but her teacher, Ms. Francine, made the story interesting and Krista could actually believe the two young people were in love with each other.

She liked boys but just wanted them as friends, at least for now, thank you very much. She didn't want to ever look as strained as Mom did around Uncle Max. If this was what "chemistry" meant, Krista wasn't sure she wanted it. But Mom did have that newer, brighter light in her eyes and her cheeks were pinker than normal. That had to be good.

The pizza was *soooo* yummy. Krista wished they had their own pizza oven. But then she was glad they didn't. This way, they could spend more time with Uncle Max. Wait until Sunday when she told Aunt Robyn, Grandma and Grandpa about tonight. They'd never believe Mom had finally let another man cook for her. Even if it was only Uncle Max.

CHAPTER THIRTEEN

"MOM TOOK SAM over to Uncle Max's and he made us pizza."

The loud chatter around Winnie's parents' Sunday dinner table immediately quieted and all eyes were on Krista. Winnie's good mood melted into her stomach.

It had been a nice weekend; really, it had. On Saturday Winnie took advantage of not having to worry about Sam being alone for so many hours. She and the girls went to a shopping center off-island, near Seattle. They'd laughed into the brisk wind as the ferry plowed through the rough water so typical of spring. Winnie didn't think about Max once—well, maybe she thought about him now and then, but she was able to push her thoughts aside and focus on the girls.

She planned to pick up Sam from Max's later this afternoon spending the day at her parents' home in Anacortes. No one had paid any unusual attention to her.

Until Krista piped up with that comment about Friday night.

Since her family never heard about her spending time with *any* man who could be remotely considered a romantic prospect, Krista's declaration had everyone staring at Winnie.

Winnie took it all in. Her mother, Barbara, sat at one end of the table, her eyes bright and her smile content as she had all her chicks in her nest for the afternoon. Krista sat between her brothers Evan and Eddie, who were across from Maeve, Winnie, Robyn and Doug. Doug, Robyn's husband, played his usual role of the strong silent type.

Evan and Eddie were studying to be Army and Navy doctors, respectively, at the Uniformed Services University of Health Sciences in Bethesda, Maryland. Evan had graduated last year and was in his residency at Johns Hopkins for gastroenterology. Eddie still had a year of medical school to finish. They'd managed to get the weekend off together and surprised her parents on Thursday night. They went back east in the morning.

"Um, sorry, Mom." Krista shot her an apologetic look. She clearly knew she'd opened a can of worms. Winnie sighed. Krista was thirteen. Thirteen-year-olds blurted out inappropriate things all the time. It was in the young-teen job description.

"*Uncle* Max?" Robyn, seated next to Winnie, whispered under her breath.

"Who's Max? The Max we knew?" Barbara's eyebrows were up, along with her maternal radar.

Crap.

"Max Ford, as in Tom's best friend." Evan spoke around a mouthful of green-bean casserole. Didn't they feed their medical residents at the National Institute of Health?

"As in Lieutenant Max Ford, the man who was your CACO?" Hugh spoke quietly from the head of the table. Winnie looked at her dad. No judging, no recrimination, just honest inquisitiveness.

"Yeah. As in my former CACO. And he's a Commander now. He had command of his own squadron."

"We know that, honey. We saw that he was injured pretty badly over there, too. On the news they said he's a hero." Good old Dad, strong and steady.

"He made you pizza? Where does he live?" Barbara faced Krista. No doubt she thought her granddaughter would be a softer target than Winnie.

Forget it, Mom. Winnie wasn't giving her a chance to interrogate Krista.

"He lives in Dugualla Bay, Mom. We went by to drop off Sam on Friday night and he invited us in for dinner. He learned how to make authentic Neapolitan pizza during his deployment to Italy."

"Why were you dropping Sam off with him?"

"When did he move back here?"

Her younger brothers assaulted her with questions in their greed to know more about Max. Evan and Eddie had idolized him ever since Tom had introduced them back in the days before Krista was born. Max and Tom were the reason both brothers had chosen the military to pursue their medical training.

Back when life was simpler—just Winnie and Tom—he'd served as a mentor to all her siblings but especially her brothers. He'd introduced them to his Navy buddies and they saw the most of Max since he and Tom spent a lot of time together off-duty. Tom and Max had taken the boys to Air Shows, video-gaming conventions and more— whatever they'd all enjoy. To Evan and Eddie, Tom could do no wrong. His death had left a big hole in their lives, too.

Yet they'd all survived, one way or another. Her brothers had dried their tears and gone to the service academies. Evan went to West Point in New York and Eddie went to the Naval Academy in Annapolis. They'd both done their first tours with squadrons and were now medical professionals.

They were smart, and incredible doctors. But they were still pains in the butt as brothers.

She swore under her breath. This was so *not* going to turn into an inquisition.

"Why I took Sam over there's none of your business. You know my therapy work is confidential."

"So Max is one of your clients?" Evan, the blond brother who always wore a smile on his face, ignored her confidentiality comment, which irked her since as a doctor he should understand better than anyone.

"He survived the attack when he saved his squadron. The paper never mentioned exactly how he'd been hurt," Eddie, dark-haired and brooding, said. He concentrated on peeling the label from his bottle of beer.

"Why are you asking me these questions if you already know the answers?" Winnie took a gulp of cold water. "As I said, it's confidential. And I never said he was a client. You assumed it."

Krista sat quietly between her two uncles, her face red and her eyes obviously wet. Winnie reached across the table to take her hand, but Krista put her hand in her lap.

"Honey, it's okay."

Krista looked out from under her long lashes. "I didn't mean to start a war. Jeez."

"Honey, you didn't start anything." Barbara squeezed Krista's shoulder, then turned back to Winnie.

Finally, Grandma comes to her senses.

"How long have you been seeing Max, Winnie?"

Or maybe not.

"I'm not *seeing* him, Mom. We're just working together on a project." Maybe this little lie would throw Mom off the trail. And it wasn't a lie; they *were* working on a project together. One that would allow Maeve to get to know her father. But she couldn't discuss her volunteer work with Max and Sam—it would be a violation of client confidentiality.

Double crap.

"A project, eh?" Barbara wasn't placated, not by a long shot. "What did he think about your family? Did he even know you had another daughter?" Bitterness laced her words. Mom had never gotten over Winnie's refusal to share information about Maeve's biological beginnings.

"He's met Maeve, and he wasn't as fazed as you apparently still are."

In fact, he'd had every reason to be a lot *more* affected, to be angry, to throw in her face the fact that he'd been there for her during her darkest hours.

But Max never threw the past in her face. Ever.

It would be easier on her guilty conscience if he'd taken his anger and disappointment out on her. He had every right to. But her mother did not.

"Mom, please, let's stop right there."

"Okay, ladies, keep it simple." Hugh held up his hands.

"It's not just Mom and Winnie, Dad. Eddie and Evan have their hands in the pot, too." Robyn came to her rescue, but Winnie noted that Doug remained silent. He'd been part of the family for more than ten years and had learned to survive by staying out of family discussions whenever possible.

"Still, it's Sunday and this is supposed to be a nice, *quiet* family time," Hugh said.

"Mommy, I don't want this dinner!" Brendan slammed his hands down next to his plate, where the tot-size silverware rested. The fork tines pressed into his fists and he wailed.

"Come here, Brendan, and calm down." Robyn reached for him and Winnie envied her the distraction from the firing squad.

"You're telling me Max had no concern whatsoever about how you had a child—apparently without a father around?"

"Mother, I'm going to ignore that for the sake of family unity." Winnie only called Barb "Mother" when she was ready to explode with anger.

Barbara knew that. She pressed forward, anyway.

"Max was Tom's best friend, after all, wasn't he? Of course he'd want to know who the father was. What did you tell him?"

Winnie bit her tongue and clenched her napkin, hidden beneath the linen tablecloth.

"What did you tell him, Winnie?" Eddie's eyes reflected his desire to know the biggest secret the family had. Winnie stared at Eddie—then made her fatal mistake.

She looked at Maeve; Eddie's glance followed. It was so obvious. Maeve had "Max" stamped all over her.

"Holy shit." Eddie whistled and shook his head.

"What?" Barb hated not being in on things.

Eddie shook his head again.

Hugh missed nothing. "If Maeve's father is someone we know, Winnie, you shouldn't be afraid to tell us."

The expression on Barb's face reflected her confusion.

"What am I not getting here? We're talking about Max, then Maeve's father, then— Oh. My. Gosh!" Her eyes grew so round Winnie was positive they were going to pop out and fly across the table.

All heads turned toward Maeve.

She started crying.

All eyes were back on Winnie.

"Max is Maeve's father." Barbara whispered the proclamation.

"Yes. Max is Maeve's father." Winnie met her mother's gaze, then cast her glance at Krista, who sat there silent, gazing at her plate.

You have to talk to her alone, away from this chaos.

"Krista, did you know this?" Barb sought verification that she wasn't alone in her confusion.

Krista slowly nodded, and Barb made a weird yelping sound as if holding back a screech of frustration.

Robyn waved her hands in front of her face. "Can we please keep calm and—"

"Carry on?" Eddie interrupted, which cracked up all the men at the table. Their laughter made Winnie want to cry. But she did see Krista's weak smile and knew that, somehow, it would all work out.

"What's the matter, Maeve? Don't you like my mashed potatoes anymore?" Barb chose to distract herself with her granddaughter. She put her face up to Maeve's, hand poised to place another heaping spoonful of the gravy-laden spuds into the child's mouth. But Maeve's mouth was puckered in disgust and her arm flexed straight in front of her as if fending off evil spirits.

"No!"

"Mom, leave her be. She needs her nap." Barb's insistence that everyone eat together, no matter what, was well-intentioned, but the heat of the crowded dining room made sweat drip between Winnie's shoulder blades. It felt like winter with the warmth of a roaring woodstove instead of spring. Except that the cool wind had blown away the morning fog, and the sun shone through the

floor-to-ceiling windows. Sunlight was in shor
supply during the winters, and it was always a re
lief when the days started to grow longer.

"Maybe Brendan and Maeve will take a nap to
gether?" Robyn elbowed Winnie, then smiled a
her as she asked the question.

"Sure, why don't we try that?" she said in relie
as she grabbed onto Robyn's lifeline.

"But by the time you get back, dinner will b
cold." Barb frowned, and Hugh kept an eye on hi
wife. Krista looked content as her uncles doted o
her. Winnie said a silent thanks that at least he
brothers realized the impact of this conversatio
on Krista's emotions.

"We'll put our plates in the microwave," Win
nie said. Robyn had already left the room and sh
quickly followed.

KRISTA REMAINED AT THE table with her uncles an
grandparents. She felt so stupid!

"How's soccer, Krista? Your mom tells m
you're a natural at it." Eddie always knew wha
she liked to talk about.

"You say that every year, Uncle Eddie."

"No, he doesn't, squirt. When you were fou
years old all we talked about was how terrible yo
were." Uncle Evan's smirk made her giggle. Bu
she still felt badly about mentioning Uncle Ma
at the table.

"I wasn't that terrible. I was only four!"

"I was Olympic-level right from age three." Uncle Evan leaned in to prod her.

"No, *you* were five, *I* was three." Eddie pointed his fork at Evan. The tines were a little too close to her eyes.

"Uncle Evan and Uncle Eddie, you're both nuts." But she couldn't keep the smile off her face. She loved her uncles. Even if she felt really stupid about "Uncle" Max right now.

"Listen, kid, don't worry about all that stuff with your mom, grandma and Uncle Max. Things work out in ways we never expect." Grandpa Hugh smiled and gave her a wink once she looked at him fully.

"Yes, I'm sorry if I upset you with my reaction, dear. It's…a surprise to me, that's all." Grandma wanted to be part of making her feel better. Krista loved them all.

Eddie and Evan exchanged a look and she squirmed. She still hated that everyone knew her business.

"THANKS FOR HAVING my back, sis." Winnie taped up the sides of Maeve's diaper and lifted her onto her feet. She'd changed her on the bed while Robyn was in the guest room bath, coaxing Brendan to use the toilet.

"No problem." Robyn spoke from the bathroom as Winnie stood up.

"Grommmeeee!" Maeve squealed.

"Don't you want a nap?"

"No."

"Okay, we'll go back. Just a minute."

Brendan ran into the bedroom, making faces at Maeve. She let out her deep belly laugh. This only egged Brendan on, and he continued to behave like a vaudeville clown. As long as his little baby cousin was chuckling, he was ready to perform.

"Don't think for one minute that I support you, though." Robyn's soft voice disguised the exasperation and anger that Winnie suspected lay just beneath her serene facade.

"What? You're the only one who's supported me through all of this!"

"Not true, Win. The whole family has supported you, including Krista. They just didn't know what exactly they were supporting."

"But you of all people understand—"

"I understand your motives, yes, but I've told you over and over that you need to come clean about all of it. Your guilt and fear have poisoned your relationship with Max. Maeve's relationship with him, too. It'll probably work out, but he's missed the better part of her first two years. Krista would have benefited from seeing Max, too, you know. She needs to see a man be a father and know that not all dads die or leave."

Robyn waved her right hand. "You can't keep expecting people to be there for you when you do the most self-destructive things, Win."

"What the hell are you talking about? You make it sound as if I had a choice about Tom's dying."

"Enough about Tom's death! He's been gone for over five years, sis. Five *years*. Krista's memories of him are happy but they're from when she was a little girl. Maeve will never know him. You need to focus on who's here now so that you can make a life for today."

Winnie stared at Robyn. Robyn's curly hair, so much like her own, was in complete disarray, a fuzzy frame around her heart-shaped face. Her eyes were wild, the look of a woman who hadn't slept in weeks.

"Were you up last night?"

"Of course I was up last night. Brendan has started to have night terrors."

"Ouch." Winnie thought back to when Krista had them—she'd been four or five, just a bit older than Brendan. Tom had been deployed on the aircraft carrier most of the scary nights and Winnie never forgot how Krista's screams had wakened her night after night.

"'Ouch' is right, but this too shall pass. How old was Krista when hers stopped?"

"Oh, I don't think it lasted that long, maybe six months on and off?" That time was a blur to her nine years later.

"Good. But back to the real issue, Winnie. What are you going to do about Max?"

"Why are you stuck on this? I'm not doing anything except what I should've done sooner. I'm supporting him as Maeve's father."

"And Krista's uncle, coach and godfather." Robyn didn't relent and Winnie remembered why she'd hesitated to tell Robyn about Max in the beginning. Robyn never allowed any wiggle room for white lies or avoidance.

"Yes, yes. Can we move on?"

"I hope you do move on, Winnie. There's a lot more to life than work and the girls, no matter how much you love both." Robyn took Maeve from Winnie's arms.

"Are you a sleepy baby?" Maeve leaned her head on her aunt's shoulder and did a long, slow blink. She'd be asleep in seconds, despite her insistence on not napping.

"You've got to give Mom and the boys time to absorb everything."

Tears burned Winnie's lids and she wished she was alone so she could release the sobs—and the pent-up frustration and anxiety she'd been holding inside.

Instead, she wiped her eyes and looked at her

sister. "Well, that's that. They know. I'll never be able to thank you enough for keeping my secret all this time. Even though you didn't agree."

"You'd do the same for me." Robyn turned to leave the room. "C'mon, Brendan, do you want a cupcake? Grandma made your favorite kind."

"Chocolate with vanilla icing and sprinkles!" Brendan recited his beloved cupcake ingredients with a hopeful expression. "I can count to twenty, Mommy."

"You're such a smart boy. Where did you learn to count all the way up to twenty?"

"On the side of the house. I painted the numbers so I'd 'member them."

Robyn's eyes widened. "You painted the side of the house?"

"Uh-huh. Grammy said I could."

"Was Grammy with you when you did this?"

"No, she went inside to put on her play clothes."

"Was Daddy with you?"

"No, you and Daddy were in the car."

"Hmm." Robyn stared at her son for a moment, then turned back to Winnie with a questioning look.

"What's that about?"

"I have no idea but I'm sure we'll find out." Robyn sighed. "Anyhow, I'd think you'd be relieved that you don't have to keep your guard up anymore. And, Win, Max seems to want to be with you and the girls. Why are you fighting it?"

"Correction—Max wants to be with the girls. Especially Maeve." Even as she said it, she knew that wasn't fair. Max hadn't shown favoritism to either girl; he'd acted as if he'd found out he had two daughters, not one.

He'll never forgive you.

"Winnie, trust me. There are ways Max could get to know Maeve better without involving you and Krista so completely. He's interested in getting to know *you* again, too."

"You can't assume that when you haven't even seen him, Robyn. You're just putting your rosy spin on things, as usual."

"Not rosy, Win, practical. You're obviously still hot for the guy or you wouldn't be so damned defensive. He wants a chance to see how things could work, so why not let go for once and see what happens?"

"I don't need a man in my life, Robyn."

"That's where you're wrong. Your girls need him, therefore you need him. It's not just about you anymore."

Where had she heard that before? "Nice try, sis, but you don't understand. Max wants to know the girls. Me, not so much. I'm the one that betrayed him, remember? Plus, we have too much history between us. How could we look at each other without all of that getting in the way? And he's going to keep flying after the Navy. I'm never getting involved with a Navy man *or* a pilot again. It's hard enough to let the girls become close to him but I don't have to do the same."

"You had a choice, Winnie. You didn't have to take Max on as a client. You didn't have to leave Sam there—all weekend. You didn't have to tell him about Maeve right away. You could have continued to avoid him—and put off his discovery of Maeve for quite a while. Whidbey's a big island, even on the base. It's easy not to see someone unless you really want to."

Winnie stayed silent. It was the only defense against Robyn when she was on a tear.

"Get real, Winnie. No one forced you to have sex with him."

Winnie sighed. "And your point is?"

"My point, sis, is that you want to let Max back in. Even if you can't admit it to me yet, admit it to yourself. You have ulterior motives. Why else would you risk the security and peaceful life you claim you've built for you and the girls? All in one day?"

Winnie was spared having to provide an answer. Barbara's shriek outside the guest-room window cut through the intensity between her and Robyn.

They both hurried to the window, and Win-

nie pulled back the sheers and cracked open the
window.

Barbara stood outside with Maeve on her hip,
one hand over her mouth—staring at a wavering
row of crudely drawn numbers.

"I told him he could do his finger painting
later," she said. "But I guess he misunderstood…"
Apparently Grandma hadn't approved of Brendan's self-teaching plans, after all.

CHAPTER FOURTEEN

"It's not a big deal, Mom. As long as you'll keep Maeve happy, Krista and I will take care of this."

Winnie had put on one of her father's work jumpsuits and stood next to Krista. A large bucket of white paint and two large paintbrushes sat between them on the tarp they'd spread on the grass.

"We owe you, and Brendan knows it." Robyn looked down at Brendan with reproach.

"I like to paint, Mommy. And I like numbers."

"Yes, but you're not supposed to paint them on walls or the sides of buildings." Robyn's initial anger had faded once she saw the huge tears in Brendan's eyes.

"The men are lucky to get out of this." Barbara held Maeve and they both giggled. The energy between grandmother and granddaughter was magical and Winnie never tired of watching it.

"Hard to believe there's a hockey game today, in this weather." It was a warm spring day, unusual for Anacortes. Spring was usually a combination of sun and clouds but always with a brisk cold breeze. The temperature had climbed into the low sixties.

"It's the play-offs." The guys had left immediately after brunch to go to Vancouver, Canada, for an evening game. The brothers were rarely home individually, let alone together, and it was male-bonding time. Doug had given Robyn a lingering kiss before he left with them, and Winnie felt a pang of wanting that for herself again.

Was Robyn right? Did she, despite her protestations, want to be with Max?

She needed to stay away from her family's Sunday meals for a few weeks if she wanted to keep her sanity.

"We've got it, Mom. You can put Maeve down for her nap if you want." Barbara hesitated; Winnie knew Mom desperately wanted to ask for details of Maeve's birth and Winnie's relationship with Max.

"Yeah, Mom. I'm going to take Brendan home now. Why don't you lie down when Maeve does?"

"Oh, no. I'll be right out to help you, Winnie."

"Mom, you have to stay inside so you'll hear her if she wakes up."

And I want to be alone with Krista.

Krista had remained silent throughout the conversation. She attacked the red numbers with gusto and splattered globs of white paint on her and Winnie.

"Whoa, girl, careful with that weapon you're packing!" Winnie tried to force a smile.

Krista didn't react.

Winnie met Robyn's gaze.

Help me. Get Mom out of here.

"Mom, let's go back in. I have to ask you something."

Finally Barb got the hint and turned back to the house with Robyn. She paused and looked over her shoulder, frowning. "Call if you gals need me."

"Thanks, Mom."

"Thanks, Grammy."

Once Winnie was sure they were out of earshot she took a deep breath. "I'm so sorry about today, Krista. This is not your fault. Or your problem."

Krista kept stroking her brush back and forth, up and down. When they'd covered the numbers, the whole wall would have to be repainted.

"Actually, it *is* my problem, Mom. Maeve isn't the only kid in this family." Her tone was acid but Winnie didn't miss the trembling in her voice. Her heart ached for Krista but Krista wasn't a little girl anymore. Her hurts couldn't be hugged away so readily.

"I know, sweetheart. I should have told you sooner about Uncle Max, maybe even right after, um, I found out I was pregnant."

"Yeah, you *should* have. Instead of all that

bullshit about 'it's someone you know but I can't tell you who it is yet.'"

"Watch your language. Your sister is a miracle—and so are you. I told you that when the time was right, we'd talk about Maeve's father. The time didn't come along until this week."

"I've missed Uncle Max. I'm glad he's back."

Here it was. Krista's real concern.

Winnie nodded. "Well, now we all know, and we're going to be spending a lot of time together. I don't want you to get your hopes up, Krista. I mean, um…" She focused on the swath of wood siding where the paint had dripped after Brendan painted 17.

"You didn't want me to think we were going to have a new dad. I'm not a *baby,* Mom. I know you had sex with Uncle Max. It doesn't mean you have to marry him. But you *did* let him kiss you in the kitchen that night."

A jolt went through Winnie and she dropped her brush. Where had Krista gotten such an attitude? Did she really understand what she was saying?

"It's best if a baby can be brought into a loving home with two parents," she said calmly, picking up her paintbrush. "Like you were. I've felt bad about you *and* Maeve not having a dad around, but not bad enough to find a man just for the sake of it." Krista was entitled to honesty.

"Or woman. Joanna's parents are two moms."

"Yes, they are, and that's fine, but I like men. So for me, for our family, it would be a man." Winnie's hand shook as she continued to paint even where it wasn't needed. She'd always been candid with Krista about sexuality and the facts of life, but it hadn't really hit her yet that her daughter was on the verge of becoming a young woman. She had an open mind and heart, qualities that Winnie admired and espoused—even if they weren't so easy for *her* at the moment.

"So why didn't you marry Uncle Max when you had Maeve?"

Here was the difference between a thirteen-year-old and a young woman. As much as Krista's brain knew that sex wasn't a prerequisite for marriage, her heart still longed for the full picture. The family she'd had before.

"Well, as I said, it wasn't time to bring a man into our lives. It was still too soon after your dad's death."

"It was over three years after he died, wasn't it?" Krista had always been good at math.

"Yes. But, honey, three years isn't very long. It sounds like ages to you now, but it can feel like the blink of an eye. I was gaining momentum with my career and you were doing great in the new school."

Winnie paused and stared away from the bright white side of the house, toward the water that lay just past the tree line on the edge of her parents' property.

"Life's complicated, honey. Adults don't deal with change as easily as you do when you're younger. I know you miss Daddy and you'd bring him back if you could, but I also know you don't have as big a hole in your heart anymore. You told me so last year."

"Yeah, but having Uncle Max around has made me realize how much I miss having a dad."

Breathe. Breathe again.

She tried to relax. She felt Krista's emotional punch physically, as if she'd been hit in the stomach. But Krista deserved to be heard and there was no right or wrong about her wishes. They were just the desires of a daughter who'd spent most of her childhood with her mother and was keenly aware of the loss of her father.

"I'm so glad you're enjoying your time with Uncle Max, honey. And it's important for Maeve to know her father. I'll never get in the way of that with either of you."

She put down her brush and looked at Krista. "You need to understand that it's not an automatic given that we'll *all* get along. Uncle Max and I will always be dear friends, but we're two very different people. We've both been through a lot. I lost my husband and, he, well, you know he was in the war, right?"

"Yeah, he told me he has DTSP."

Winnie's lips twitched. "Uh, that's PTSD." She paused, watching Krista for any sign that this was too much information for one day. When she saw nothing to indicate an overload, she pressed on.

"Yes, Uncle Max has some injuries to work through. He's done well recovering from the shrapnel wounds and he's physically strong again. He just needs more time for his brain to heal from the shock of everything he saw and experienced."

"He said it's like when you go to a rock concert or listen to your MP3 player really loud. When you can't get the songs out of your head. But his songs are a lot quieter now, he said, and most days he doesn't hear them anymore."

Leave it to Max to put something so complex into terms a teen could comprehend.

"Yes, and he's working with Sam to help him get rid of the remaining 'noise.'"

They'd finished painting over Brendan's numbers and Krista became quiet. A bee buzzed near the rhododendron bush next to them, and its hum seemed to loosen the tense knot in Winnie's neck.

"I'm really sorry, Krista. I love you so much and I never wanted to hurt your feelings. You know that, don't you?"

Krista nodded, her gaze lowered. Winnie took in the dejected expression on Krista's face.

"Come here, honey."

Krista stepped forward and Winnie hugge
her tight. She'd already messed up by not tell
ing Krista more about Maeve from the start. Sh
didn't want to risk losing her because of anythin
as stupid as her own stubbornness.

Krista hugged her back, and that made up fc
every swearword uttered by her eldest daughter

"Thanks, Mom." Krista pulled away and ges
tured at the side of the house. "We did a good jol
didn't we?"

"Yes, we did," Winnie agreed, not adding tha
someone else would have to run a roller over th
whole thing. "High five!" She held her hand u
and Krista slapped it in celebration.

"Is it time to go see Uncle Max?" So much fc
a moment of serenity.

"Yes, when Maeve wakes up from her nap.
Winnie refrained from mentioning that it wasn
"time to go see Uncle Max" but "time to pick u
the dog." Right now, she needed all the momm
points she could get.

THEIR PLANS TO LEAVE hit a snag when Maeve didn
wake up on her own.

"She's pooped from such a long morning an
then the meal. Let her sleep as long as she need
to." Barbara went to the stove to prepare anothe
pot of tea.

"No, thanks, Mom. We have to get going. It'

a school night and we have a forty-five-minute drive ahead of us."

"I never woke you kids when you were little." Barb tried another trick. "Never wake a sleeping baby."

"I'll just get her up and into her car seat." With any luck, Maeve would doze until they got to Max's.

"Good luck with that one. She's cranky when she's tired."

As if Winnie didn't know her own daughter. Actually, Maeve was a pretty easygoing baby. For the most part. When she ate her regular diet of veggies, protein and milk. Not so much when she'd had all kinds of high-carb treats at Barb's.

"She's probably still sleeping because she crashed after that sugar high from dessert." Winnie herself had avoided the sweet gelatin-and-canned-pineapple concoction, along with the cupcakes. Barb always overdid the sweets.

"Nonsense. All you kids ate it. You're turning into a health-nut whack-job, Winnie."

"Thanks, Mom, I appreciate that." She smiled at Krista. "I'll be right back. Krista, go and load the stuff in the car, will you?"

"Sure." Noticeably sunnier since their talk, Krista bounced about the family room gathering up their things.

Soon after, Krista was buckled into the backseat next to Maeve's car seat, where Winnie had placed her, still sound asleep.

She turned to the driver's-side door.

"I'm sorry you didn't feel comfortable enough to tell us who Maeve's father was before, Winnie."

"Mom, don't do a guilt number on me now. I'm sorry I worried you or stressed you at all. But I just wasn't in a place to share any more of my life—with anyone."

Barb sniffed. "I suppose we can talk about it at another time." The closest thing to an olive branch Barb would ever offer her.

Winnie leaned forward and gave her mother a quick peck on the cheek. "Okay, let's do that. Thanks for a great meal today and please don't obsess over this, okay, Mom?"

"I don't obsess, Winnie. I'm just concerned. I'm a mother."

"I know." She got in the car and started the engine. Maybe she should've moved after Tom was killed. She could be living anywhere else in the country, away from this constant family involvement.

But that would never have been right for Krista. Or for *her,* truth be told. This was where she'd been born and raised. Where she'd had her babies. The mountain views, water and strong winds were a part of her. They were in her blood.

And now in her daughters'.

THE DRIVE DOWN TO WHIDBEY and into Dugualla Bay was quiet. Maeve slept on, and Krista listened to her MP3 player.

She's thinking about our conversation.

A lump formed in Winnie's throat and her tears made the road waver. She blinked.

She'd get through this, damn it. She had to.

Problem was, she'd taken on too much during the past eighteen months. It was her own fault. Keeping secrets took a lot of energy and energy wasn't something she had to spare these days.

"You okay, Mom?"

Krista's worried voice jarred her out of her thoughts.

"Just digesting the day, sweetheart. You know I'm sorry, right?"

"Yes, Mom, you've said that a million times. But don't ever block me out again."

Winnie drew in a breath, then let her shoulders relax against the seat.

They pulled into Max's drive twenty minutes later and Winnie shut off the engine. She wished she could keep it running and fetch Sam in a quick pit stop. But nothing with Max was ever going to be quick again. Not as long as Krista and Maeve had anything to do with it.

Heck, even her family—her parents and siblings—posed a threat. She wouldn't put it past them to come down here and subject him to an inquisition.

They wouldn't, of course. At least not tonight…

Max opened the front door as she climbed up the steps and Sam came racing out to greet her.

"Hi, big boy! Were you a good boy?" She rubbed his ears and chest, and his tongue lolled to the side in canine ecstasy.

"He was great. We walked for a few miles yesterday, and went on another long one this morning. He really flakes out when he gets back into the house." Was that a note of pride in Max's voice?

Sam's tail thumped next to her foot as he gazed adoringly up at Max.

"I'm glad you enjoyed your time together. I won't take any more of it, though. Maeve's asleep in the car and Krista's watching her. We have to get back—it's a school night."

"She doesn't look asleep to me." Max nodded toward the drive and Winnie turned to see Maeve banging her yellow stuffed rabbit against the window. Krista waved.

"Oh." *Of course* Maeve was awake. "We still have a half-hour drive home and, like I said, tomorrow's a school day. I need to go."

"Let me buy you all ice cream. I'll follow you into town and we'll stop at Dolly's."

Winnie opened her mouth, the refusal ready

to fire. They'd eaten at her parents', and the girls didn't need a second dessert.

She shut her mouth. And bit her lip.

"Ouch!" She winced.

Max frowned. "You okay? I don't mean to upset you, Winnie. I just thought it might be fun to take the girls out for a treat." He stared at her. "You look awful. What happened with your parents?"

"They found out you're Maeve's father."

He whistled. "So you never told them, either."

"Of course I didn't. I wouldn't tell someone else and not tell you. Except for Robyn."

He stood silent for a minute. She looked down at the ground. Then his arms were around her before she could protest and he embraced her in a big bear hug. "It's going to be okay, Winnie. One step at a time."

His strong arms held her tight, his chest warm against her forehead. There was nothing sexual in his gesture—just a friend's comfort.

Until she turned her head and laid it on his shoulder, for the briefest moment. The scant inch it drew their bodies closer was too much. Winnie heard his heartbeat and felt his chest move as he breathed.

She pulled away from his warmth before she wanted, *needed,* more than a hug. A glance at the car revealed that they had a rapt audience.

"I don't need your sympathy, Max."

"It's not sympathy, Win. Trust me. I'm just showing some compassion and concern for the mother of my child. Now let me buy you an ice cream."

If Krista ever learned that Uncle Max had invited them out and Winnie had refused, it would only cause more heartache than Winnie could stand.

"Okay. Thanks," she muttered. "You'll follow us?"

"Right behind you."

"See you there."

HE WATCHED HER CLIP on Sam's leash and walk him to her car. He knew she felt beaten down and emotionally exhausted. He'd been there; hell, he was *still* there. It'd been a long week. But in spite of the stress and the difficult transition, he knew one thing had never changed between them.

Max wanted her in his bed, and as much as Winnie might deny it, she wanted it, too.

Their situation wasn't as simple as merely dating a single mother. He'd done that. This single mom was Winnie. She was complicated and they had a tangled history—because of Tom, because of that night two years ago. Max never turned down a challenge, but even though he wanted to go to bed with her again, he didn't want the complications that would undoubtedly ensue.

He followed her station wagon and pulled in beside to her at Dolly's Dairy Delight. Time to work on the friendship. Forget any hope of being a couple. And yes, forget the sex!

CHAPTER FIFTEEN

WINNIE STARTED THE DAY the same way she'd started every day in the weeks since Max had learned about Maeve. Had it been an entire month already? Since she'd told Max he was a father, since she'd been fighting her constant attraction to him?

She saw that Krista was awake and carried Maeve into the kitchen, where she made her mandatory cup of coffee. After she'd filled her mug and topped it with organic half-and-half, she allowed Maeve to play in the family room, in sight of the kitchen and back deck.

As routine as it all was, her life had taken on new purpose. She found joy in the mundane. Today Maeve had awakened as her usual cheerful self and hadn't protested one bit as Winnie changed her. Krista's muted, "Thanks, Mom," from under the covers carried the simplicity of a child's love for her mother. The cup of coffee was spectacular—even more so because she enjoyed it on her deck while Sam took care of his morning business in the yard below.

She could finally relax. The constant worry over when to tell Max about Maeve was gone.

Not the guilt, however, that weighed on her each time she looked at Max and saw the absolute delight and reverence he held for Maeve. She'd kept this from Maeve, not just Max. Krista, too, benefited from Max's presence in ways Winnie hadn't really considered.

"Stop it. You had every reason to protect him from unsettling news. He was at war." She spoke to the empty deck. Maeve glanced up from her toys to see what her mother was whispering about.

But Max wasn't at war anymore. He was here, back in her life in the biggest possible way. As Maeve's father.

Since she was being completely honest with herself, she admitted that there was nothing she'd like more than to go to bed with Max. But it would make their relationship too intense, too involved, and that would affect the girls. It would risk setting them up for a fall. As much as her body needed sexual release there was no reason it had to be with Max. In fact, there was every reason it *shouldn't* be with Max.

He was planning to fly. She couldn't go back to censoring everything she said, everything she felt, just to protect him from any upset, just to ensure that he could keep his mind clear for his flights.

He was angry with her over Maeve, might always be. But she knew he still looked at her with the same desire they'd shared the one night they'd made love.

"Damn you, Max," she whispered as she sipped her coffee and gazed out at the trees in her yard. Of all the careers he could've pursued after he retired from the Navy, he had to pick one as dangerous as flying small aircraft? Especially in the often-harsh weather conditions and challenging terrain of the Pacific Northwest?

What are you going to do then? Never speak to him? Never let the girls talk to him unless he's not flying the next day?

"Hey, puppy."

Sam looked up at her from where he sat, near the patch of tulips she'd planted last fall. They were close to full bloom.

"Okay, pooch, let's go. Good boy," she praised him as he loped across the lawn toward the deck steps. He took the five steps in one leap and slid across the deck to her feet.

"You're a silly guy, aren't you?"

Sam rolled on his back for a belly rub.

"Mom, phone!" Krista's shout had her up and in the house in seconds. Maeve sat in the middle of her pile of soft blocks, still trying to stack them with no regard for size or shape.

"Who is it?"

"Uncle Max." Krista smiled.

Crapola.

"Hello?"

"Good morning, Winnie. How's it going?" The husky tone of his voice reached through the phone as if he'd physically touched her.

He wasn't even in the same room.

"Great, everything's great. I'm about to get the girls off to school, though. Will this take long? If so, I can call you back in about thirty minutes."

"No, no, I just wanted to ask if you can join me for lunch on Saturday. But just you this time. Do you have someone who can mind the girls?"

"Ah." Her voice caught and she cursed herself for being so vulnerable. She opened her mouth to turn him down.

Aren't you tired of running?

"I'll ask Robyn and let you know. Anything else?"

"No. Just make sure you're dressed for a bit of a hike. I'll pick you up at noon."

"Um, fine. If you don't hear from me otherwise."

"And, Winnie?"

"Yes?"

"Chill out. It's not a date." He hung up.

She put the phone back. The flicker of anticipation that his call had sparked blew out as if blasted by gale-force winds.

"So Uncle Max is taking you out on a date?"

The smirk on Krista's face should have annoyed her. Instead, she hardly noticed.

"No, definitely not a date." Winnie had to smile in spite of herself. It really was amusing, the way she got worked up over anything to do with Max. They *could* do this, be good friends while raising the girls together. No complications. Maybe this hike or whatever it was would provide the respite they needed to make a fresh start....

"Just two friends meeting for lunch," she added.

"Yeah, right. You made a baby together, Mom."

"Krista, there is absolutely no excuse for you to be so rude to me. I'm your mother, and don't forget it."

Krista's huge sigh echoed across the kitchen but Winnie ignored it.

"Yes, Uncle Max and I had Maeve together," she went on. "So it's up to us to raise her together, and you're included in this since Max loves you, too. But sometimes we need to have adult conversations away from you kids, just like any other parents do, married or not."

"Moooommmeee!" Maeve had come up the two short steps from the sunken family room and brought several of her cloth blocks with her. She dumped them on the floor by Winnie's feet.

"Thank you, little girl." She bent down and hugged Maeve, who hugged her back.

"Luff Momma."

"Love you, too, sweetness."

Winnie straightened up and caught Krista staring at them. "Did you understand what I said, Krista? Is everything clear?"

"Sure, Mom."

If Winnie kept her relationship with Max equally clear and he did the same, they'd all be okay.

"THANKS, LAURA." MAX took the large brown paper bag from the owner of his favorite island deli.

"No problem, Max. Are you sharing it with anyone I know?" Her query was innocent enough, but Max remembered a time when he might have had an interest in Laura. She was a former pilot who got out of the Navy and bought the deli a few years back. They had shared a lot in common. On paper, anyway.

She's nothing like Winnie.

"No, just a friend." It was his way of keeping his privacy and averting any island gossip about Winnie. Whidbey was a large enough place that Laura probably didn't even know Winnie, but you could never be too sure.

"Enjoy it. I put in extra-large pieces of my apple pie."

"Thanks! See you later."

Once back in his truck, Max took out the picnic

lunch he'd purchased and repacked everything in his backpack.

This was the first time he and Winnie were going to get together for a reason other than Maeve or his therapy with Sam. He wanted it to go well.

It had only been a month since he'd found out he was a father, that he'd been told one unforeseen night of passion with Winnie had made a beautiful baby girl.

It felt like years.

The grief over missing Maeve's birth and her first year came at him like a sucker punch as he drove down to Winnie's place.

How ironic that he'd been there for Krista's birth more than thirteen years ago, when Tom had been out doing touch-and-goes with an aircraft. Touch-and-goes were local Naval aviation events, taking a plane out and landing it for a few seconds before once again taking off. It exercised the aircraft's function as well as the pilot's acuity.

Tom had been radioed to come back from his last touch-and-go and he'd landed at N.A.S. Whidbey just as Krista arrived, two weeks earlier than expected.

Max had picked up Winnie from their house and driven her to the base hospital. He'd left her side to do what Winnie had asked him to—he got Tom there as quickly as possible. When he'd come back to the hospital with Tom, he'd expected to be happy for his best friend. He hadn't expected to be in awe of the tiny infant, and how strong Winnie had been. He often thought of her as Tom's nagging wife back then, but his hard stance had softened after Krista's birth.

Tom's expression had been one of sheer joy when he entered the room and saw Krista in Winnie's arms.

That's a memory you need to share with Krista.

He had a history not only with Winnie but with Krista. And now, Maeve. The connection between him and Winnie was fraught with pain, from Tom's death to Winnie's betrayal in not telling him about Maeve. Their unique shared history didn't have a lot of bright spots to date, except for the girls.

And the night of the Air Show.

He pulled into Winnie's driveway and reminded his libido that this wasn't about rekindling anything they'd experienced that night. It was about forming a strong partnership in which to raise the girls.

Winnie opened her front door, wearing a teal fleece vest over a white turtleneck. Black tights hugged her legs. Her figure was fuller than it had been before Maeve, sexier. The urge to press her against the wall hit him as hard as his anger had just moments ago.

"Hi, Winnie."

As strong as his sexual attraction was, wh
caught his attention more than anything was th
light in Winnie's eyes. She was no longer a your
woman whose only concern was herself. No lor
ger a Navy wife who resented every minute h
husband spent at work and with his friends. N
longer the grieving widow he'd stood next to whe
all he wanted to do was punch a wall in grief an
frustration that his best friend was dead.

This was a woman who knew who she wa
and where she wanted to go. More important, sh
knew she was capable of getting there.

"Hi." She gave him a half smile and he wishe
her eyes would stay connected with his. Instead
she turned aside and waved him in.

"I'm just getting some last-minute things done

"Hi, Max." Robyn walked up from the sunke
family room, grinning widely. "Where you tal
ing my sister today?"

"Don't mind her, Max. She's nosy."

Max smiled back at Robyn. "I'm going to mak
her work for her lunch. Lots of hiking."

"Sounds like fun. At least the weather i
cooperating." Robyn winked. "Although if it ge
cold I'm sure you know how to handle it, being
nature guy and all."

Max chuckled.

"Really, Robyn? How old are you, twelve?

Winnie wasn't amused as she grabbed her bag and called out, "Come give me a hug, girls!"

Maeve crawled up the steps from the family room and then toddled over to Winnie, but went right past her mom to Max.

"Hi, baby girl!" Max lifted her up and planted a kiss on her cheek. He'd never tire of her sweet scent, the chubby hands that patted his face.

Krista came up and watched the family scene.

"Hi, Krista." Max balanced Maeve in one arm and held open the other in invitation.

"Hey, Uncle Max," she said, readily accepted his hug.

This is what it can be like.

"Where're *my* hugs?" Winnie stood with her small backpack and waited for her daughters to remember that she was part of their family, too.

"Sorry, Mom." Krista grinned and shot Winnie a sheepish look before she hugged her.

"Be good for Aunt Robyn and—" Winnie pulled back "—help her with Maeve, okay?"

"Okay."

Winnie held out her arms to Maeve. Reluctantly, Max let her go.

Sam sat by the front door, his gaze alert.

"Bye, baby." Winnie bent down and kissed the top of Maeve's head, then handed her to Robyn.

"You're making the rounds today, sweetie."

Robyn smiled at Maeve and then looked at Max. "You'd better go now before the wailing starts."

Max laughed. "I don't believe it. These girls are the best behaved I've ever met."

On cue, Maeve began to fuss.

"Let's get out of here." Winnie collected her hat and hurried toward the door.

"Have fun, you two." Robyn had to shout the last two words as Maeve's displeasure at her parents' leaving turned into all-out sobs. "Sorry, Sam, you're staying home today."

Winnie closed the door behind them and paused on the front step. "Phew. That's always tough."

"I had no idea. Does Maeve usually get that upset when you leave?"

"Most times she does. And of course Krista's not so thrilled, either. They sense we're going to have fun, do something without them, and they don't like it. They're kids."

"Will you be okay?" He didn't want her worrying about the girls all through their afternoon together. This was an opportunity to forge their new friendship; Winnie's anxiety wouldn't help either of them.

"Are you kidding? This is my freedom! Race you to the truck!"

He followed a step behind and watched her hips sway in her hiking clothes. He shook his head. Winnie was unpredictable as hell.

"If I'd known we were going back up north I could have met you at your place." She'd watched his profile as he drove through Oak Harbor and then past Dugualla Bay. He looked more relaxed than he had in five weeks—since she'd first gone to his house with Sam.

"Isn't it time someone did something for *you*, Winnie?" He shot her a brief smile before returning his attention to the road, keeping an eye out for deer. Although smaller than the average North American deer, the Whidbey Island variety was big enough to cause a deadly accident.

"I don't need anyone to do anything for me." She heard her own words and cringed. "That sounded too harsh, didn't it? What I mean is that I'm okay with meeting you halfway. I don't expect you to cater to me. If anything, I should be doing more than my share after what I did—or rather, didn't do."

His eyes narrowed but he didn't take his gaze off the road. "Today's not about what either of us did or didn't do. It's about us working on a friendship that we're going to need to get through raising a daughter—*two* daughters—together."

"All right." She exhaled. It wasn't really all right, but she couldn't argue with him. And the disappointment she felt at his declaration that this wasn't going to be a "date" was something she didn't want to examine at the moment.

Let it go.

"You really don't know how to relax, do you, Winnie? You're always 'on,' whether it's for the girls or your work with Sam or your business. You didn't really answer me earlier. When's the last time anyone did anything for you?"

"My family does a lot for me."

"Really?" His eyebrows arched. "I'll concede the fact that Robyn is babysitting today, and your parents obviously help with the girls from time to time. But how often do they come to your home to do it? And how often does anyone drive *you* anywhere?"

"Why should they?"

"It's not a matter of 'should,' Winnie. It's about allowing someone else to do something nice for you." He pressed on the brakes as the traffic slowed to a stop. His glance took in her expression.

"I'm not talking about the touchy-feely stuff I've learned in counseling—that we all have to take care of ourselves first. That's a given." His gaze dropped to the curve of her breast before he turned back to the traffic.

This was never going to work if he looked at her like that again.

"I'm talking about letting yourself be pampered, indulged a little bit. Getting a break. How many dates have you been on since Tom died?"

Her head jerked back. "Dates? How can I have time for dates when I'm taking care of so much, as you say? And this isn't a date—you made that clear." The air seemed to close in on her and sweat dripped down her back.

The line of vehicles started to move again and Max shifted into gear. "Exactly. So relax, Win. We're going to have a nice afternoon together and do what friends do. Talk. Maybe even laugh."

Relax. Everyone was telling her to relax.

"Okay, got it."

As a younger woman she might have interpreted the cold, then hot, sensation in her gut as anxiety. Or fear. But she knew beyond a doubt what it was.

Sexual tension.

She looked at him as he drove. Max was steady as ever, driving and shifting gears. No beers at a pub this afternoon, no reminiscing about Tom today. They were here together, for the girls.

But the girls had nothing to do with how alive she felt as she sat next to him in his truck.

MAX TURNED INTO THE entrance to Deception Pass Park and pulled into an empty spot. He shut off the engine and turned toward her. "I thought we'd hike for a bit, work up an appetite, then eat on one of the trails on the other side of the bridge."

"Fine with me." She really just wanted out of

the truck; it was too close and she needed fresh air to keep her head clear.

They locked her purse in the car and headed over to Deception Pass Bridge, which spanned the narrow river that divided Whidbey and Fidalgo Islands, and connected the Strait of Juan de Fuca to Skagit Bay, which lay to the east of Whidbey.

"You know why Captain Vancouver named this Deception Pass, don't you?" Winnie stopped at midspan, taking in the sheer drop to the water below. Cliffs covered in rich green firs framed either side of their view all the way to the Cascades.

"Because it's deceptively calm water?" Max's reply made her smile.

"Are you joking or do you really not know?"

"I'm not kidding." His straight face convinced her.

"Because until then he, I mean Vancouver, thought that Whidbey was a peninsula."

"I'm sure the natives could have set him straight."

"They set a lot of settlers straight over the years," she said, referring to the instances of conflict between Native Americans and settlers. Whidbey's history wasn't as idyllic as the current panorama implied.

"I never get tired of flying over this—it's magnificent from the air. You've seen it, right?"

"From the air? No, never. I drive to Bellingham

or Seattle to catch any flights. I'm not a small-aircraft kind of girl."

"They're safer than driving off-island to the mall."

"Maybe so, but I feel better staying on the ground whenever possible." She didn't want to talk about her flying phobia with Max. It had affected too much of her life already.

There was a silence between them. Then, although she hadn't planned to, Winnie asked, "Do you miss flying, Max?"

He gently grasped her elbow and started them walking forward again. They fell into a brisk but comfortable pace.

"Sure I do. But I'm still doing some flying. It's only the Navy missions I'm done with. Even when I get a clean bill of health I'll be too senior to fly for the Navy anymore."

They continued to walk.

"I fly at least two or three times a week," he said.

"You have your own aircraft?"

Max smiled. "Aircrafts. I have one Cessna I like to get up in to see the sights, and I have a seaplane that'll eventually be part of my fleet of interisland aircraft." He paused. "I've been on my own all these years, Winnie. I have money for my toys."

Neither of which sounded like any fun to Winnie.

"Which direction should we take?" He switched the conversation back to their walk.

They'd reached the other side of the bridge and Winnie knew some trails but not many. She never brought the girls here; it was too dangerous, with steep drops just inches from the edge of some paths.

"What do you suggest, Max?"

"Let's head down to the left, and wind our way back into the forest a bit. We can find a bluff to sit on and eat our lunch."

"Do you hike a lot?"

"Not like I used to, but yeah, walking's helped keep me limber and I think it's helped me heal."

Winnie held on to tree trunks as they followed a narrow dirt path that twisted through trees and underbrush. The woods grew dark and shadowed, and they both stayed silent as if taking in the serenity. After a half hour or so, she could imagine there was no water around them—until they climbed up a sharp incline and arrived at a substantial ledge.

"Careful as you come forward." Max reached back for her hand and she grabbed it. Heights still scared her. She was generally okay if it was a familiar path but she'd never been this way before.

"Okay, just a few more feet." Max's voice steadied her enough to remain focused on the beauty around her rather than the threat of a sudden sheer drop.

They cleared a clump of trees and the ledge opened into a small meadowlike area. But as Winnie walked beside Max, she saw that it was an illusion—the meadow didn't roll into the distance. Instead, after a few yards, it dropped off to the sparkling water below them. They faced the northern tip of Whidbey with the bridge to their right and the Cascades to their left.

"Here, sit down." Max had shrugged off his backpack and removed his outer fleece layer, which he spread on the ground.

"Wait, let me take off my vest, too. We had quite a good workout and I'm hot!" She unzipped her vest and laid it down, then joined him on the ground.

"I'm afraid to look over the edge. Does it go straight down?"

"Not exactly, but close enough."

"Okay, I'm going to look, but I'm crawling over. Don't make fun of me."

"I wouldn't dream of it." He opened his backpack and started to pull out their meal.

Winnie crawled forward on her hands and knees, and got herself into a push-up position on the edge of the grass. She lowered herself to the ground and peered over.

"Oh!"

Max hadn't exaggerated. It wasn't a straight drop down—there were other similar ledges under them, although smaller and narrower, like little steps down to the rocky beach below. At the moment, it was shrinking, being overtaken by the tide.

She saw that they'd descended almost three-quarters of the way down the edge of the Fidalgo Island southern cliffs. She could all too easily imagine falling down the cliff's side. Winnie closed her eyes to shut out the feeling of vertigo.

Max's hand rested between her shoulder blades. "You're safe here, Winnie. Come back from the edge." His voice and touch chased away her dark thoughts.

Winnie pushed herself up and, with Max's arm around her waist, returned to their picnic site.

Max poured her some sparkling water. "I thought of bringing some wine but I think water is better for this kind of hike."

"Thanks." She accepted the paper cup and took a long gulp. "And you're right about water versus wine."

"Now, do you want brie or blue cheese with your baguette?" He smiled, and she knew she'd remember this moment forever. His eyes glinted with the brilliant sunshine, and the only tension

between them seemed to come from her own attraction to him. She'd get over that, wouldn't she?

They were friends. And friends they would remain.

THEIR LUNCH IN THE IDYLLIC setting was perfect.
Winnie couldn't recall a time she'd been so relaxed since Maeve was born, if not earlier.

They talked about the girls, of course, but also
about each other. Winnie's fiber business and
Max's dream of his own miniairline. Winnie tried
to ignore the ache in her gut when he talked about
the kick he got out of flying a small aircraft in
challenging weather conditions.

"We've discussed just about everything, Winnie. But we haven't touched on one of the most
important."

She swallowed. "Okay. You go first."

"We still have this chemistry between us."

"Maybe. But it's nothing we can't ignore until
it goes away, is it?" She turned to face him. He
looked up at a bald eagle that made lazy circles
in the middle of the pass.

"I sure hope we can. We're going to have to."

She agreed with him but it didn't stop the
twinge of sadness she felt at his words.

"The night of the Air Show was a surprise to
me on so many levels. I tried to rationalize it—I
thought maybe it came out of our talking about

Tom and bringing up the old hurts. But it's still here, and I have to tell you I'm not comfortable with it. Tom was my buddy, my colleague, and Navy rules are clear—you don't mess with your shipmate's girl."

"Your shipmate is dead and I'm not a girl." Had she just said that? She heard his sharp intake of breath and held up her hand. "Hold it."

She took a deep breath. "I didn't mean that I disagree with you. It's weird for me, too. You were Tom's best friend, and I put you in the 'brother' category for many years. That night we made love, was equally…shocking for me." She paused for a few seconds. "Even if we didn't have the history and the Navy connection, I don't ever want to bring another man into the girls' life on a casual basis."

"I'm not casual, Winnie."

"You know what I mean, Max. I'm okay with you being around them as a father figure. As more, no." Why were they even having this conversation when he'd never forgive her for her betrayal and she'd never be able to get over his choice of a career?

In his silence she read his anger at her, his resentment that she'd compared him to a mere acquaintance.

"Max, you know I'll never be serious enough about anyone to make him part of the girls' lives."

"I believe you have the best intention for them, yes." He spoke quietly, with purpose. "Do I believe you'll never meet anyone that you'll want to spend your life with, make a commitment to? No. There's no way you can predict that, Winnie. If we've learned anything from what we've been through, it's the unpredictability of life."

The easy peace they'd shared was gone and replaced by the friction caused by regret and hard cold facts.

"It's a miracle we're even out here together, that we're working through this." She whispered the words but he heard her. She knew from the way he grasped her shoulder.

"Yes, it is."

She turned to face him, expecting to see a grim look of distrust.

Instead, she caught a brief glimpse of his mouth before he leaned in and kissed her.

HE'D SWORN HE WOULDN'T kiss her, wouldn't touch her as more than a friend. But when he'd seen the look of complete remorse on her face, he moved to comfort her on instinct.

That instinct was going against every rule he'd set for himself with Winnie. But rules didn't matter when he had her tongue in his mouth and her head cradled in his hand.

She whimpered under his kiss and he pulled back a fraction of an inch.

"I'm sorry, Max." Her eyes gazed into his and he realized the salty taste of her lips was from her tears. He knew she regretted her uninhibited response to his kiss.

"So am I. I'm sorry I started this." He bent back to her, needing her, needing to feel her against him.

"No, Max, we can't." She kept her hands on his chest with a light pressure.

"We *are* doing it, Winnie."

"I know, but…it's only going to make things too complicated, and it's not good for the girls."

The girls.

"Right." He drew back and made sure she was firmly seated before he dropped his arms.

Without a word they packed up the remainder of the lunch and started their hike back to the car. He wanted to punch his fist against a tree trunk, or throw a large rock down into the water.

He'd promised her he'd be her friend. That he didn't need more.

But his desire had ruined his plan to set the foundation for their partnership as parents.

He glanced over his shoulder to check that Winnie was keeping up with him. For the first time in ages he wasn't in any physical pain as he forged ahead on the wild path before them. For once he had energy to spare.

Energy that he'd rather have spent making love to Winnie.

THE FIRST FEW MILES of their ride back to Coupeville were quiet. Winnie was both horrified that she'd been so needy with Max and humiliated that she'd practically begged his forgiveness.

She didn't deserve anybody's forgiveness, least of all Max's. Not after the way she'd betrayed him. She might tell herself that they should forget the past, focus on the future. But she wasn't convinced it was possible.

And if he'd continued to kiss her, had resisted her request to stop, they'd still be out there on that cliff, lying in each other's arms.

"Max, we have to make this work. For Krista and for Maeve."

"We *are,* Winnie. Not as smoothly as I hoped, but trust me, we will make it work no matter what. They need me, and I need them."

As always, she warmed at his use of "they." He accepted Krista *and* Maeve as his daughters, his to love. She also noted that he didn't include her, which was a good thing, right?

"After today we won't be tempted to do anything so stupid." She waited for his response, certain that he'd agree.

Max said nothing.

They entered her driveway and he idled th
truck engine.

"Do you want to come in and see the girl
Maeve is probably down for her nap but she'll b
up soon, and you could visit with Krista."

His face looked set in stone but his eyes re
vealed an inner torment she couldn't identify.

"Not now, Winnie. I need some time to regrou
Tell them I'll see them at soccer." He placed hi
wrist on top of the steering wheel and stared o
the windshield. "I'll see you sooner, with Sam?

"Yes, on Tuesday." Opening the door, sh
stepped down from the truck. "Thanks for lunc
Max."

"You're welcome."

She shut the door. He backed down the driv
but didn't look at her again as he maneuvered th
truck onto the road.

Winnie didn't realize there were tears pourin
down her cheeks until he was out of sight.

CHAPTER SIXTEEN

"KRISTA, YOUR UNCLE Max is here," Mom shouted up the stairs. Krista yanked her sweatshirt over her head.

"Coming." Uncle Max was taking her and Maeve out for a Saturday-afternoon treat. It'd been a month since Uncle Max and Mom went on their lunch hike and they'd seen a lot of him on their own. Mom seemed to trust him, and Krista loved it. But it might be even more fun if all four of them did things together every now and then.

Krista didn't get it. Uncle Max was around almost every day, and Mom seemed happier. They'd all adjusted to the fact that "Uncle" Max was also "Daddy" to Maeve. But there wasn't anything going on between Mom and Uncle Max and that puzzled her. As much as it grossed her out, didn't grown-ups *need* to be together, alone? Didn't Mom and Uncle Max even *think* about being a family?

"C'mon, Krista. Do you have your shin guards?"

"Yup." She hoisted her backpack higher. "Bye, Mom."

"Bye, sweetie. Maeve, be good." Mom kissed

Maeve on the cheek before she handed her over
to Uncle Max. He'd bought a car seat so they
wouldn't have to switch the one from Mom's car
all the time.

"Great. Let's go, baby girl." He hugged Maeve
to him. "We'll be back later this afternoon."

"Oh, I thought I'd take Sam for a good run on
the beach. I can meet you at the soccer fields down
there in a couple of hours."

Mom had that stupid fake smile on her face
again. Maybe there was something between them,
after all, but not the way Krista had hoped. She'd
hoped for a family, a family with a dad.

With Uncle Max.

Uncle Max was taking her and Maeve to City
Beach. He was going to kick around the soccer
ball with her and then they'd go to the playground
so Maeve could have fun, too.

Once they got to the park, they ran all over
the soccer fields. There were a few other families
out there since it was Saturday. Krista hated the
way the wind whipped her breath away but loved
how much better she'd learned to control the ball
since Uncle Max had been working with her as
her coach. But she really liked being one-on-one
with him, too. They talked about everything, not
just soccer.

He jogged up to her, Maeve at his heels.

"Wheeee!" Her tiny giggle made Krista laugh.

And a little jealous. She'd loved her dad and would never forget him, but being able to call Uncle Max "Dad" would be neat, too.

"What's got you in such a funk, Krista girl?" Uncle Max tugged at her ponytail. She felt safe and protected when he was beside her.

"Nothing."

"I can see it on your face, honey. Something's eating at you."

"Come here, Maeve." Krista didn't answer as she bent over to pick up her baby sister. Maeve immediately wriggled, asking to be put back down.

"She wants to run, don't you, pumpkin?" Uncle Max took her from Krista and set Maeve on his shoulders. "Let Daddy help you get there, and then you can run all you like."

"Uncle Max, do you think we could all go camping together, you know, with Mom, too?"

Uh-oh. Uncle Max looked way too serious.

"I'm not sure," he said cautiously. "We can ask her and see what happens. It's tough to get all our schedules synchronized."

Krista stayed silent.

"You didn't answer my original question, Krista." They'd drawn even with the playground and had a bit more of a walk before they reached the soccer fields.

"I don't want to ruin what we already have,

Uncle Max," she finally said. "But I'd really like it if you were my dad, too."

Uncle Max stopped and stared at her. Krista didn't like the feeling in her stomach, so she shifted her gaze to the water. She'd blown it, and now she'd scared Uncle Max off.

She snuck a glance at his face and couldn't read it. He was looking out at the water, too. Even Maeve was quiet as she sat on his shoulders and played with Uncle Max's short hair.

Krista wanted to cry.

MAX'S CHEST ACHED FROM trying to take large gulps of air without letting Krista or Maeve see his distress.

Winnie is going to kill you.

No kidding. Winnie had spent the better part of their hike making it "clear," as she said, that their relationship wasn't going to be anything but a friendship. She didn't want any false hint to the girls that he and Winnie were ever going to be more than coparents.

Krista couldn't hide her disappointment at his lack of response. Max groaned.

"Honey, you've given me the biggest compliment ever. Your dad was a great man and the fact that you even think of me in the same way fills my heart with so much happiness."

He watched Krista's expression carefully. He

didn't have a lot of experience with kids. None, in fact. Other than playing with Krista when she was still a toddler and for a few months after Tom died.

But Max knew he had to honor the commitment he'd made to Tom. To be there for him no matter what. Since Tom was gone, he'd be there for Krista. And he'd be damned if he was going to do anything to hurt her.

"Maeve's my biological daughter, yes. Ouch!" Maeve's fingers pulled his hair. Krista didn't even smile.

"But I've known you since you were born, Krista. I made a big mistake when I didn't keep in touch with you, especially over the past few years. But I'm here for you now. I want you to always feel comfortable with me."

A single tear fell from Krista's left eye. The sight of it was more painful than any of the shrapnel that remained in his body.

"Aw, honey, come here." He lowered Maeve from his shoulders onto his hip and pulled Krista close with his free arm. Maeve's attention was on an errant seagull that ran back and forth in front of them, squawking.

"Bird, bird!" Maeve seemed oblivious to the angst her older sister was going through.

"Krista, I never want to hurt you. What have I done?" He kissed the top of her head.

She sniffed, and he wished she wasn't so stiff

and tense, resisting his hug. But she didn't step out of it, either.

"It's not you, Uncle Max. It's me. I want a full family for us, with a dad. I think Mom's happy around you and I don't get why she won't let her control-freak self go, so we can all be happy together."

"Wait a minute, gal." He leaned back and raised her chin so he could meet her eyes. "Your mom loves you and Maeve more than herself. You're her life. She's not going to do anything she feels could put either of you at risk, emotionally or physically. You understand that, don't you?"

"Yeah, but—"

"No *buts*, Krista. Your well-being is your mom's number-one driving factor. If it wasn't, you could be living a very different life." He couldn't tell Krista, who was fairly sheltered, about the single parents he'd seen go the other way—sleeping around, bringing home stranger after stranger, exposing their children to God knows what kind of partner and situation. For a very brief time, Winnie had almost gone that way. She was human like anyone else, she'd been grieving and desperate, but she'd made the choice to put her girls first.

"Just because Mom doesn't sleep around doesn't mean our well-being is number one for her."

"Krista! I never want to hear you put your

mother down like that again. Let's chalk it up to
the emotions of the moment, okay?"

When Krista didn't respond but stared reso-
lutely at the gravel path, Max gently squeezed her
shoulder. "Okay, Krista?"

"Yeah, okay." She wiped her nose with the
sleeve of her hoodie. "Now you think I'm a complete jerk."

"Honey, never." He kissed her forehead. Her
hair smelled like strawberries and girl sweat. How
could he have let himself miss so much time in
her life? He was her godfather, and her father had
died. Guilt sank a nasty claw in his gut.

"I want Mom to be happy, too, Uncle Max. I
just don't know if she even knows what makes
her happy."

Max forced back a smile. He'd thought the same
thing.

"Tell you what, Krista. Let's not worry about
the details, but keep enjoying our time, together.
You and Maeve are the most important people in
my life."

He didn't add that Winnie fell in there with
them. He couldn't. He had to be honest but use
discretion with Krista. She was a kid.

"C'mon, little gal. Let's go play!" He jogged
with Maeve in his arms and Krista ran alongside
them toward the soccer field.

"SAM, STOP IT." WINNIE jerked on his leash and Sam got the message. He stopped trying to drag her over to the beach.

He'd spotted Max and the girls sooner than she had and was relentless in his quest to join them on the rocky sand. She should have stayed home a bit longer but the weather was too nice.

Max and the girls looked so natural together on that beach. As though they'd been a family forever.

They have. No thanks to you.

Her eyes filled with tears. True, she'd readily agreed when Tom wanted Max to be Krista's godfather. Her brothers would've been honored to be named, but they wouldn't have appreciated it as much as Max. Nor did either of them know Tom as well as Max did.

Now she'd let Max into their circle, not just for Maeve but for Krista, too. It would be perfect if she and Max could work it out. But there was no "it" to work out. He'd seen her as Tom's wife and could never see her as the woman she felt she was today—very different from what she'd been fifteen and five and even two years ago.

You're not so different if you can't accept the choice a man makes for his career.

Sam's sharp bark jolted her from her thoughts. His tail wagged restlessly and he kept looking at the water, then at her.

"Okay, let's go throw the ball and then if you want you can take a dip." Sam loved the water as if he were more Labrador than German shepherd.

You're just killing time until you can be with Max.

They hadn't discussed their physical attraction for each other again, not since their hike almost a month ago. They'd fallen into a routine of short phone calls to plan his time with the girls. As much as possible, they didn't do things together. Winnie told herself this was so she could have more time to herself as Max, among others, had suggested.

But nothing erased her body's response to him or the fact that she felt most alive whenever she was near him. She wished she could get rid of her anxieties, but they were like Max's PTSD—they'd never be completely gone. And she couldn't, wouldn't, bring another man into that with her. Hadn't she hurt Tom enough with her fears and complaints?

MAX LOOKED UP AND WHEN their eyes met Winnie saw his unspoken apology.

"What?" she asked.

He shook his head and turned his attention back to the girls, who were up on the grassy fields.

"Is it okay to let Sam off leash or are you still doing soccer drills?" Sam sat ramrod straight. He knew he was moments from free play. His astuteness always astonished her. The experts said it was all about obedience training but she felt a deeper connection with Sam. Always had.

"Sure, go ahead. We're wrapping up." Max called out to Krista, "Do you think you can give me one more length of the field with the side dribble?"

"I'll try." Krista's grin was a mile wide. She'd not only try, she'd excel. Her soccer talents had flourished under Max's tutelage. Winnie didn't doubt Max's abilities as a coach but she also thought Krista pushed herself harder in order to impress him.

Why shouldn't she?

Winnie leaned down and unfastened Sam's leash. He immediately ran up to Max, greeted him, then raced after Krista. She laughed and shouted at him as he tried to take the ball away from her.

"I didn't realize he was adept at athletic training, too." Max stepped up beside her.

The heat of his body didn't surprise her anymore, but that didn't make it any less disconcerting.

"Do you ever wonder if we're both missing out on something extraordinary, Winnie? Something between us?" he asked in a low voice.

She opened her mouth but no reply came. She

bit her lip. "Max, we—we have an agreement," she stuttered.

"Agreements can be renegotiated."

"Really? Suddenly you're not concerned about breaking your promise to Tom, breaking the Navy 'code'?"

"I'm more concerned that it was so easy for you to keep Maeve from me. What else would you hide?"

Ouch.

"Even with that, I'd like to think I have an open mind. We're building a friendship here, aren't we? Couldn't we eventually move beyond that?"

"*You're* building a relationship with the *girls,* Max. Let's just focus on that."

He surprised her when his hands covered hers, clenched on her crossed arms.

"Can you just consider it, Win?"

She looked at him and wanted to give in, wanted to pretend the past no longer influenced the present—and, more important, that he wasn't going to put them at risk every time he went up in his tiny aircraft.

"No, Max, I'm afraid I can't."

He gazed at her for a moment, then dropped his hands.

"Well, that's that. I need to tell you what Krista and I talked about."

"What happened?"

He pursed his lips and sighed. "First Krista asked if we could all go on a camping trip together. Then she said she'd love it if we were more than just four people hanging out. If we were…a family."

"She did?" Anxiety gripped her. She felt as though she was gasping for air. *No, no, no! It was so* not *going to play out like this.*

"Yeah, she did."

"We're the adults here, Max. *We* make the decisions."

"It takes two of us to make 'we,' and you're the only one throwing out the decisions."

He stood a foot away and his hands remained at his sides but it felt as if he'd slapped her. Tears stung her eyes and she blinked.

"No one's ever dared to tell you that maybe your way isn't the only way, right, Win? With the occasional exception of Robyn, everyone's too busy tiptoeing around you."

"That's not true!"

"Oh, but it is, babe." He stepped closer, into her space, and Winnie had to fight to stay put. Her legs trembled and she wanted to take a step back.

No, you don't. You want to grab him and kiss him right here on City Beach.

"I never asked for your opinion, Max."

"You did the minute you let me back in your life, Win."

"So now you're attacking me for having integrity?"

"Hardly. This isn't an attack, Winnie. You won't accept any help or consider any other approach. It's an observation. And judging by your reaction I hit it right, didn't I?"

"Let's remember who needed the help most recently, Max." She watched his expression go from triumphant to shocked to completely guarded.

Winnie felt sick to her stomach. She'd never thrown anyone's disability at him like that. And *she'd* been the one to volunteer to work with Sam and Max. He didn't ask for her help.

"That's what it'll always go back to, is it?" The growl in his voice shook her out of her defensiveness and the remorse that ran through her made her shiver in the bright sun.

"Max." She put her hand on his forearm. "I didn't mean it like that."

"Right." His lips were set in Navy Commander mode.

"Mom, Sam's going crazy!" Krista and Maeve were in front of them, winded from running.

"What?" Winnie had a hard time moving through the fog of pain she'd just imploded on herself and Max.

"Over there! Don't you hear him?"

Winnie followed Krista's gesture and saw Sam

nearly a quarter of a mile away, his front paws on a tree trunk. His yips carried across the field.

"Is it a bird?" Winnie lifted Maeve to her hip and started walking, Krista behind her. Max followed more slowly. Winnie couldn't bear to look at the anguish on his face.

"No, Mom, it's a cat. It ran up a tree and Sam saw it and went nuts. He even tried to climb the tree after it."

"Great."

"Down, Momma. Down."

"Not right now, Maeve. We have got to get to Sam."

"I've got her." Max's strong hands took Maeve from her hip before Winnie had time to come up with a response. Winnie didn't hesitate as she broke into a jog.

"Sam!" The wind tore her words away but she knew the dog heard her. He'd been trained on her voice.

Good dog that Sam was, he pricked up his ears at her call, and sat down on his haunches by front of the tree.

The soccer fields abutted a recreational vehicle and RV park, where travelers and tourists kept their homes-on-wheels for a few hours or several days as they took in the beauty of Oak Harbor.

Winnie's apprehension was realized when a

blue-haired woman scurried across the parking lot, cell phone in hand.

"Your dog chased my cat up that tree. She's afraid of heights!"

Winnie took a deep breath. If the worst thing this woman had to worry about was her cat...

Stop it. You'd be the same if it was Sam.

"I'm sorry, we'll help you get your cat down." Winnie didn't ask the obvious: What the hell was her cat doing outside in a strange town? And she didn't point out that Sam had *found,* not chased, her cat.

Winnie looked over her shoulder at the tree and at Sam. Max and Maeve had joined them, and Max's neck was exposed as he stared up into the branches.

Her hand itched to stroke his nape, to massage his temples. To tell him she was sorry.

"What's your cat's name?"

"Henry the Eighth."

"We'll get Henry back down, even if we have to call the fire department."

"It's 'Henry the Eighth.' Not 'Henry.'" The woman's lower lip jutted and showed the faintest hint of a tremor.

Are you kidding me?

"No worries. We'll get him back in your arms in no time." Winnie didn't want another trauma on her hands.

"Sam!" Sam responded by quickly trottin
over and sitting down next to the woman's fee
He looked up at Winnie with complete alertnes
Winnie swore he winked at her.

Damn dog.

"Sam, stay." Winnie turned to the woma
whose expression was already softening even a
she tried to keep up a brave front.

"What's your name, ma'am?"

"Dolores."

"I'm Winnie. Sam, stay with Dolores." She co
veyed her alpha status through her eyes but als
gave Sam an extra pat the head. It was her sile
way of letting Sam know that he was under stri
orders.

She went over to Max and the girls. "Where
this cat?"

"Take a look. He's to the right of the crow
nest."

Winnie leaned over and Max's hand was on he
shoulder, his voice in her ear.

"Look up the main trunk. See where the kno
is? Now look over to the left. There's the crow
nest. See the next branch, on the right?"

Winnie nodded. She thought she deserved
prize for not reacting to Max's nearness, espe
cially so soon after she'd blown their relationshi
to smithereens. She shivered again.

"Cold?" Max's taunt was unmistakable.

"Mom, how can you be cold? It's hot as heck out here in the sun." Krista brought her back to reality. She wasn't alone with Max, and her girls were watching every move.

"Just from sweating after that run, I guess," she murmured as she kept scanning the tree. "Oh. Oh, my gosh!"

"Yeah, he gives *fat cat* new meaning."

Henry the Eighth deserved his name. Even from fifty feet below it was clear that he was huge. A big mass of fluffy white and maybe gray fur splayed out from the boughs of the old tree.

"How on earth...?" Winnie knew that even the fire department might not be able to get him down.

"I have someone I can call." Max continued to balance Maeve on his hip while he fished in his pocket. He made short work of dialing and his Naval Officer voice took over.

"It's Max. I've got a bit of a problem down here at City Beach. Huge cat in a very tall tree. Can you help?" He listened for a moment.

"Roger." Max shoved his phone back in his pocket.

His gaze met Winnie's. All business. "Ten minutes."

"Will the cat jump and hurt himself?" Krista asked anxiously.

"Probably not. I doubt he'll budge." He glanced at Winnie as if to imply that Henry the Eighth wasn't the only stubborn creature around.

CHAPTER SEVENTEEN

MILES SHOWED UP IN A blaze of glory. He rode into the RV parking lot on his Harley and Max couldn't help the grin that spread across his face. Miles was his own man, always had been.

He also loved animals and had been known as the dog whisperer in his combat unit. What few people knew about Miles was that he'd lost his working dog when he lost his leg. The dog saved his life—he alerted to the IED but it detonated before it could be disarmed. One step closer for Miles, and he would've died in the desert with his beloved companion.

"Warrant!"

"Yo, boss." Miles had left his helmet on his bike, along with his gloves. He strolled up to the group at the base of the tree and raised an eyebrow at Max. "These are a lot of people to disappoint, boss."

"You can do it. Your talents are infamous."

Miles let out a short laugh and gazed up at the tree.

Max held his breath.

"Who are you and what do you think you're going to do?" An unfamiliar angry voice pierced the silence.

Max turned to see an attractive brunette with a protective arm around Dolores as she glared at Miles.

He ignored her. He just kept looking up at the tree as if measuring the firepower of the enemy.

"Is it your cat, too?" God Bless Winnie, who stepped in to defuse the situation.

"No, it's my mother's cat." The woman gestured toward Dolores. There didn't appear to be any family resemblance.

"I'm Winnie."

"Roanna."

"This is Max." She lightly touched Max's upper arm. "And his friend…"

"Warrant. That is, Miles." Max nodded at Miles, who was in his save-the-cat frame of mind and didn't respond.

"Who is this guy?" Roanna had apparently observed the same thing they did. Miles was unreachable as he focused on Henry the Eighth.

"My colleague. We're both in the Navy," Max said in an authoritative voice.

"So am I. Funny, I've never seen you around here." It was a simple statement but her doubt was evident.

"We've both been deployed quite a bit." Max

kept his face impassive. "Miles is an expert dog-handler and has a way with animals."

"That's great, Max, but in case you haven't noticed, it's my mother's *cat* up in that tree. A dog could never climb that high!"

"That's not accurate. A trained combat canine can scale walls and buttresses no man could ever do on his own." Miles's voice interrupted them.

He hadn't missed a word, and now his gaze was on Roanna. Was Max crazy or did he see them both straighten as they sized each other up? Roanna frowned. Miles held his ground, looking down his nose at a woman nearly a foot shorter than he was.

"You should know better than to let your cat get out. And maybe we haven't met because there's about twenty thousand active-duty folks on the island."

Max had only known Roanna for a minute or two but he'd swear she looked like she was going to explode all over Miles. He tried not to grin.

"My mother is visiting in her RV. I live in town. My dog hates cats, so Henry the Eighth stays in Mom's RV—if it's any of your business. And I don't need a demographic lesson, *Warrant*."

"You can call me Miles. The safety of this animal *is* now my business. If you want me to help. Or we can call out the fire department and your mother can be presented with a nice bill from the town."

"I can afford to pay the bill, but—"

"Ro, honey, no. Let the man get Henry the Eighth." Dolores admonished her daughter as no one else had dared to.

Roanna squeezed her mother's shoulders. "Okay, Mom, we'll give it a try." The look she threw Miles, however, was every bit as icy as her tone had been.

"With your permission, I'll make every effort to get your cat down." Miles met her anger head on.

She nodded abruptly and Miles turned back toward the tree. Max had no doubt Miles would get the fat cat out, but he had no idea *how* he'd do it.

"He's got to be almost sixty feet up," Max murmured, keeping his eyes on the cat, not revealing that he was having a conversation with Miles.

"Yeah, he's in a pickle all right. But I'll get him down."

Miles was dressed in a T-shirt, leather jacket and jeans. He shed his jacket and put his arms around the tree.

"It's sturdy enough. Wait here, will you?" He didn't glance at Max but went back to his bike and opened the storage compartment.

"What's he going to do? Pull a trampoline out of there for the cat to jump on?" Winnie's comment made Max smile but Winnie didn't know Miles.

"I've learned never to underestimate him."

"Uncle Max, is he going to shoot the cat down?" Krista's voice carried and before Max could respond, Roanna and her mother visibly jerked.

"No, no, he's not going to do anything of the sort," Max reassured everyone.

"Sam, Sam!" Maeve held her hands out to Sam, who'd obediently taken his position at the foot of the tree in a down-stay.

"It's okay, honey." Max jostled to maintain his grip on the child.

"I'll take her. You help Miles." Winnie took Maeve from him and walked away, then she let her down to run off some steam.

Miles walked up with an assortment of climbing equipment.

"You rappel?"

"And climb."

"Since—" Miles had never mentioned rock-climbing with his prosthetic device.

"Yes, since I lost my real leg. But this one is just as good."

"Okay, whatever you say."

"Watch my back, will you, boss?"

"Sure thing."

"Krista can you take Sam away from here? I don't want any extra commotion."

"But I want to see him get the cat!"

"I hear you, Krista. But I've got to stand guard

for him and I can't take Sam. Your mother has Maeve."

"Oh, all right. C'mon, Sam." Krista's sulky teenage expression would have been comical if Max wasn't so annoyed by her initial refusal.

She's a kid, not a sailor.

He let out a breath. And this was Miles's show, not his. Hell, if it'd been up to him, he'd have sided with Roanna and called the Oak Harbor fire department.

He chanced a quick look at Winnie. She was standing several feet away, swinging Maeve between her legs. But she glanced up as if she felt him watching her. Winnie's eyes met his and after a moment she smiled.

WINNIE WASN'T SURE WHAT to think about Max's friend Miles. They were both in the Navy and she assumed they'd known each other when they were in the war. But Miles didn't act like the kind of guy either Max or Tom would have hung out with. Miles or "Warrant" seemed a lot more relaxed and ready to let life roll whichever way it needed to. She didn't bother to ask if Miles was indeed a "Warrant" in the Navy—a Chief Warrant Officer. It didn't matter.

She liked his smile and his practical manner. He was attractive—downright hot. A fact that

Roanna hadn't missed, if her surreptitious glances were anything to go by.

While Miles went to work assessing how to rescue Henry the Eighth, she played with Maeve.

And watched Max.

He caught her staring at him and she sucked in her breath.

"Wheeeee!" Maeve squealed as Winnie swung her up and then back down. Winnie was grateful for the excuse to look away from Max. But not soon enough... He smiled back at her.

Her stomach fluttered—the type of flutter that always preceded her bouts of anxiety. There was no longer any reason to panic, though. He knew Maeve was his daughter and had accepted it, reveled in it. Most of the time, he even appeared to have forgiven her.

His manner with Krista was miraculous. He could stop a teenage sulk in midstride and even elicit a giggle.

He'd kept their relationship where it needed to be, except for his comment today.

Max fit into their family too easily....

As she swung Maeve down low again, her eyes caught Max's sneakered feet. She straightened up and held Maeve close. Maeve twisted to see him.

"Daaaad!"

Winnie's heart stopped or felt as if it did. Then

it started back, thumping like Sam's tail on the hardwood floor.

Max's reaction was equally surprised but full of a joy that she'd never witnessed in him before.

"Maeve, honey! Yes, I'm your daddy." He reached out his arms and Winnie let go as he scooped her up.

"Well, she knows who you are, no question."

"Yes, she does, don't you, sweetie pie?" Max looked at Maeve as if memorizing her every feature.

Winnie smiled in spite of herself. After all that Max had been through, after all they'd been through together, he deserved this happiness.

She just didn't want *his* happiness to involve any emotional risk on her part.

Impossible.

"Well, should we go see how Miles is doing?" she suggested.

"Since I told him I'd have his back, yes, we'd better."

KRISTA SCRATCHED SAM behind the ear. "We've both been told to stay away, Sammy." She loved Sam. He understood her moods. Unlike Mom, who acted like she was supposed to stay young forever. Or even Uncle Max, who said he wanted to get to know her and be there for her, but really, who was he kidding? If he hadn't found out that

Maeve was his kid, he wouldn't be hanging out with them.

Sam barked.

"It's okay, boy. We've got to wait it out." She looked in the direction Sam had barked. That friend of Uncle Max's had climbed halfway up the tree to get the stupid cat.

Krista sighed. "I don't think the cat's stupid, not really. I just wish he hadn't gone up there. You found him, didn't you, boy? Good dog."

Krista loved how Sam leaned his weight against her as they sat and watched the show.

Uncle Max and Mom were standing near each other. She saw their lips moving, so she knew they were talking. But she couldn't tell from their gestures or positions what the conversation was about. Maeve was sitting on the ground.

"If Mom wasn't so stupid, Sam, she'd see that Uncle Max is perfect for our family."

Sam panted in the sunshine, his coat shiny and clean.

"Are you hot, boy? Let's get you some water." She stood and walked Sam over to the park's dog water fountain. Sam drank straight from the fountain, noisily lapping up the water.

Krista wanted to walk closer to the scene, but she couldn't take Sam over there. Not until the cat was down and back in the arms of that old lady.

Krista felt sorry for the woman. She looked confused and very angry at Sam.

"You didn't chase him up there. Nope, you just noticed he was there. You actually saved him." She had a sudden thought—maybe Sam could bring their family together. Uncle Max wasn't seeing him for therapy anymore, but he and Sam were buddies now.

"You need another guy in the house, don't you? Fat chance of that with Mom around." She sat down next to him again and they waited.

CHAPTER EIGHTEEN

WINNIE STOOD BESIDE MAX, Maeve in her arms. Maeve wanted to be with Max, of course, but since Max was Miles's backup, it wasn't an option.

She shielded her eyes with her free hand and looked up into the branches. Miles had shimmied up the tree without a problem, as though he did it every day.

Thank God for military training.

If Henry the Eighth didn't make it back to his owner in the next few minutes Winnie was afraid there'd be a medical emergency. Possibly two— Henry's owner would stroke out and her daughter would assault Miles, then probably come after Sam.

"You've got it. I'm right here, holding steady." Max had a set of rappelling ropes in his hands and his eyes never left Miles.

Winnie held her breath as she watched Miles loop his rope around a thick bough and pull it tight. Now he could make a grab for Henry the Eighth.

The cat stared down at him as if to say, "Come one inch closer and I'll go even higher."

This could be a long afternoon.

"How can we be sure he knows what he's doing?" Roanna fretted next to her mother.

Winnie offered her a smile as she extricated Maeve's hand from her curls. "He sure knows how to climb a tree. I'm guessing he'll be able to bring your cat, er, Henry the Eighth—" she glanced at Dolores "—back safely." She didn't really know if it was true but it seemed like the appropriate thing to say.

"He's my baby." Dolores started mumbling again, and Roanna put an arm around her.

"It's okay, Mom. We'll get him down."

Winnie blew hair off her face. She understood the woman's fear. If anything happened to Sam she'd be devastated. Even though she'd gone through the greatest loss of her life when Tom died, Sam was still a member of their family.

"I hope you're right." Roanna's voice was infused with anger as she shot Winnie a scathing look.

Winnie bit her lip. "C'mon, Maeve, let's go see what Krista and Sam are doing."

She made the short walk across the parking lot to where Krista sat in the grass field with Sam. With Krista's face buried in Sam's neck, they resembled two partners in crime. Sam's single free ear rotated in Winnie's direction.

Krista pulled away and looked up at Winnie. "They get the cat yet?"

"No, it's going to take a bit of coaxing." Winnie put Maeve down and she immediately buried her fingers in Sam's coat.

"Duh."

"Krista, watch your tone!"

Krista responded by rolling her eyes.

"Why do you think you can behave like this with me? Would you do this to one of your teachers at school?" She felt like adding "or to Uncle Max" but didn't want to hear the answer.

"No, but my teachers at school wouldn't…" She trailed off, mumbling in teenage lingo Winnie's hearing didn't catch.

"Would you like to speak up, please?" With one eye on Maeve and Sam, she did her best to look Krista right in the eyes.

"You don't think about anyone but yourself." Krista's lower lip was out in full pout.

"Oh, is that so? What's eating at you, daughter-of-mine?"

"You don't want to have a father in our family, but what about Maeve and me? What about what *we* need?"

For the third time in ten minutes Winnie felt sucker punched. First Max had brought up their

shared attraction. Then Maeve had called hi
"Dad." Now Krista was throwing a fit about n
having a father.

"Did Max put you up to this?"

"He didn't have to. He wants to be part of ou
family. *You're* the one who won't let him in."

"Krista, if and when I ever bring another ma
into this family it will be *my* decision. This ma
seem all romantic and perfect to you, but wh
about the first time he tells you not to do som
thing? How will you feel then? It's not all pizz
and soccer games, you know."

"So what? At least Maeve and I would have
dad."

Fury made Winnie's head buzz and she fougl
to keep control of her emotions. But she was goir
to kill Max when she had the chance. He'd had r
right to say any of this to Krista!

"You did have a dad, Krista," she said tersel
"I'm sorry he passed on so early. But your fath
gave you everything while he was here."

"How does that help me now?" Krista stoc
and stormed toward the beach.

"Krista!"

But Krista stalked off, refusing to turn bac
toward Winnie. Winnie crouched beside Maev
and Sam.

"What am I going to do, guys?" The consta
drama created by a thirteen-year-old exhausted he

"She'll cool off."

Winnie jumped at Max's deep voice.

"What did you say to her?" she snapped, then looked past him to Dolores, who held a fluffy white mass in her arms. Roanna was reaching out her hand to Miles.

"You got the cat?"

"Warrant got the cat." He slid his hands into his pockets. "And I didn't say anything to Krista. But she was full of determination this morning that she and Maeve need a father figure."

"And she said she wants it to be you. Fine, it is you. She has her father figure. Isn't that enough?"

"Don't throw that at me, Win. Of course she's attached to me, as I am to her. It's only natural she'd think there could be more, for all of us. She's thirteen. Don't you remember being thirteen?"

"When I was thirteen, I had two parents. My father was still alive."

In the silence that fell between them Maeve giggled. She'd pulled off her shoes and socks, and the grass tickled her feet.

"Didn't you just prove her point?" he asked softly.

Max was close—she felt the warmth of his body and the resulting awareness that chased up her arms, down her spine, to her belly.

The weight of his hands on her shoulders was a relief. It grounded her, made her able to think.

Her sensual awareness of him remained constant, but at least when he touched her she could draw from his strength.

"You take on too much. What did you say I had to do if my work with Sam was going to help? 'Keep an open mind. Open your heart to the possibility of healing.'"

She didn't even bother to wipe away the tears that spilled down her cheeks. She turned into his embrace. "Do you have your eye on Maeve?" she asked.

"Mmm," he murmured into her hair.

"Because I need to cry." She allowed her arms to go around him and pressed her face into his shoulder.

"Cry all you want, Win."

She pulled back and looked up at him. True to his word, his eyes were fixed on Maeve. Winnie glanced over her shoulder and saw Krista walking toward them.

"This doesn't change anything, Max," she whispered. "We're friends, family friends. That's good. It's enough."

She didn't imagine he'd reply right away, but the last thing she expected was his bark of laughter. It turned into an all-out belly laugh as his hands grasped her shoulders and pushed her back.

"Do you really think that's it? That all's well and we'll go on from here?" he demanded.

"I—well, yes, I do."

"No touching?" He dropped his hands and took several steps away, no longer sheltering her. The immediate chill from the brisk wind seemed to emphasize his absence.

"You can wipe it off your face, Max."

"Wipe what off whose face?" Krista piped in, obviously over her most recent trauma-drama. "Are you okay, Mom?"

"I'm fine, honey. Max was giving me his shoulder to lean on," she said with a slight smile.

Krista didn't seem impressed. "Hmm. Whatever."

"Good news, Krista. We might be able to do that camping trip you asked about." Max grinned at Krista, who smiled back, but cast Winnie a guarded look. "Being family friends and all."

"Really, Mom?"

Winnie decided to keep the peace and go along with the camping plans. "It might even be fun, as long as we get a cabin. I don't do tents."

"Cool."

Winnie nodded. Taking the path of least resistance, she'd given in as gracefully as she could. Between Max and Krista, she didn't stand a chance.

CHAPTER NINETEEN

"Mom, why can't Maeve have her own sleeping bag?"

Krista's face was flushed. She'd been rummaging through the small amount of camping equipment stored in the garage. It was Friday of the three-day Memorial weekend, and Krista had looked forward to the trip since the cat incident at City Beach three weeks ago.

Max—but mostly Krista—had spent two weeks cajoling Winnie, but they'd finally convinced her to go camping. They'd be staying in a cabin, so Winnie had agreed. Tent-camping, she claimed, was not in her genetic makeup.

"Because Maeve is going to sleep with me to stay warm." And serve as a good chaperone to make sure she didn't get any ideas about Max in such close quarters.

"C'mon, Mom, it's not like we'll be in a tent. *You* insisted on a cabin."

"Are you *sure* you want to go, Krista? Because your tone sounds more like that of someone who'd like her mother to just say, 'Forget it.'"

Honestly, if they made it to the Cascades with everything they needed before noon tomorrow, Winnie was going to buy a lottery ticket. Luck was all that would get them packed in time to be at Max's by 7:00 a.m. Saturday.

Why had she agreed to this? Oh, yeah. Because she and Max would have chaperones. Because Krista had wanted to do this for the longest time and Winnie had never had any desire to take the girls and go with either of her brothers, who were hard-core backpacking wilderness campers. Because she'd never do this on her own. She knew her way around a campsite and wasn't afraid of the forests or of getting lost, but—despite their beauty—she didn't like the unpredictability of the mountains.

She rubbed the back of her neck. "We've got to get the car packed before Aunt Robyn brings Maeve back. We'll never get anything done after that."

"Can I take my MP3 player?"

"Yes, but only for the car ride up and back. Not in the mountains—there's no point in going if you don't appreciate the nature around you."

"We have nature around us here, Mom." Krista's expression was earnest and still...young.

"Come here, you." Winnie held out her arms. Krista didn't hesitate to come into her embrace.

"I love you so much, my daughter. You know that, don't you?" She squeezed Krista's shoulders.

"I know, Mom."

Winnie stroked Krista's hair while keeping both arms around her. "I know I've been so overwhelmed since Maeve came."

"Mom, it's okay, really."

"That's not the point, honey. I don't want you to think I love you any less than I ever have. I love you so much more every day. A mother's love isn't something I can explain. I just hope you get to experience it yourself someday."

"I love you, too, Mom." Krista pulled away. "And I really think you've done an awesome job with Maeve."

Winnie held back a smile. A teenager's approval of her child-rearing—could there be higher praise?

"Thanks, honey, I appreciate that. Now let's get this finished so we can go to bed early. I don't want to keep your uncle Max waiting."

ONCE AT MAX'S Saturday morning, they reloaded all their supplies into Max's SUV.

"Are you sure we have everything we'll need for the weekend?" He cast a sidelong look at her after they'd lifted the last box of food into the back. His lips twitched on the verge of a grin.

She ignored the sarcasm. "I know how to camp,

Max. I just choose not to for the most part. These girls eat a lot more than you realize."

She threw in a bag of dog food as Sam waved his tail.

"There're a lot of things you're good at, Winnie, that you choose not to do."

Winnie's brain screamed at her to run but her feet remained firmly planted, just inches from Max's.

"The trip isn't going to work if we start out like this." Her words sounded saner than her desire to grab Max's head and pull his lips to hers, grin or not.

Max laughed. "We're chaperoned, right? We won't have a minute alone. What's wrong with some harmless flirting?"

Everything.

She walked away and got settled in the backseat with Maeve and Sam. They'd decided she'd sit in back so that Krista could have some one-on-one with Max as he drove.

Krista was also learning to use a map this trip—her generation had been brought up with GPS and Max felt map-reading was a necessary life-skill. Winnie agreed.

She leaned her head back for the ride, with Sam curled up at her feet. Maeve usually fell asleep before they'd even crossed Deception Pass Bridge and she thought this time would be no exception.

Winnie drifted off until she heard Krista's high-pitched excited voice.

"Mom, look! There's a glacier! At the top of the mountain. It's such a pretty blue."

Krista glanced over at Maeve, sleeping as predicted, then shifted her gaze out the side window. Her breath caught.

They'd climbed into the densest layer of fir trees and forest, yet there were glimpses of the mountains. One in particular spread out ahead of them—Mount Baker, with its telltale glacier clinging to its side. The deep hue of the glacial ice contrasted with younger layers of white ice and snow, even in this warmer month.

"Spectacular." She spoke quietly so as not to wake Maeve. She met Max's eyes in the rearview mirror. He hadn't appeared so relaxed, so at ease, since their hike. Sexual longing rose from deep inside her.

She'd never manage to be only friends with Max. Why was she still hanging on to that illusion?

"Where does the map say to go next, Krista?" His low, soothing voice reached back to Winnie's ears and for a moment she wished she could listen to it forever.

But nothing was forever. She'd already learned that in the most painful way.

Still, it would be nice to unwind for a few days.

To give up being constantly in control. To rely on a partner to help with her children.

MAX RELISHED THE TIME they all spent together in his old truck. He realized that he'd never be satisfied with just a weekend here and there with Winnie and the girls. They fit together like a family. Hell, they *were* a family.

He'd been patient, waiting for Winnie to come around to his way of thinking, but his patience was wearing thin.

He shifted into low gear as they took the Jeep up into the mountains.

"We should be there in half a mile, Uncle Max."

"This last bit is going to be the steepest, and then it'll level out where we'll be staying."

"I think it would've been cool to pitch a tent here, don't you?"

"Krista, we've been over this," Winnie said from the backseat, but her voice lacked its usual bite when it came to keeping her teenage daughter on track. Max was glad. Finally Winnie was letting things just roll.

"Your mom's right, Krista. We all felt that a cabin is the best way to go since Maeve's still so young." He felt Winnie's eyes on him but didn't risk confirming his hunch in the rearview mirror. He had to stay focused on the winding mountain road.

Max loved the crunch of the pinecones under the SUV's wheels and the pungent scent of the forest that blew in through the half-open windows. He felt better than he had in the past year. His joints didn't ache anymore, unless a cold front was coming in. While he'd never have the physique he'd had as a young pilot, he was in the best shape of his life, especially considering what he'd been through.

His health wasn't all that had improved; his state of mind was equally vibrant. Winnie was the reason. Winnie and her girls.

He couldn't pinpoint the time or day it had happened, but his anger at Winnie, the resentment he'd harbored over not knowing about Maeve, had disappeared.

The road leveled out and within several hundred feet it opened onto a wide plateau. Max followed the signs and drove into a gravel parking lot by a log cabin that had an Office shingle hanging out front.

"We're here!" Krista's excitement was infectious.

"Not quite. We have to check in here, get our keys and then get ourselves to our cabin." Max smiled at Krista's enthusiasm. Imagine—without music blaring in her ears or a computer in front of her, Krista was having fun.

"Hi, baby girl." Winnie's voice caressed his ears as she spoke to their daughter.

Their daughter.

Pride still welled over and flooded him with warmth. He wanted to shout to the world that he had a daughter and that he was a survivor.

Must be the mountain air playing with his sanity. He was proud to be a father, yes, but…it was as if his emotions had been freed.

"If you want to wait here with Maeve, Krista and I can go get us set up. We should only be a minute or two." He turned around to face Winnie.

"Sure. Once we take her out of her seat…" Winnie smiled, eyebrows raised in expectation.

Max wiggled Maeve's foot, which elicited a bubble of joyful laughter.

"Do you want to be out there with the bears, baby girl?" He smiled at Maeve until she smiled back, then hid her face playfully against the side of her seat.

He looked at Winnie. Her expression was one of open warmth and admiration. His insides tensed in reflexive defense. He forced himself to exhale.

Hadn't he told *her* to relax?

"We're blessed, aren't we?" He risked posing the question and risked even more using the plural.

"Yes, we are," Winnie said quietly.

The air between them grew taut with wonder, with need.

Max let out a breath and shook his head. "I'll get the key now, Win."

He heard her soft chuckle before he shut the car door.

THE CABIN WAS BARE-BONES as expected. They'd brought enough blankets and warm clothing to get them through a week, let alone the two nights they'd actually stay here. Max arranged firewood in the pit and they pulled out their folding chairs.

"So it'll be ready and waiting when we come back from our hike."

"Sounds good to me." Winnie liked the idea of not having to do much prep work once they returned from the two-mile hike that Krista had mapped out with Max's assistance.

"We might want to take our hiking sticks with us, since there's a pretty rocky part near the end of the hike, according to my guidebook." Krista held two pairs of hiking poles in her hands.

"I have yours and mine, Mom. Uncle Max, did you bring a pair?"

"Sure did, kiddo." Winnie watched Krista's expression go from content to ecstatic.

Even out here, in the planet's serenity zone, she still had to work at turning off her controlling tendencies. Maybe Max was right. If she let go, she might be surprised at how much easier and joyous life could be.

She was so weary of keeping up her guard around Max. But he was hell-bent on his future career as a small-aircraft pilot, and putting herself through the misery of worrying about him each day wasn't something she was willing to do. It would be so nice to forget about all that, if just for this weekend.

As soon as Maeve had finished her midmorning snack, they loaded her into the new backpack Max would wear to carry her. Winnie had Sam on his leash and Krista held the map. Winnie and Krista each had carried a knapsack with water, juice and lunch.

The trail started just a few hundred yards from their cabin and wound into the tree-canopied mountainside. No one talked for a while as they all settled into a comfortable rhythm. Maeve held on to Max's hair but he didn't complain. Birds of all species flew across their path. At one point Max stopped suddenly, his hand up.

Krista and Winnie stopped behind him. Sam's ears were cocked; he remained silent and alert.

Max turned around to face them. "There's a doe with her fawn up ahead, a little to the right of the trail. Look around me. Can you see her?"

Krista stepped up next to Max on his right. Her gasp of delight carried back to Winnie. She motioned urgently. "Come here, Mom!" Her voice was a breath above a whisper.

Winnie gave Sam the hand signal for *stay* and *silent,* then moved close and had to lean against Max to keep her balance. As she inched forward to catch a glimpse, Maeve shot out one hand and grabbed her hair.

"Owwww!" She pulled back.

Maeve's scream of victory echoed across the path. Winnie could make out the white flash of the doe's tail before she disappeared with her fawn into the safety of the forest.

"Way to go, Mom." Krista sounded upset but when Winnie glanced over, she saw her smile.

"More like, 'Way to go, *Maeve.*'" Winnie rubbed her crown. "Don't pull Mommy's hair, Maeve."

"Why did you do that, huh?" Max reached behind him and held Maeve's hands in his. They made a perfect circle with their arms—Maeve's held straight in front of her, over her head, and Max's behind him.

"Doesn't that hurt your shoulders?" She knew his shoulders had taken the brunt of the IED blast, which had exacerbated the arthritis caused by years conducting carrier launches.

"Nah, not when it's this munchkin."

Winnie noted that he released Maeve's hands and shook his arms out after he'd lowered them.

"Good dog, Sam." She'd almost forgotten to praise him.

A two-mile walk would normally take Winnie forty minutes with Krista walking beside her and Maeve in her stroller. But the rough terrain made the journey much slower.

"Do you want a break from her?" Winnie saw Max wince a bit when he shrugged out of the carrier. They'd found a nice spot to eat their lunch, at an overpass that provided a startling view of both Mount Baker and the valley below.

"I should be okay after a little rest. Besides, she won't be as good if you carry her."

"True." Whenever Winnie tried to, Maeve let out gusty howls of protest. For some reason she liked to be on Max's back, no doubt due to the better view and the sense of a stronger carrier.

"I'm still new," he said. "It'll wear off."

"Daddy." Maeve stood in front of Max and reached for the grapes he'd pulled out of the backpack.

"Here you go, honey." He bit the grape in two before giving her half. He even had the safety part of being a parent down pat.

Winnie studied them for a moment. She took a bite of her ham-and-cheese croissant and chewed thoughtfully.

"What's on your mind?"

"We've known each other for a long time, Max. And then we didn't see each other for years. Yet here we are, almost as though no time has passed."

"Yeah, this reminds me of the old days."

Winnie nodded. The four of them—she, Ton
Krista and Max—had spent afternoons a lot lik
this one on summer days. Something Max woul
bring his girlfriend of the moment....

"Except now you two have a daughter." Krista
comment threw down a gauntlet in the midst of a
of them. Maeve perched on Max's thigh while sh
ate her lunch. Winnie crossed her legs and sippe
her water. Let him deal with this one.

And he did.

"Yes, we do, Krista. But we had you long be
fore Maeve. I may be only your godfather but I'v
always been part of your family. Consequentl
you've always been part of mine. Even when
wasn't with you, I never forgot you."

Winnie watched the color creep up Krista
neck and cheeks. She sighed. Max knew tha
Krista hung on his every word.

"Yup." Krista nodded and stared at her sneal
ers.

Max must have felt Winnie's observation be
cause he looked at her over Krista's bent hea
He raised a brow as if to ask, "What do you e:
pect me to say?"

Winnie simply smiled.

She wasn't taking the bait, not this weekend.

CHAPTER TWENTY

LATER THAT EVENING the shadows grew long across the campsite and the bugs came out in full force. The fire kept them at bay close to the flames. It took Maeve and Krista about five minutes after their gooey roasted marshmallow, chocolate and graham cracker treats to start looking sleepy.

"Krista, why don't you two go lie down inside?"

"Okay, Mom."

Winnie turned to Max. "I'll clean up these plates and get the girls ready for bed. I'll come back out for a bit if the fire's still going."

"It'll be here." Max stoked the flames with one of the sticks they'd used to roast the marshmallows. His features seemed etched in the orange glow.

Winnie had the girls get into their pajamas and then directed them to their bunks. Maeve insisted on crawling into Krista's.

"I don't mind, Mom." Krista really was tired; she usually pitched a fit if Maeve wanted to sleep with her, as Maeve's kicking woke her up during the night.

"Okay. Thanks, honey. I'll get her when I come in."

Winnie finished the brief kitchen cleanup and grabbed a bottle of new wine and two plastic glasses to take out to the fire. She and Max could enjoy a glass before bedtime.

When she looked at the girls one last time, they were snuggled together, sound asleep. She bent over them and kissed their cheeks.

Max wasn't there when she came back out; neither was Sam. She figured they'd gone for a brief walk.

She wiggled her Swiss Army knife out of her jeans pocket and flipped up the corkscrew. Once the bottle was open she set it down to breathe.

The sound of twigs breaking and a loud panting alerted her to Max and Sam as they reentered camp. She looked up to see man and dog, walking side by side as though Max, not Winnie, was the one who'd raised Sam from a pup.

"I see you've made good use of those acrylic wineglasses." He sat down in the camp chair next to hers. Sam trotted up to the cabin's small stoop and lay down.

"This is a treat for me. I don't usually get to have a glass of wine unless I'm out with Robyn or a girlfriend." She paused. "Or you."

She poured the wine. "It's not Montepulciano but I hope you'll like it." She was grateful for the dark so that he couldn't see her hand tremble.

Max chuckled. He took the wine bottle from her and read the label in the firelight. "Chilean— nice. Believe it or not, I probably haven't had much more of a chance to enjoy a decent glass than you these past months. Getting better and staying healthy has occupied my time recently. Before that, around-the-clock flying and working didn't leave a lot of room for partying."

"Cheers, then. To our health."

He leaned toward her and tapped her glass with his. The plastic made a dull noise compared to crystal or glass, but it was music to Winnie's ears.

After a sip, Max stared into the fire. "We've come a long way, Winnie."

"Yes, I suppose we have. We're not bickering every time we see each other for one thing."

"No, but I don't just mean over the past several months. I'm talking about how we've known each other since we were nothing more than kids, really. Since before you and Tom got married."

"I didn't know you were talking about *ancient* history, Max."

"Not ancient, but shared. That's something a lot of people don't have anymore."

A warning buzzer went off somewhere in her brain, and it had nothing to do with the wine. If Max started in on his theory that they should be *more* than friends…

"And before you go getting your panties in a

wad," he said, using an old-fashioned expression she'd heard from her parents, "I'm not talking about us as anything other than family friends— at the moment."

"Of course." She swallowed, then brought her glass to her lips.

You're not disappointed, are you?

"You're right," she began. "We've known each other longer than a lot of friends, a lot of—" She cut herself off. Her face was hot and not from the fire. Max was finally seeing things her way and she was going to argue with him?

"Married couples? It's okay to say it, Win. I know you're not implying that we're an old married couple or ever will be. I get it."

His words should have been soothing to her. She should be relieved. And, in a way…she was. Underneath his tone, she sensed amusement.

She managed to laugh. "You really do get it, don't you?"

"I've been telling you this for how long now?"

She couldn't keep the smile off her face. This was the Max she used to and could relax with. The Max who listened, offered an opinion here and there and made no judgments.

"How bad was it, Max?"

He turned to her then, looking at her before he angled back to the fire. She didn't have to expound on "it." She referred to what they'd never really discussed, not in any detail. His war injury and how it had happened.

"The whole experience wasn't as bad as it could've been. Yes, it was stressful. I spent days worrying about different crews flying different types of missions. Especially if they were going into known danger zones. Which, to be honest, includes every mission. Nothing is certain over there.

"We were in the midst of our last two weeks of a seven-month deployment on the ground, in country. It's a notoriously tough time—and if anyone's going to do anything stupid or careless, that's when they do. Going home is so close you can taste it. We were all proud of what we'd accomplished, but your body—anyone's body—can only take so much of the constant adrenaline rush."

He gasped out a short laugh.

"You'd think I have a glamorous story to tell, something like you've seen in a movie. But it was as normal a day as you get in a war zone. I was walking from my barracks to the canteen. I knew most of the squadron would be there for breakfast, since we were having a safety stand-down that morning. No flights, nothing operational.

"I saw her when she was still twenty yards from the guard shack. Covered from head to toe in black, with just a small opening in her burka to see out of. She was moving slowly but very deliberately toward the base gate. On my other side I saw dozens if not hundreds of my squadron walking toward me, toward the mess tent."

He rubbed his eyes as if the memory burned them.

"It was pure gut instinct. I didn't see anyone else stopping her, making her wait before she went forward through the cars that were lined up at the gate. So I yelled as I rushed the gate and tried to get one of the guards' attention—he was checking under a vehicle for explosives. Hell, *she* was the explosive."

His eyes seemed to search the flames in front of them.

"I shouted at the kids walking toward me to turn and run back. They didn't hesitate. I meant to run back in their direction, too, but she detonated herself before I was clear of the frag zone."

He paused, shaking his head. "I don't remember a whole lot after that. The reverberation from the blast knocked me out for twenty minutes, I'm told, but it felt like a year. When I came to in the medical unit, a doc was stitching up my thigh and my head hurt like hell. Once they'd determined that my head injury wasn't life-threatening, they sedated me for a day or so to give my brain and body a chance to heal more effectively."

He looked at her again. "That's it, Winnie. That short time of about—" he glanced up at the darkening sky "—two or three minutes is what's haunted me for the past year. It can still make my bones and muscles ache from the shrapnel that couldn't be removed."

"Why do you act as if it was no big deal, Max? Of course it was!"

"Sure. I've been through all of that with my therapist. I'm not ignoring what you said. I'm just trying to emphasize that I didn't do anything anyone else wouldn't have. My aircrews, who flew through enemy fire to complete their mission, the ground crewmen who suffered through hell in order to keep the planes flying. They did the extraordinary. They never complained, never tried to back out of their commitment to complete a mission. Ever."

"It's hard to imagine what you were thinking through all of it. All we get here in the States is news coverage by reporters who can only guess at what you're going through, unless they're imbedded with your squadron."

"We both know that's not going to happen, not with our platform." He meant the classified nature of the EA-6B's mission, which involved communications and electronic surveillance.

"Mmm. Tom would've loved to be part of it all." She remembered how excited Tom was before any deployment, but he always tried to hide it from her. She understood that he didn't want to leave her or Krista but that he loved his job, protecting his country. It was his calling.

"He *was* part of it, Winnie, and in some ways still is. He trained so many of the men and women who were out there flying missions with me. He did all the preps for deployment. He made the squadron ready to go on a moment's notice. Nothing he did was in vain. Nothing any of the sailors who give it their all is in vain."

"That's tough to prove to the families left behind."

"I know. Despite what I did, what I'm doing, it's been tough for me to accept losing Tom and every other service member we've sacrificed."

"Max, you understand this is the biggest reason I need us to remain just friends? I can't go through it again. And I refuse to put my girls at risk of suffering because of my choice in a life partner. I know you're getting out of the Navy, but you're still going to fly...."

Max didn't reply. Winnie waited.

Finally he said, "That's all well and good, Winnie, and I applaud your intentions."

"But?"

He shifted in his camp chair and she wondered if sitting so low to the ground was bothering him. He'd said he needed to move around a lot to keep the aching to a minimum.

"But you've already put them at risk. The day

you decided to tell me about Maeve, the day you said okay to me spending time with both girls—that's when you made your decision."

He got up and stood there for a moment, arms stretched overhead. Winnie was relieved to be able to call it a night.

Are you, really?

Max lowered his arms and reached out to her. She hesitated, then grabbed his hand and let him haul her up out of her canvas chair.

They were inches apart and, despite all her resolve, her body wanted one thing.

"Max." She swayed toward him. It would be so easy. Feel so right.

"I'm not done yet. You put the girls at risk because if anything happens to me, they'll be hurt. Sad. They'll miss me. But the deed is done, Winnie. They're getting to know me and trust me. Like a dad."

She breathed in sharply.

"They—the girls and I—we're having a blast. We're enjoying our time together."

He leaned in and the warmth of his breath caressed her face.

"The only person who's not having any fun here, Win, is you. You're still trying to orchestrate everyone's life. Do you even know what you want for yours?"

He pulled back and rubbed his upper arms.

"Have a good night. I'll wait here while you use the restroom and get settled with the girls. Then I'll go in, too."

Winnie stared at his retreating back. He sat down next to Sam on the stoop. Seconds later, Sam rose to curl up against him.

CHAPTER TWENTY-ONE

NOT ONLY DID MAX RESPECT Winnie's wishes that first night, the next day he appeared to enjoy every single minute with the girls and with her but never made another move to bring anything sexual into their time together.

Winnie appreciated it. Or tried to.

I'm not sulking. I'm not disappointed. This what I want.

Their second day of hiking was longer than the first. It included a ride in a motorboat Max had rented. They navigated a mountain lake to a floating lodge, where they had lunch, and came back ashore near a meadow that was ripe with spring wildflowers and early berries.

When they returned to the cabin, it was time for dinner. To Winnie's surprise, the girls were still chatty after they'd eaten.

"Uncle Max, can you tell us a scary story?" Krista had placed her camp chair next to Max's. She'd been on a paranormal reading kick, so her request didn't surprise Winnie.

"Honey, it can't be too scary for your sister."

Maeve snuggled in Max's lap, her head leaning back on his chest so she could watch the fire.

"I'll keep the first story tame." Max playfully shook Maeve's foot. "If Miss Munchkin drifts off, I can make the second one scarier."

He started to recite Beatrice Potter's classic story about Peter Rabbit, one of Maeve's favorites, from memory.

She immediately clapped.

"Yay, Daddy!" Winnie blinked back tears. Max had read the book often enough in the past couple of months to know it by heart. Since March, when he'd met Maeve, until now—only a short time but it felt as if they'd been a family forever.

Max's eyes lit up, glistening in the firelight. Even in the darkness Winnie saw his pure love for Maeve.

Unconditional.

As he told the story, Winnie relaxed in her camp chair and watched the three of them. Maeve reveled in the story, safe in her daddy's lap. Krista's expression reflected her enjoyment of the tale she'd heard hundreds of times in her childhood. It didn't seem to matter that she was thirteen.

Winnie closed her eyes and listened as Max's voice carried across the fire and the campsite. She'd rest her eyes until Maeve fell asleep and then put the baby to bed....

"Win." His breath caressed her lips, her cheeks. She wanted to wake up but it was so cozy and warm here by the fire.

The campfire.

She bolted up and banged her head on Max's chin.

"Oww." Max sat back on his heels.

"Sorry! I forgot where I am, was— Oh." She looked at him. "Are you okay?"

"I'll live."

She glanced around the campsite.

"The girls are safely tucked together, just like last night. They're already asleep." He answered her before she'd even asked.

"Thanks. I'm sorry, Max." And she was. As much as he wanted to participate as a parent, she never wanted him to think she was taking advantage of his good intentions.

"Nothing to be sorry about." He was still on his haunches, his hands on her thighs. His eyes were unreadable as he blocked the remaining light from the fire.

"I can't see your face at all. Did you mind doing—?"

"No, Win," he interrupted. "I love taking care of the girls." He paused. "I'd love to take care of you, too, Winnie."

"I thought you finally got it, Max. You've been a complete gentleman all weekend." She heard the teasing note in her voice. And the huskiness that had nothing to do with the wisps of smoke from the smoldering fire.

"I do get it. That's what's got you so messed up." He lifted one hand from her thigh and stroked her cheek. It was like striking a match to a kerosene lamp. "You want this—" he moved his hand from her cheek to cup her breast "—as much as I do."

"I do." She leaned in and placed her hands on either side of his face and pulled him down until his lips were touching hers. "Max, I need you to make love to me."

"I think I can manage that." His whispered reply ended abruptly when his tongue traced her lips, then entered her mouth with an excruciating slowness that sent a tremor of need through Winnie. She was up and out of her camp chair.

Her momentum forced Max onto his back on the soft dirt.

She straddled him and kissed him as if he were the last man on earth. Max *was* the last man, the only man, for her, and this was where she wanted to be.

In his arms.

Max grabbed her hips and pushed, positioning her pelvis directly on his erection. Even through their jeans, the contact shot flashes of delight behind Winnie's closed eyes.

He reached up and held her head to keep her lips on his, then rolled them both over. His hands still cradled her head, his chest crushed her breasts and the weight of his hips prompted her to wrap her legs around him.

When Max stopped kissing her, Winnie opened her eyes. He stared at her, his eyes reflecting the dancing flames from the campfire, his face alight.

"I love you, Winnie."

She couldn't deny his declaration or fight her response. She pulled him back to her, and this time she teased his lips with her tongue, kissed him on his eyelids, his nose, his strong jaw.

Max groaned. "Let's get in the sleeping bag, Win."

"We can't go in the cabin, Max."

Max smiled in the dim light. "We don't have to. I've got a sleeping bag in the truck." He rolled off her, and she felt an immediate chill that had nothing to do with the temperature. She needed Max to feel complete, alive.

You haven't been fully alive until now.

She blinked, sat up, looked around. Night had fallen while she and Max kissed. There were countless stars that blinked down from the deep plum sky, framed by the tips of fir trees that surrounded them. The log cabin's windows, with a small light inside, looked inviting. She saw Sam's

silhouette where he lay at the front screen doo
guarding the girls.

All this beauty, her girls, a man who wante
to make love to her. Not just have sex, but *mak
love*. Stay with her and the girls. Provide for then

He was her anchor.

She sought him out in the dark. She heard th
car door close, and then his tall figure was back i
view. How had she resisted all of this for so long
How had she convinced herself that she couldn
have Max as her lover and certainly not as he
life partner?

He smiled, a smile that was genuine but shor
lived. Max was a man on a mission.

He rolled out the sleeping bag. He turned an
looked at her as she sat on the ground.

"Are you going to watch me or make love t
me?"

"Both." She stood, but didn't go right to hin
Instead, she raised her shirt over her head an
tossed it on a camp chair.

Max was silent, but she heard him take a breat!

Winnie maintained eye contact with him as sh
pulled her bra straps down, releasing the cup
When her breasts were free she unhooked the br
and it joined her shirt.

She kicked off her sneakers, then unbuttone
her jeans and shimmied out of them. Her pan
ies were a practical bikini cut but from Max's re

action they could have been a diamond-studded thong. He drew her to him and bent his head to suckle her breasts.

"Oh, Max." She bit her lip to keep from screaming out her need. The girls and Sam were quiet, asleep. She didn't want to change that.

Max made short work of her panties and with no warning put his hand, his fingers, inside her. Her wetness clamped onto him and the resulting orgasm made Winnie cling to his shoulders. Her knees sagged against his legs as she whimpered into his neck.

She couldn't catch her breath before Max urged her down on the quilted bag and tore off his clothes. Winnie would have enjoyed undressing him but they were beyond seduction.

He put on a condom and joined her on the ground, enveloping her with his musk, her own scent still on his fingers.

"Win…" He filled her with one thrust and she felt the start of another climax. But he wouldn't let her come again that easily—he made her work for it. He shifted over her and took his time, alternating deep thrusts with shorter, less satisfying ones that brought a scream to her throat, a scream she knew would erupt if he didn't finish, he didn't stop torturing her.

"Max, please, please."

"Please what, Winnie?"

"Please...make...me..."

"Come?" He thrust hard and so deep that she thought she felt their hipbones touch. He swallowed her scream with his mouth, his tongue and lips taking in her passion as he let go of his own. Never before had Winnie actually lost all sense of time and space in a man's arms.

With Max, she did.

"I WAS AFRAID YOU'D get bruised but I couldn't hold back, Win. Are you okay?" He felt stones and sticks through the sleeping bag as he lay with Winnie close beside him, her head against his shoulder.

"I'm more than okay, Max. I'm in complete bliss. Shh, don't talk. This is perfect."

He laughed and pressed her closer to his side. "Your skin is the softest thing I've ever felt."

"Mmm."

"Win?"

"Shh."

"No, Win, we need to talk about this, once and for all. Work things out."

She grew still. Fear sliced a tremor into his chest.

"Work what out? We seem to be doing just fine."

"I'm serious. I want us to be more."

Quiet.

Then a long, martyred sigh. "I suppose we can figure it out. I have been rather unyielding on the idea of making this 'more,' haven't I?"

She rose up on her elbow and looked at him. Her eyes caught the last glimmer of light from the embers of the waning fire. "This is hard for me, Max. I'm not good at change or compromise."

"Let me help you."

He pulled her to him and kissed her.

Hours later he woke her in the predawn and made love to her as if both their lives depended on it. Slow, purposeful. He wanted her to know he'd be true to his word and be not only a father to the girls but also the man she needed.

WINNIE WOKE TO THE SMELL of coffee and to aching muscles. She snuggled deeper into the sleeping back, wanting just a few more minutes of warmth, of Max.

He was gone. She opened one eye and saw him with the tin coffeepot, boiling water on the portable propane stove. He was completely dressed so she quickly got her own clothes on.

After she'd used the campsite restroom, she walked back to the cabin, smiling at him. It was still early for the girls, thank God. The fresh air and constant activity of the past two days had caught up with them last night.

"Hey." She stepped up behind him and slid her arms around his waist, pressing her body against him.

He grabbed her hands and turned around. She anticipated his kiss but instead he simply stood there, watching her.

"What?"

"I have to tell you something, Win."

"What, Max? You have another child? Another woman? What?"

His lips twitched. "No, nothing like that." He sighed. "I'm in love with you, Winnie. You have to trust that I know what I'm doing and that I'd never do anything to hurt you or the girls."

Her stomach squeezed and she took a step back. "But you're still determined to start your airline," she muttered. "Still determined to put yourself in danger."

"Flying is what I do—it's in my blood." His words were spoken quietly, but they severed the newfound bond of trust and love between them.

"I can't deal with this right now, Max."

"Don't. Give it some thought. There's too much at stake here."

She stared at him. What he said made sense. She ought to think carefully about it, not panic.

"Mom!"

Maeve's cry ended the conversation. With a last glance at Max, Winnie took a deep breath.

"I'm right here, sweetheart." She went to Maeve.

SHE COULDN'T DO IT.

She waited a week before she forced herself to call Max and ask to meet him. At a neutral place—not at either of their homes.

They met at the Coffee Klatch again.

"I can't, Max," she said with virtually no preamble. "I can't put myself through it again. You can tell me a thousand times that you're a safe pilot, that you'd never risk your life in bad weather, whatever. But like you said, it's in your blood to be a risk-taker. It's who you are. And it's in my blood never to go through that kind of anxiety again. I can't function under those circumstances. Krista and Maeve deserve more from me. *You* deserve more, Max."

"They deserve a father. You deserve a husband."

She couldn't respond, couldn't bring herself to look into his eyes. Until he said, "Ultimately, it's your call, Winnie. It always has been. I'll continue to be part of the girls' lives, but we can't do as much with them together. It's just…too hard."

At last, she glanced up from the Formica table that stood between them and was arrested by the expression on his face. His eyes were red-rimmed with proof of a sleepless night and the gray tinge to his skin reminded her of how he'd looked when Sam first started spending time with him.

"Has this triggered your PTSD?"

"PTSD?" He grunted. "Honey, PTSD has nothing on my broken heart." He let it sit there a minute before he visibly gathered himself and sat up straight. His face revealed no emotion.

"Thanks for at least giving us a chance, however brief it might have been." He stood and pulled his khaki cover out of his belt.

"I'll pick up the girls for soccer practice later today. You don't have to come out. Just have them ready to go at five-thirty."

He turned and strode out of the coffee shop. Winnie waited for the wash of relief, a lessening of the knot in her stomach. It didn't happen.

"I've come clean, and I'm doing what's right for me and the girls. No more pleasing everyone else." She whispered the words to herself. No one else was in the café at this hour; it was the lull before school let out and teenagers and elementary kids' moms stopped in for a shot of energy.

She steeled herself to look out the picture window and saw Max's retreating back as he walked through the parking lot toward his Jeep. She watched a petite woman get out of a small dark car she'd parked next to Max's. They started talking to each other.

She recognized Sandy, a woman Max had been involved with on and off for years, before he went away to war.

The bile that rose in her gut wasn't from jealousy. It was from knowing how Sandy felt as Max talked to her.

Like she was the only woman in the world.

"SO YOU'RE OKAY WITH all of this? Even when he comes to the house to get the girls?" Robyn popped another Gerbera daisy from its seed pot and placed it in the terra-cotta-style planter she'd bought as a surprise for Winnie.

"Of course I am. I love daisies."

Robyn cast her an exasperated look. "Funny, sis. You know what I'm talking about. Max. And not being with him. Heck, you two act like perfectly civilized divorced parents. He picks the kids up, brings them home. You drop them off with him for a weekend here and there. Doesn't it kill you to see him and not jump him?"

Winnie handed Robyn an English ivy plant. "I think this will look nice next to the orange daisy."

"Mmm. Answer the question, Winnie."

"What do you want me to say? Am I lonely? Sure, sometimes. Do I wish I could spend time with Max? Of course. Am I going to? No. I'm not setting myself up for another crisis in my life."

Robyn put down her trowel and rested her

hands, still in gardening gloves, on her knees as she squatted on the deck.

"Your *life* is a crisis, Winnie. You have your destiny staring you in the face and you're turning it down."

"Did it ever occur to you that my destiny is to be alone?"

"No, it hasn't. Do you want to know why? Because you attract friends. You are a loving, beautiful woman. And you've been blessed with two men in your lifetime who are willing to love you for *you*." Robyn took off the muddied canvas gloves and wiped her forehead. "For such an intelligent woman, you sure are stupid at times."

"Thanks a lot." She felt a wave of exhaustion—and sadness. "I'm all for the girls having a father figure. I'm not even against having male companionship from time to time. I just don't have it in me to lay it all on the line again. I know Max is going to do whatever he needs to stay in the girls' lives, and I'm grateful for that. But let's face it, Robyn. If it weren't for Maeve—and okay, Krista, too, at this point—Max would've been out of here. I'd never see him. He's made it clear that he doesn't want to be only my friend. I've said no to being—"

"You say that like it's a crime!" Robyn burst out. "Of course he wants to be more than a friend. He *is* more than a friend."

"No, he isn't. He can't be, Robyn." Her headache was going to blossom into a full migraine, she knew it.

"Newsflash, sis. 'Friends' don't help you raise your kids practically 24/7. A friend listens to you, does you favors, but a friend doesn't get you pregnant and then still want to make love to you and—oh, yeah, want to spend the rest of his life with you. Max is the answer to what you've been missing. He challenges your control-freak habits, he lets the girls go wild and have fun and he wants to do whatever it takes so you'll see him as more than a friend or fill-in parent."

"Are you done yet?"

"No. I want to know what the hell you're waiting for, Winnie. What will it take for you to realize that the pot of gold at the end of your rainbow is Max?"

"I'm not waiting for anything, Robyn. I'm living a solid, responsible life."

"You're not living, Win. You're surviving." Her words hit Winnie in the stomach.

"Stop now, Robyn. Put down your shovel and step away from the hole."

Robyn didn't even offer a ghost of her usual grin.

"Winnie, you're my sister and I love you. But you're the biggest coward ever. Surviving can look really nice. But it doesn't keep you warm at night, it doesn't nourish your dreams. And it doesn't teach your kids to have dreams of their own."

"I'm going to remind you of this when you're having your next mommy crisis."

"I'm not going to let up on this until you see that you deserve more than what you're allowing yourself to settle for."

Winnie squeezed her eyes shut and rubbed her temples. She felt Robyn's kiss on the crown of her head.

"I love you, sis. I'm here for you. But I wouldn't be doing my job if I just played along with your disastrous life-planning."

"Thanks, sis." Winnie's head and stomach hurt too much to argue.

"Take a couple of ibuprofen and get some rest."

"Thanks."

After Robyn left, Winnie sat in the deck lounger for a long while, eyes closed, breathing in the cleansing aroma of the fir trees. She was relieved to be alone. She needed the time to think.

But thinking only took her back to what Robyn had said, and she was so *done* thinking about her relationship with Max. Let Robyn claim she was a coward. At least her heart *would* remain intact. Her daughters', too, as much as Max's situation would allow. And the girls had a stability they'd never have if Tom had lived and the Navy moved him every couple of years.

Her stifled laugh ended in a sob. If Tom were still here, she'd never have fallen in love with Max, and she wouldn't have Maeve.

CHAPTER TWENTY-TWO

TWO WEEKS AFTER HER conversation with Robyn, three weeks after the fateful camping trip, Winnie walked into the N.A.S. Whidbey Navy Relief office. She was going to meet with a caseworker to see how many clients Sam could take on in the next couple of months. Max's official work with Sam had been over weeks ago and she needed the distraction of new clients.

The air outside was still, a bit unusual for Whidbey Island at this time of year. Since the island was poised at the entrance of the Strait of Juan de Fuca, there was always some sort of breeze coming in from the Pacific.

"Hi, Kat." She smiled at the receptionist, who gave her a little wave from her perch behind the curved counter. Kat was busy, on the phone, but Winnie knew where to go.

As she walked toward the caseworker's office, a tall man strode toward her.

"Winnie! Nice to see you again. You remember me, don't you? I'm boss's friend, Miles."

"Boss? Oh, you mean Max."

"Yes, I meant Max." He grinned like a school-boy caught doing something with fireworks. "I can't call him Max, you know. He'll always be 'boss' to me."

She leaned her weight on one foot. "Why is that, Miles? Why is Max your boss?"

He laughed. "Oh, no, he's not my boss. I mean, I've never worked for him. We didn't get to know each other until we were both back from down-range." He didn't have to fill in the rest—Winnie knew. They'd met in rehab, after they'd both survived horrific ordeals.

"I call him boss because he *is* the boss in the best way. Not many senior officers I've met in my Navy career have been as down to earth and real as him. He's not one for appearances, you know? That was important to me, especially before I started wearing and getting used to this." He knocked on his lower thigh and Winnie heard the sound of knuckles on plastic or metal.

"You lost your leg?"

"Yes, ma'am. They weren't sure I was going to even walk again, much less have not one, but two great legs." He winked at her. "I have another one for sports that's made out of titanium. It's killer."

She blinked and took a deep breath. "What a minute. You mean to tell me you climbed that huge tree to save that persnickety old woman's cat and you only have one leg?"

He laughed, and her cheeks flamed at her obtuseness. "I'm sorry, Miles, I really am a boor."

"Don't worry." He patted her upper arm. "Yeah, I climbed that tree pretty good, didn't I? And Miss Roanna, the daughter of the woman, she didn't think I'd be able to do it. She thought I had two regular legs." He smiled at the memory as though he'd pulled a fast one.

"So did I—and I thought you were nuts to climb the tree at all, especially in those boots you wore to ride your bike. But now I get it. You have better traction with them than sneakers would've given you. Am I on the right path?"

"Smack dab on it!"

"Well, I know I speak for everyone who was there that day when I say thank you again for all you did. I doubt even the fire department would've had as good a result."

"They might've kept the gals a bit calmer," he said, referring to Roanna and her blue-haired mom. Was that a blush she saw under his tan?

"So have you see Ro since?" She kept the focus on Miles. If he changed the subject to Max and asked her if she'd seen him lately, she'd die. She didn't want to admit that while she allowed him full access to her girls, she didn't let him any closer to her than necessary.

"Ro? No, that was it. I don't figure I'll see her

again. She didn't take kindly to me just taking over the situation that day."

"Well, I'm sure she's grateful for how it all turned out. You could always call to see how the cat's doing."

A twinkle sparked in his eyes. "I suppose I could. In fact…it might be the right thing to do. The polite thing." A second later, he looked away and shoved his hands in his pockets. What shadow had crossed his path?

"So what about you, Winnie? Have you seen Max recently?"

"No, no. He spends a lot of time with the girls, which is great. They love him."

"But what about you?"

She squirmed. She needed to get to the caseworker's office and she did *not* want to have this discussion with Miles. After all, except for Max's high praise of the man, she didn't really know him.

"Um, I'm here to get more clients to work with my therapy dog, Sam. You met him the day you rescued the cat."

That brought the grin back to Miles's face. "Sure, I did. He's the one who got that cat up the tree, isn't he?"

"No, actually, Sam's the one who noticed the cat was even there. He rescued Henry by alerting to

him. Otherwise, I think his owner would've bee
looking for him for quite a while."

"Yeah, she wouldn't be able to hear the cat cry
ing for her."

"I'm not sure the cat *was* crying for her. Seeme
to me he just got bored and once he was out of th
RV he bolted. Can't say I blame him!" She gav
him a quick smile.

"Yeah, that's probably true."

"Well, I've got to get going. Nice seeing you.

"The pleasure was all mine, Winnie. Tell bos
I said hi, okay?"

As she walked to the counselor's office, sh
sensed Miles's charisma. She admired him. R
spected him. And *he* respected Max beyond mea
sure. Pride and gratitude welled up in her ches
reminding her why she kept coming back on bas
to help the returning sailors.

It wasn't that she felt she was repaying a de
to the Navy for taking care of her and Krist
after Tom's death. It didn't hurt anymore, eithe
to come back on base so regularly.

With a jolt she realized she'd recovered fro
Tom's death some time ago. She'd always lov
him, but it wasn't Tom she'd betray if she and Ma
became a permanent couple.

No, she'd betray the woman who'd been s
deeply hurt. She'd promised that woman—he
old self—not to ever let that happen again.

But what about her *new* self, the woman she'd become since Maeve's birth? Since Max's reentry into their lives?

Winnie's insides shook. Was she really being a strong mother and protecting her girls, or was she allowing her fears to keep them all from being happy?

CHAPTER TWENTY-THREE

"UNCLE MAX SAID he'd wave to us."

Winnie pushed Maeve in her stroller. Krista loped beside them as they crossed the tarmac at the Naval Air Station. It was the annual Air Show, the weekend thousands flocked to Whidbey Island to witness aircraft of all types in flight.

This same weekend two years ago was when Maeve had been conceived....

"Wave to you from where?"

"From his plane."

Fear iced Winnie's neck. "Do you mean on the ground, in a static display of the EA-6B Prowler?"

Krista cocked her head in confusion. "No, I mean from the plane he's flying today. Something about the World War II demonstration."

"Honey, Uncle Max doesn't fly for the Navy anymore, and he certainly doesn't fly *antique* airplanes." She adjusted the brim of her visor. The sun was brutal but meant the viewing would be great later on.

"Besides," she added, "he said he was going to

meet us at three." It was one-thirty now, and no planes were scheduled to go up until two.

"He's flying as a passenger, Mom. He said they only do a quick flyby, then land on the far runway."

Winnie gripped the stroller handles tightly. It was the only way to keep from shaking. "Did he say what type of aircraft he'd be in?"

"Some kind of bomber, um, with a number."

"A B-17." Max's favorite airframe. He had a beautiful print over his mantel—a B-17 during combat operations in 1943 Europe. She'd always known about his love for WWII history.

Today he'd get to live a piece of it.

Be happy for him. It's not about you.

Besides, he didn't have to ask her for permission.

But he could have warned her for the girls' sake. What if Krista got upset, thinking about her dad crashing…?

Winnie sighed. If that was really a worry, she wouldn't have brought Krista here to begin with. Krista, who loved anything to do with aviation. Despite Tom's death, her adoration of flight had never really gone away.

Krista had gotten angry with herself when she was nine, about two years after her father died, and had shoved all her toy planes and miniaircraft models under her bed. Skateboarding and computer games became her new hobby.

But over the past few months Winnie noticed that some of Krista's collection had reappeared. On her desk, her windowsill, her bathroom counter. She'd even found the model of an EA-6B clutched in Maeve's chubby hand. She hadn't asked about it. Whether Maeve retrieved it from under Krista's bed or Krista had given it to her didn't matter.

Aircraft and flying. They were in her daughters' blood.

That call to flight was something Winnie believed Tom had been born with. She hadn't, but both Krista and Maeve seemed to have it. As young as Maeve was, she never missed the sound of a jet or a prop overhead, and was forever staring up at the sky, pointing to airplanes.

Can't you see this as a chance to have faith in Max?

"Mom, look!" Krista showed her a merchandise stand that was chockful of aviation-related T-shirts and ball caps. There was even a sport duffel bag with an EA-6B imprinted on its side.

"You could use a new bag for your soccer stuff. If you like it, why don't we see how much it costs?"

"Thanks, Mom!" Krista bounded over to the table and picked up one of the flattened duffel bags. She checked it over and spoke to the vendor, then put it down and came back. Winnie kept Maeve parked in the shade of a large umbrella.

"Mom, it's not that expensive! And if you don't want to buy it for me, I have enough saved from my allowance."

Krista told her the price and Winnie was surprised that Krista actually knew what she was talking about as far as value was concerned.

"Here, honey." She fished out her wallet from the diaper bag and handed Krista the money.

"Yay! Thanks—I'll be right back."

Winnie looked around the shady refuge while she waited for Krista. There was a stack of programs on a small stand and she grabbed one.

Sure enough, on the center of page one, she saw a description of the flyby at 2:15—three historic planes, a B-17, P-51 Mustang and P-40 Warhawk. She bit her lip. So Max was going to be in the B-17. Fine. Whatever. He was an adult and could make his own decisions. Take his own risks.

She knew from being around the Air Show for so long that the pilots of these aircraft were most often older, retired Navy or Air Force flyers, who dedicated their lives to Second World War re-enactments so no one would forget the sacrifices made by so many. It used to be that exclusively WWII vets flew the planes, but as their numbers had dwindled in the past decade, it was now the next generation, the children of those WWII heroes, who flew the aircraft.

Krista came back the proud owner of a Navy duffel bag with a silhouette of the Air Station and the aircraft that flew from Whidbey embroidered on it. The EA-6B Prowler electronic reconnaissance platform was emblazoned next to the P-3C Orion submarine hunter.

"I'm glad you're happy with it, honey." Winnie smiled at Krista and got a surprise hug.

"Yup, sure am. This is perfect for my sports clothes and I can use it for sleepovers and campouts, too."

"Now, let's find a comfortable place to sit. We just need to steer clear of the sun. It may feel cool but those rays will still burn."

"We put sunscreen on, Mom." Krista's patience with her was vanishing rapidly. She'd already forgotten that Winnie had bought her a new bag.

"Yes, we did. But you can't expect it to last through all day in the sun."

Before Krista could protest further, they heard the announcement.

"Ladies and gentlemen, welcome to the annual Naval Air Station Whidbey Island Air Show!"

"C'mon, Mom! Let's get up close for when Uncle Max flies by. We can go back under an umbrella later."

Winnie fought the apprehension that rattled her

stomach and put her sunglasses on. "Fine. But stay close and remember we've got the stroller."

They headed out and reached the crowd gathered along the flight line a few minutes later. Winnie couldn't help smiling as she looked around.

People from all walks of life had come to see the show. Of course, many in the crowd were from local military families, but there were also civilians who'd driven hours to see the demonstration.

"This is gonna be great!" Krista bounced up on her toes next to Winnie.

"Maaaammeeee." Maeve was awake.

Winnie bent down under the stroller's umbrella top. "Hello, sweetness. Are you up?"

"Hi." Maeve gave her a lopsided grin.

"Here, let Mommy change your diaper now so we won't have to worry about it later."

Maeve wasn't so thrilled but Winnie changed her diaper in the stroller before she could complain too loudly. Soon the drone of engines would drown out any crying, but for now the crowd was hushed in anticipation of the National Anthem.

"That's a good girl." She lifted Maeve onto her hip and handed her a sippy cup full of watered-down apple juice. "When you're hungry I have some yummy snacks for you, honey." She kissed Maeve's tousled mop and then put a sunbonnet on her. Maeve's fingers were too busy with the cup to try to yank off the hat.

Winnie and Krista sang along to "The Star Spangled Banner." Krista put her hand over her heart, and Winnie couldn't stop the tears that spilled over her bottom lids. Her sunglasses would keep Krista from seeing them, thank goodness. She didn't want her daughter to think she was upset.

Quite the opposite.

To watch Krista, who'd lost her dad too soon and too young because of his dedication to the Navy and his country, place her hand over her heart in such a patriotic gesture was a source of pride and joy. Tom might be gone, but he lived on in Krista. In her interest in flying and the shape of her eyes and the sound of her laugh, sure. But more than that, Winnie saw Tom in Krista's dedication to doing what was right, regardless of the challenges thrown her way.

"Here they come, Mom!"

Maeve clapped, picking up on her older sister's energy. "Yaayyy!"

"It's so exciting, isn't it, baby?" Winnie didn't have to distract Maeve at all. Maeve was enthralled. When a P-3C Orion and EA-6B Prowler flew in formation over the field, the crowd went wild. They were the two aviation platforms that had been on Whidbey the longest and continued to be deployed.

Winnie's breath caught as Maeve squealed in

her arms and Krista bounced next to her. The symbolism of the moment triggered so many memories.... Saying goodbye to Tom before deployments. Greeting him six, sometimes seven, months later. Cheering up friends whose husbands were deployed.

No one here had been untouched by war. It would never have been her choice to lose her spouse to war, but she would never have wished it on anyone else, either.

"Okay, Mom, Uncle Max should be next."

"Ladies and gentlemen, please pay attention to our next set of demonstrations. They remind us of the sacrifices made by the Greatest Generation during World War II. Today you'll see a B-17 Flying Fortress..." The announcer went on, introducing each pilot and giving a brief description of each plane's history.

Winnie ignored her anger that Max was up there, risking his life in an ancient aircraft.

"Mom, look! There's the B-17 he's in!"

In the distance she saw the unmistakable four engines on the huge but graceful old gal. The flyby wasn't as fast or glamorous as that by a supersonic jet, but Winnie bet hers weren't the only wet eyes in the crowd.

"Do you think he could see us?" Krista asked excitedly. "I told him I'd have this orange shirt on." Krista was wearing one of her favorite

T-shirts decorated with her current favorite band's logo on the front.

Winnie smiled and sought out the graceful bird one more time before it disappeared over the horizon. The B-17 would require a much larger flight path to turn around and make an approach back to the runway than a smaller plane.

Winnie saw the bird fly higher before it left her field of vision.

"Look, Mom. See how fast this one is!" Krista pointed out the P-51 Mustang, whose single Merlin piston engine shook the ground with its reverberations.

For the next fifteen minutes their attention was focused on aircraft after aircraft. They were in the midst of observing a French acrobatic pilot perform a loop-de-loop when Winnie noticed a pair of red fire engines. They raced across the flight line, followed by other emergency vehicles, all flashing their lights.

The French acrobat must have been alerted via his headset; the small plane instantly righted itself and flew out of the flight area.

Winnie's heart sank. She saw black spots in front of her eyes and lowered herself to the ground. Her grip on Maeve was all that kept her from completely losing it.

"Mom, what?" Krista grabbed her shoulders.

Winnie shook her head. Then she couldn't speak. They needed to listen to the announcer.

The sound system remained oddly silent.

Krista sat down beside Winnie and took Maeve into her lap. "Mom, are you okay? Why did they stop the show like this?"

"There's a problem—didn't you see the fire trucks?"

"No! Wait," Krista stood quickly, keeping Maeve in her arms.

It might not even be Max's flight, Winnie told herself.

But her instincts screamed otherwise. It was as though she *felt* his concern.

Winnie's hands shook so badly she grasped her knees to still them, sitting on the hot cement. The crowd's murmurs floated above her and she barely noticed the passage of time.

Still holding Maeve, Krista returned from her perusal of the activity. "You're right. There's a lot of flashing lights. Do you think the French pilot's hurt?"

"I don't know, honey. Let's just wait and see if the announcer says anything."

Of course, it could be as simple as the French pilot needing to land early. But the emergency vehicles were already on their way before the acrobat was waved off.

Finally the announcer began to speak. "Ladies

and gentlemen, please be patient while we take an unexpected break in our program. Our old gal the B-17 is making an emergency landing, but no problems are anticipated. The mishap vehicles are a precaution."

Winnie stood on shaky legs, her stomach heaving. She gasped huge amounts of air and concentrated on the far runway. The vehicles were still there, the lights still flashed.

All she and the girls could do was wait.

And pray.

"Mom, what are you thinking?" Krista stood next to her, not completely aware of what they might face.

"I'm thinking you're a great daughter and a wonderful big sister," she said, hugging Krista and Maeve together.

And if your uncle Max walks off that plane alive, I'm going to kill him.

CHAPTER TWENTY-FOUR

MAX NEVER MISSED A CHANCE to fly with World War II and Vietnam vets when they brought the old planes out for Air Shows. The guys who'd agreed to take him up in the B-17 this morning were no longer WWII vets as they'd been when he was a junior officer fifteen years ago. One of the pilots was a Vietnam vet and the copilot was a civilian who'd always loved flight.

It was a clear day, perfect for the Air Show.

He knew Winnie wasn't going to be happy with him when Krista told her he was up in this plane, but they didn't have any agreement, other than that he'd continue to be a father to both girls.

You still hope she'll change her mind.

Maybe, but he couldn't dwell on it or wait for Winnie to come around.

"Welcome aboard, Skipper." The lead pilot, Lieutenant Jimmy Rahal, retired and a Vietnam vet, shook Max's hand with vigor.

"Thanks, sir." Max swore his heart swelled whenever he had the honor of working with these old guys. They were the backbone of American history.

"This is Ross, my copilot." Jimmy put his hand on the other man's shoulder. Ross looked younger than Max by a long shot.

"Hi, Ross. I'm Max."

"Skipper. Great to have you with us this morning."

"Okay, we're going to get buckled in. Roanna, a P-3C flight observer—" Jimmy nodded to the familiar brunette on his right "—and you need to sign the paperwork. No signature, no ticket." Jimmy laughed.

As Jimmy pulled out his pilot notes to prep for preflight Max turned to Roanna.

"Nice to see you again. How's your mother's cat?"

"Fine, thanks."

She handed him a release form, and as he started to read it, he listened to the copilot give his spiel.

"Sir, ma'am, I know you're excited to come up with us, but legally I have to remind you that this is an antique aircraft and the head pilot is over retirement age. By signing, you acknowledge this and agree not to hold the crew or their family members liable for any mishap."

"Got it." Max read over the form. If he'd had

any fear of flying with these people, he wouldn't have requested this flight to start with.

He signed and then listened to the preflight brief. This was nothing like the briefs before a combat mission, because their "mission" that day was to get out, enjoy the air and show off what the old bomber could do. And, he hoped, inspire some of the people watching to learn more about World War II.

"Skipper, you'll be on a headset in the waist gunner position. Roanna, you'll be in the nose turret."

"Roger."

Max walked over to the waist of the airframe; it was not only in the middle of the craft but also where the fuselage narrowed slightly, and the overhead was too low for a gunner to stand upright. This necessitated the small step below the gun, so the shooter could brace himself while aiming.

Max's height didn't help. He put his headset on and prepared for a cramped but thrilling flight.

Takeoff was uneventful, and within a few minutes he was looking out his window as Whidbey Island's northern tip emerged below him. Linked to Fidalgo Island and the town of Anacortes by Deception Pass Bridge, the island was covered in dark green firs. Deception Pass twisted under the high bridge and its relatively smooth surface reflected the clear skies.

Staring down at the bridge reminded him of tl day he and Winnie had hiked Deception Pass and the kiss that had followed.

He wished he could share this view with Winn and the girls. Krista would have a blast up her If he wasn't mistaken, she was a pilot-in-trainin judging from her attention to every aircraft th flew over the soccer fields and her incessant que tions about flying.

"Winnie, why do you have to be so damne stubborn?"

He spoke the words aloud, but no one could he; him over the audio system unless he pressed tl talk button on his chest piece. The decibel lev of the engines made ordinary conversation in possible.

It didn't matter, anyway. There was only or person who had to hear him and she was on tl ground fifteen hundred feet below.

"We're coming back around for the flyby. A stations check in, please."

Max listened to the pilot, copilot and flight er gineer check in. Two other observers checked i too, and then Max gave his status. "Waist Pos tion, all secure."

There wasn't anything to secure, as the Brow ing fifty-caliber machine gun that had once stoo there had long since been removed. Still, it w:

exciting to feel the power and imagine the missions this plane and her crews had lived through.

"Okay, crew, we're going down to two hundred feet for our low-altitude flyby. Wave at the kiddies!"

Max chuckled at Jimmy's enthusiasm.

He enjoyed the image of Krista and Maeve smiling up at him. Then his mind flashed to an image of Winnie, scowling at his foolhardiness for getting on such an old plane. Especially after he'd survived the suicide bomber attack in Afghanistan.

"Ah, Winnie, you'll see. It's not all tragic."

MAX HAD TO RETRACT HIS own words a few moments later.

A loud *bang* and resulting shudders rolled over the airframe. He waited for it to steady and when it didn't he went into emergency mode.

He pushed back from the window and looked up toward the cockpit.

"Bird strike!" He read Roanna's lips.

"Son of a bitch!" Max ripped off his headset and ran forward.

He yanked open the door to the cockpit, careful to use it as a body shield in case there was flying glass or plane parts. He met with a rush of air. The flight engineer, Roanna, yelled above the roar. She'd climbed up from the nose/bombardier position. He could make out the words, "Take the throttle."

His eyes couldn't handle the air coming in through an open windshield. He glanced furtively around the radioman's area and saw a vintage leather helmet that hung in the corner. He reached for it.

The helmet had a set of old, yellowed goggles attached. He pulled them off and shoved them on his head, then over his eyes. They certainly weren't polarized but gave him the protection he'd need.

He went into the cockpit and relied on Roanna for the casualty assessment.

"We've got to get Jimmy out of the seat and you in there!" He barely made out her words but saw that Jimmy was completely incapacitated—if not dead. His copilot, Ross, held a dustcloth over his eyes, blood seeping out. His other hand was pulling back on the yoke, but he was losing the battle with the aircraft.

As Max got to work lifting Jimmy's dead weight from the left seat, he saw that only the pilot's windshield had blown out from the strike. The other remained intact, for now.

It felt like forever but they managed to wrestle Jimmy out of his seat. There was no time to worry about spinal injury. If Max didn't get into the pilot's seat and fast, they were all going to die.

He slid into the seat and grabbed the yoke. As soon as he had the controls, he yelled at Ross. "I've got it!" He proceeded to level out the plane.

The B-17's controls were nothing like a Prowler, but as Max was fond of saying, "You could teach a monkey to fly," because the fundamentals of flight were the same across all aircraft.

He looked over at Ross, who still had his headset on in spite of the windshield shards that must have hit his face.

Not that there was a chance of talking to him. They had to bring the plane in. Max wished he could hear someone from the tower, at least, to talk him through the landing.

He looked out the hole where the windshield had been and saw that they'd overshot the landing pattern and lost a lot of altitude—too much to land safely.

"I've got to circle her around one more time," he yelled to Ross. Roanna was tending to Jimmy in the area behind the cockpit where they'd dragged him. He still had a pulse—Max had felt it under his fingers.

"Make it tight." Max thought that was what Ross said, but he didn't know for sure. It was too loud, and Ross wasn't in any shape to be yelling.

Max pulled the throttle to starboard and turned the plane, his entire focus on staying level and landing it on the tarmac.

And walking the hell away from it.

Winnie. He saw her the way she was when he'd made love to her. He saw her as she held Maeve, Krista at her side. *Winnie.*

He was going to see them all again. If this bird held up...

MAX HAD NEVER LANDED without landing gear. He cursed to himself. "I can't get the hydraulics back," he muttered, praying that Ro had Jimmy and herself strapped down. At least he knew the bird was solid, that she could withstand a belly landing. How many vintage reels of WWII footage had he watched, in which the B-17 did just that? More than any other bomber in history, she was built to land on her belly, with her wings at the bottom of the fuselage.

Could he do it and save the aircraft, too?

If this wasn't such a critical time he'd laugh. Was he *really* worried about saving the bird?

Sure. Save the bird, save all of us. Be with Winnie and the girls.

"Let's do it!"

He shouted to no one. Ross sat slumped in his seat. Max hoped he was just unconscious but couldn't tell.

Roanna would know what to do when they landed. She was probably strapped in back there, next to Jimmy.

He knew from hours of Navy training on Whidbey that Runway 7 was going to come at him hard and fast once he cleared the water.

His hands tightened around the yoke and he eased up on the rudders. Focus and landing an aircraft were two of his most polished skills and he drew on them as he'd done each time he landed on an aircraft carrier, each time he'd flown a combat mission. He took the turn over the water and caught sight of the runway just beyond the shore.

The altimeter indicated he was under two hundred feet. He had about another fifteen seconds over water.

Runway 7 lay in front of the nose in a perfect lineup. Not bad considering that he was used to flying much smaller aircraft. The grass on the side of the runway beckoned; it would make for a much softer landing and might save the bird. But he'd end up on concrete for a bit, no matter what, as 7 crossed the other runway, 1, in the center.

"Come on," he whispered under his breath, and prepared to hang on to the yoke while he pulled up with all his might at the first jarring hit to the ground. Mud, muck and grass flew at him and into the cockpit, but he kept the pressure on, waiting for the gal to slow to a stop.

The journey across the concrete X of the two runways was horribly loud, and he hated to see the sparks that flew up in front of the cockpit but it did slow the plane down, enough so that he knew they'd stop in the dirt on the other side.

The plane came to a shuddering halt that lifted Max from his seat. He waited a split second and listened. No more engine noise, no more scraping.

They'd made it.

Now to get out before anything caught on fire or exploded.

"MOM, HERE IT COMES! Look!" Krista was still bouncing. Maeve was eating a snack of oat cereal. Winnie was hanging on to the last of her sanity by watching Maeve eat the cereal, one little "o" at a time. If she allowed her mind to go anywhere else, she was going to scream.

"Mom, look!" Krista grabbed her arm.

Against her better judgment, despite all her memories of losing someone from an aviation mishap, Winnie looked.

The runway shimmered in the sunlight. Except for the emergency vehicles and their flashing lights, it was quiet. She didn't see anything.

Until she looked up. Over the tree line, against the cerulean sky, was the B-17. The old bird didn't appear any different and was, in fact, flying toward the runway in what seemed to be slow motion. Ever so slowly she came closer to the ground, and Winnie wondered if she'd make the runway at all.

But just as the bomber became perpendicular to them, Winnie saw what the problem was. The collective gasp from the crowd said they saw the same gaping hole in the windshield that she did. The smooth plane of glass that would normally reflect the sunshine was missing.

There was a pilot in the cockpit, and although it was way too far to know who it was, she swore the shape of the head was Max's.

"Please, please…" She couldn't stop her fingers from digging into Maeve's jacket sleeves.

The plane finally closed the distance to the runway. In that instant she saw the reason for all the precautions and emergency equipment. She hadn't noticed that the landing gear wasn't deployed—she'd been focused on the cockpit.

No sign that the landing gear had deployed. Not good. She couldn't help holding her breath.

A huge dirt cloud hid the plane from view within seconds of its reaching earth.

Of course, Max had decided to touch down on the grassy verge beside the runway. It made for a much softer landing. But he'd have to cross cement at some point—the two runways on Whidbey met in a cross formation.

Unless he could stop the plane sooner and avoid the fire risk. Her heart skipped a beat, probably two. She took deep breaths to keep herself as steady as she could, as if by staying in the moment she'd will Max through it, too.

She saw the sparks under the belly before she heard the screech of steel, tons of it, scraping the cement runway.

The emergency vehicles swarmed the craft and she saw streams of fire-smothering foam as the firemen sprayed the scene.

Miraculously there was no smoke. The engines had simply stopped. No flying propeller parts, no fire, no explosion.

She eased her grip on Maeve and sent up a silent prayer of thanks.

So where were the passengers?

THEY WERE MET BY RESCUE crews who brought out stretchers for each of them. Max and Roanna didn't need them, but both Jimmy and Ross were unconscious and nonresponsive. Max stood with Roanna as the paramedics rushed the pilot and copilot to the waiting ambulances.

"Jimmy's tough. His pulse stayed strong the entire time. I really think he's got a good chance." Roanna's arms were crossed in front of her chest and her hair flew wildly about her face.

Max nodded.

"I can't thank you enough for saving my life, Skipper. Great landing."

"We walked away from it. That's all." Max saw

she was starting to shiver a bit. "You need to have the doc take a look at you. You're a little edgy."

Her eyes were glazing over, but then she snapped out of her daze. "I'm okay." She rubbed her upper arms. "But I'll have him check me out, just in case. You, too, Skipper."

"Will do."

The fact of the matter was that he felt great. Sure, there'd be some soreness tomorrow—hell, maybe a lot of soreness—but he was happy to be alive, to feel anything at all.

Only one thing was causing him pain at the moment.

He had to get to Winnie and the girls.

CHAPTER TWENTY-FIVE

"MOM, COME ON!" KRISTA was two strides ahead of Winnie, pushing the stroller through the crowds with Maeve happily enjoying the fast pace.

"Don't worry about me, just get to him!"

Winnie's strength surged back as soon as she saw the crew come out of the aircraft. There'd been a man on a stretcher but she refused to think it could be Max. No, she told herself, it couldn't be; her heart wouldn't take it.

You're in it for the long haul. Face it—you can't live without him.

She was ready to acknowledge that now. She wanted to laugh, to cry, but she had to breathe regularly, steadily, to keep up with Krista. They were well past the crowd now, on their way to the hangar where the flight crews were prepping for the Air Show. She had to get to Max. All of them did.

"Krista, wait, maybe I should go back for the car and drive up to the hangar. It would be faster."

"No, Mom, we're almost there. And Uncle Max will know it's us when he sees my shirt."

Winnie glanced at Krista's neon orange shirt. The color of caution, of warning.

Please don't let it be an omen. Let it be a beacon.

Her mind jangled with her disjointed thoughts and worries, but in this moment it was her heart that ran the show.

"I'm sorry, but I have to ask you folks to go back. This area is off-limits to spectators." A civilian guard stopped them a good distance from the hangar.

"We're family of one of the passengers on the B-17."

"Who's that, ma'am?"

"Commander Max Ford."

"Just a minute." He tapped on his radio button and spoke into the mic.

"I've got the family of Commander Ford here. Do I have permission to let them in?"

Winnie wanted to shove the guard aside and make a run for the hangar. She needed to see Max, to touch him. If he was the man on the stretcher, even more so.

"Could I see your ID cards, ma'am?"

"For heaven's sake," Winnie muttered as she bent over and dug through her purse in the storage basket under Maeve's stroller seat. Her hands shook and she fumbled for her wallet. She cursed her shaky fingers, unable to get her military identification card out of its compartment.

"Uncle Max!" Krista's scream pierced her nervous frenzy. Winnie stood slowly and held on to the stroller handles for extra support. Suddenly the tarmac didn't feel so steady.

The guard's attention was no longer on Winnie but on Krista and Max. Krista ran up to him and nearly threw him off-balance with her exuberant embrace.

"Krista, girl!"

He was okay. He was alive.

Max stood ten feet in front of her and Maeve, holding Krista in a bone-crushing hug.

"Did you see us? Could you see my shirt?"

Max laughed loudly. The sound sent waves of relief over Winnie.

He's still alive.

"Daddy!" Maeve screamed from her stroller seat, wanting in on the reunion.

"Hang on." Winnie bent down again and unbuckled Maeve's restraint belt. Maeve wriggled out of the seat and as soon as her feet hit the asphalt she dashed toward her daddy.

It's like a homecoming.

Winnie had greeted Tom when he came home from countless deployments. She'd witnessed other families reuniting after six or seven months apart. It was the Navy way. It was Navy life.

This was life, too. Feeling similar intense emotions—and one emotion she'd shut out for too long. Her love for Max. It was time for Max to come home, time for all of them to be together.

"Maeve, my baby girl!" Max swung Maeve up into his arms and gave her a smacking kiss before raising her above his head. She giggled with pure childish joy, oblivious to the life-altering event that had just occurred.

Sheer gratitude overwhelmed Winnie as she watched Krista stand next to Max, her arm around his waist, while he held Maeve on his hip and smiled at his baby daughter.

He's their father. And the man I love.

As if he read her thoughts, he finally met her glance.

If it were possible to share everything that had ever passed between them in that one glance, they did. Winnie saw the naked love she felt for Max reflected right back at her. Their youthful days of friendship. Max's unrelenting support of her and Krista when Tom died. Max's suffering from his war experience. His shock and then joy at discovering he was Maeve's father. Her betrayal and his forgiveness. Their mutual discovery of how much they meant to each other...

"It seems that you're done with your therapy. You handled that perfectly."

"Here, honey, go to Krista for a minute." Max

handed Maeve to her older sister, who eagerly took the toddler in her arms.

Max turned toward Winnie but she was already there. She'd narrowed their separation to less than a foot. He stepped closer and put his hands on either side of her head, his fingers under her hair, and pulled her to him.

Their lips met in mutual relief, love and acceptance. Just when the kiss would have sparked their passion to the "inappropriate in front of the girls" stage, Max leaned back and looked into Winnie's eyes.

"Yes, Max. I've been a fool. Can you forgive me? Will you marry us?"

Max's grin lit up his face and he turned to the girls. "What do you think, girls? Should we get married?"

Krista screamed, "Yeah!" and Maeve clapped.

Max looked back at Winnie.

"Yes."

EPILOGUE

Three months later

THE FRIDAY OF LABOR Day weekend brought its usual perfection to Whidbey Island as the sun shone on one of the warmest days of the year.

A sizable audience was gathered to watch Commander Max Ford retire after twenty years of service to the United States Navy.

Winnie noticed Robyn and her parents, also seated in the front row. Unfortunately, her brothers hadn't been able to get time off from their medical training. Her gaze continued along the second row, behind her. She saw the two men, Jimmy and Ross, who'd survived the B-17 crash landing with Max, and farther down the second row was Roanna. She wondered if Ro and Miles ever met up again.

Winnie relaxed as she held Maeve on her lap, feeling a profound sense of peace. She'd found a man to love, a man who loved her for the woman she was. Max supported her wholeheartedly with her fiber company and she'd overcome her fears

to support him with his commuter air business.
Winnie reflected that they weren't entering into
their relationship with the naiveté of youth, which
made it somehow deeper and even more special
to her.

A huge, billowing flag hung from the rafters
of the aircraft hangar and served as the backdrop
for a stage on which Max stood alone at the podium. His guest speaker, Chief Warrant Officer
Miles Mikowski, had just finished a short speech

Winnie was proud of Max. He'd shown his
true humility and sense of duty when he'd asked
Miles to be his guest of honor. Usually officers o
Max's stature invited a more senior officer, often
an Admiral, to be the guest of honor at their retire
ments. Miles and Max had bonded as they healed
Max's deep respect for Miles made him the per
fect choice.

Miles saluted Max and Max returned the salute
Winnie knew that this moment, with the two Nav
men in their Service Dress Whites, Max wearin
a sword at his side, would stay in her memory for
ever. She didn't have to turn around to know the
probably wasn't a dry eye in the hangar.

Max was saying goodbye to the Navy.

He looked out over the audience and his gaz
sought out Winnie's. She sat in the front ro
with Maeve and Krista on either side. She kne

they were all that mattered to him. They were his world.

"I want to thank everyone for coming out on this beautiful day. I'm not going to speak for long—I had my chance to do that at my Change of Command ceremony a couple of years ago. My career has meant everything to me. I've never been prouder than when I've served the U.S. Navy. Until…" He paused. "Until I found out I was a father."

He smiled.

"All great things come to an end. My time in the Navy is over. But my life is just beginning. A new life, a great life, with my new family. Winnie, I can't thank you enough for finally agreeing to marry me. Krista, you're a daughter to me and I know your dad would be so proud of you. Maeve, you'll never remember this day or my time in the Navy, but we'll raise you with the knowledge that others are sacrificing every day so you can enjoy the good life we'll do our best to give you."

The audience murmured its approval and Winnie didn't bother to wipe her tears away. Let them fall—she'd earned them. Tears of joy.

"I'll now read my orders."

Max proceeded to read his official orders, at the end of which he stood back from the podium. It was silent in the hangar. He walked to the red carpet that ran between two rows of sailors, side boys, who stood at attention. The announcer stated, "Commander, United States Navy, departing."

The sailors all held their salutes while the ship's whistle piped Max "ashore" as he walked through the side boys. He left the stage and went to Winnie and the girls.

The crowd stayed silent.

"Are you ready, Winnie?"

"Yes."

"Girls?"

"Let's go, Dad!"

"Daddy!"

The four of them walked onto the stage. They took their place, as a family, at the head of the red carpet.

Max looked at Winnie and smiled. "To our new family."

She smiled back at him.

"And our new life."

They'd moved his furniture down to her house the week before and hired a contractor to build an addition so Max would have a place to escape all the women in his life.

Max nodded at the announcer. "Navy Commander, retired."

Max, Winnie, Krista and Maeve walked through the line of sailors together and were greeted by thunderous applause from their guests.

Max kept Winnie's arm linked in his and smiled

at her. "How does it feel to be Mrs. Ford, wife of a retired Navy man?"

She answered him with a kiss.

*   *   *   *   *